STREET
VENGEANCE

Also by Evie Rhodes

THE FORGOTTEN SPIRIT

OUT "A" ORDER

CRISS CROSS

EXPIRED

Published by Dafina Books

STREET VENGEANCE

EVIE RHODES

DAFINA BOOKS
http://www.kensingtonbooks.com

DAFINA BOOKS are published by

Kensington Publishing Corp.
850 Third Avenue
New York, NY 10022

All Kensington titles, imprints, and distributed lines are available at special quantity discounts for bulk purchases for sales promotion, premiums, fund-raising, educational, or institutional use.

Special book excerpts or customized printings can also be created to fit specific needs. For details, write or phone the office of the Kensington Special Sales Manager: Attn. Special Sales Department. Kensington Publishing Corp., 850 Third Avenue, New York, NY 10022. Phone: 1-800-221-2647.

Dafina and the Dafina logo Reg. U.S. Pat. & TM Off.

ISBN-13: 978-0-7582-1668-7
ISBN-10: 0-7582-1668-8

First Printing: July 2008

10 9 8 7 6 5 4 3 2 1

Printed in the United States of America

Street Vengeance is dedicated to The Lord Jesus Christ for the lesson, "Let he who is without sin cast the first stone."

and

Street Vengeance is dedicated to James Rhodes for loving, believing, and always giving!

Acknowledgments

The Lord Jesus Christ—simply for being You!

James Rhodes, husband—always for the dream, the vision, the struggle, and the belief.

Rakia Clark, editor—for your editorial insights.

Kensington Publishing Corporation (Dafina)—for the publishing experience.

Robert G. (Bob) Diforio, agent—for your literary services.

Karen Thomas, former editorial director—for acquiring the story.

Jemal Freeman, a good brother—for picking the signature photo, and for always supporting my writing.

For the gangs, the street life, and all of those who have been affected—for your struggle. I wish for a positive change.

"The Lost Generation"
Rap Lyrics

Written by
Evie Rhodes

Rollin in the streets
players playin for keeps
take your life
in the matter
of a heart beat
driveby's cruising
God we're losin
Spillin our blood
Neighborhoods
being run by
HUD
depression
heaped upon
pain and despair
frustration and anger
gots to go somewhere

Death before dishonor
payin props for your
peeps

Losin your soul
demon snatchin
no fear for not
restin in peace

No souls to The Lord
in his kingdom
for him to keep

Now I lay me down
to sleep
I pray The Lord
my soul to keep

No spoils from my
flesh for The Grim
Reaper to reap.

No more existence
from Society's child
for the world to keep.

The lost generation
doesn't someone care
respect is for the dollar
and the dollar rules
beemers and benzs
gold and jewels
but when you're laying
in the gutter and
your blood is
running out
take a nuther nuther

Lord that's not what
it's about
but if the guns
don't get me
slow death by
economic clout
the lost generation

like the city of
Atlantis
disappeared without a trace
as though
it never had a place

Speakin of place
heed my case
Wake up to the chase
You ain't never had
a place
never put your foot
on the startin' line
of this race
maybe you ain't feelin
it but on this I rest
my case

The one who wants
you
you don't hear his
cry
callin from the
wilderness
for you and I

No carrot to dangle
in front of you
like Satan's lie
Deceived, played, and
hoodwinked, just in
time to die

The lost generation/it makes
me wanna cry/the lost generation/
what a loss/to you and I.

The lost generation
one by one
the lost generation
dyin by the gun
the lost generation
mackin in the streets
the lost generation
layin up
buying death for keeps

now I ain't gonna preach
You'd just think I've
breeched
if it ain't what you
feel
I won't even try to
teach
I know about the game
that tries to keep
ya just out of reach

Plenty of contenders
tryin to draw you out
playin wit your mind
Nah
that's not what I'm
about

Holla, if ya hear me
cuz inside ya
know what it's
about
a playa's got his
instincts
if you feel me
just give a shout

I'm a take the road
I've been given
despite all
the doubt
narrow is the way
but that's what
I'm all about

The Lord has given
me power,
and on that
I'll stand
shinin
like Standin In Da Spirit
cuz that's who I am
a ram in the bush
The Lord said I AM

Satan can't play me
cuz I understand
Holla, if you hear
me those of you
who ran

The Lord is full of
mercy, come on back
to his plan.

I am who I am
and on that I'll
stand but I only
learned after the
devil made his
grand stand.

Now I'm telling
you, so you can

feel the real
I AM

The lost generation
from which
no
I cannot hide
A two-year-old boy
was shot down
in the street
a girl age nine
was raped
yeah
and beat
it's Wild Wild West
time
in the hood
eliminatin
yeah for good

When you're on your
way out
reapin that flash of
last doubt
now you might wanna
give The Lord a shout

the lost generation
gone for good
the lost generation
legacy of our hoods

Lost by lack
of knowledge
I'm not talking
college

lost generation
death of a strong
nation
the lost generation
say good-bye
the lost generation
ruled by
the wrong high
the lost generation
gone for good

the lost generation
gone
not only our legacy
but our pride
for good

The lost generation/it makes
me wanna cry/the lost generation/
what a loss/to you and I.

Chapter 1

The last blow of the nightstick to Q's spine was the one that caused his paralysis. He was immediately incapacitated. Excruciating is too mild of a word to describe the pain that exploded through Q's limbs or the sparks of light that shot through his brain.

He saw a black boot descend through the air, speedy and vigilant, before it connected with his head. At the same time, he heard his friend Brandi's horrific scream followed by deadly accusations hurled at the LAPD. Her voice was filled with animosity, pain, and confusion. It was all she could manage from her restrained position to yell and make known to everybody within listening distance the police's mistreatment of Q.

Mercifully, Q blacked out. His mind was singed with dark, black waves of pain, and his body was unable to withstand even one more blow and still be alive.

There's a reason the Lord created unconsciousness.

Q's body seemed to drift to a place that distanced him from the pain and suffering. Like the surfing of television channels, his mind skipped around and finally settled on the time and place he'd been in right before his current predicament.

It seemed like only seconds before that he and Brandi had been jamming to the X-Masters with the rest of the hyped-up crowd. The group's suggestive lyrics and flaunting bodies danced across the stage, gyrating aerobically to every beat.

Brandi Hutchinson had been the bomb and she knew it. At eighteen years of age, she was smart, hip, and black as well as fabulously beautiful. She was dressed from head to toe in the hottest street gear. Her long, shiny black hair swung from the hip cap that she wore with the X-Masters's name emblazoned across the front.

Her hands were in the air, and her body became one synchronized movement to that phat beat the X-Masters had developed and then mastered, giving them claim to their name.

The X-Masters were considered musical masters, lyrical geniuses, and they were at the height of what music production was all about. As they rose up in the music industry and stacked platinum records, the group had had little competition. They were the crowned high princes of Hip-Hop with their sleek, sinewy rhymes and moves. And they held down the charts as though their very names were permanently engraved there.

Grooving to the X-Masters right on Brandi's hip was her best friend, Tangeline Parker. Tangie still held a grudge against her dead mother for giving her that stupid name. Who in the hell ever heard of somebody called Tangeline? And somebody black, at that? What had her mother been thinking?

So Tangie went only by Tangie—unless somebody wanted to be treated to one helluva nasty attitude. Almost always even-tempered, a shout of "Tangeline" was the one, surefire way to get her blood boiling.

Tangie was a close replica of Brandi in terms of their dress code. But Tangie had smooth dark skin and Brandi's was caramel colored. And Tangie was barely five feet tall, whereas Brandi stood five feet eight inches in her stocking feet.

Tangie was eighteen years old, too, but her attitude was eighteen going on forty. There was a maturity about her that belied her age.

The X-Masters's concert had been organized by Tangie's older brother, Fishbone, whose reputation preceded him wherever he went. Niggas were known to cross the street just so they wouldn't be walking on the same side as him.

He had once beaten a dude so badly with his bare hands that the dude was in critical condition in intensive care. It had been touch and go for a while, but the guy eventually pulled through. Fishbone stayed low until he was sure that he wasn't going down for no attempted murder rap. That was too much time.

But as fearsome as his reputation for physical violence was, he was even better known for getting in people's heads with psychological manipulation.

At twenty-eight years old, he was the head of the gang called the L.A. Troops, and he marshaled a small army under his leadership. The L.A. Troops were the ones bringing the noise at the concert and letting it be known that they were in the house.

Fishbone's public appearance at the rap concert was a bit out of character for him. He generally kept an extremely low profile and liked to stay under the radar. It was one of the main reasons he was still alive today. He had grown wiser as he'd gotten older, and he knew that illusions and appearances went a long way. That and paying off the right people. It was a simple strategy that worked.

But his boys were mostly young thugs and they needed to get out sometimes. There were a few at the top of the helm with him, like Maestro, who had been down with him since they were snotty-nosed kids. But most of them were young. The concert was a good way to release energy for them. Plus, he had wanted to keep an eye on Tangie and Brandi.

As word had spread on the street that the L.A. Troops would be putting in an appearance at the concert, some of the other gangs in the city decided to avoid this particular outdoor concert.

Brandi yelled over the noise to Tangie, "Girl, I told you this was going to be a slamming concert! It is da bomb!"

"You ain't never lied, girl."

Fishbone interrupted their conversation. "What you know about slamming, little buck?" He reached over and pulled Brandi's cap over her eyes so she couldn't see.

She slapped his hand away affectionately, pulling her cap back into place with the stroke of a young woman who knew exactly what she wanted.

Brandi exuded a powerful presence for one who was so young.

Tangie stretched out her arms between the two of them as though warding off a war. "Hold up. Chill with that noise, will y'all?"

She knew those two could go on all night. They were similar in personality, and they loved to rile each other up at times.

Brandi always refused to come up short just because Fishbone was older than her. She was not feeling that. Age wasn't nothing but a number. Her mama had taught her that.

Fishbone looked over at Tangie, shaking his head in the negative. "I'll be calling the shots here, shorty. Don't forget I'm your big brother. Now shut up before I have to spank you in front of all these people and send you home. And I know you ain't feeling that," Fishbone joked with his younger sister.

Tangie gave him her sassiest look and poked him in the chest. "I ain't no baby and you ain't gonna be doing no spanking or sending anybody home. You ain't got no kids up in here. I don't think so. Do you feel that?" She poked him harder this time.

Brandi howled with laughter, unable to resist kicking it off with Fishbone.

"See," she said, instigating. "He shouldn't have gone there, but girl, *yes,* he did. It wouldn't be me."

She turned to Q, who was seventeen years old and who

had been her very best friend since they were running around the schoolyard in elementary school.

They had also lived next door to each other for as long as they could remember.

Q was tall, lean, wiry, and good-looking.

Q had the girls chasing because he had curly hair, light skin, and green eyes fringed with alluringly thick lashes.

He also possessed a penchant for being extremely childish at times.

His mental age was about thirteen, and at times it showed. It still didn't put him at a disadvantage with the girls, though, because what he lacked in mental maturity, he more than made up for in looks.

Heck, Q, he had young women older than Brandi and Tangie trying to hit on him. Yet, he was loyal to a fault—at least when it came to Brandi. And Brandi loved him as if he were her blood brother. She couldn't have loved him more if he was, and vice versa. That was just the way it was with the two of them.

Brandi pointed to Fishbone. "Fishbone ain't right. You know that, Q. He done dissed my girl. And not in private, either. You heard it, right?"

Q laughed. "Yeah. And you know that. Even over all this noise I heard that dismissal. Tangie, you better get straight chasing for home, girl, before you turn into a ghetto pumpkin. Cinderella ain't got nothing on you!"

They all joked at Tangie's expense. She joined in their laughter good-naturedly, and poked her brother in the ribs with her elbow for bringing the noise and starting the mess in the first place.

Suddenly, Lyrical, the lead rapper for the X-Masters, ran to the front of the stage. He immediately drew everybody's attention with his lyrical mastery. He was a very fascinating rapper and knew how to entrance a crowd.

In fact, Lyrical was one of the few coveted rappers with a voice that the microphone loved in the studio as well as onstage live. Lots of rappers had one or the other, but Lyrical had both. You couldn't pay for that. You couldn't learn it, funk it, or fake it.

He was a music producer's and engineer's dream. And he knew it. That sensual, gritty quality to his voice made record label executives see dollar signs, and that was no easy feat in itself.

In the studio his voice as well as his lyrical flow (hence his current moniker) was as smooth as silky cream. He was magically able to carry that cream mixed with a hard-edged grit live onstage, transmitting it to very excited audiences.

When it was his turn up to the mic, the crowd went wild at the sound of his voice. He pumped them up, sweating and prancing across the stage.

He lashed out lyrically:

> *"Blood spilled*
> *Another killed*
> *Trigger happy*
> *Yeah*
> *They didn't chill*
> *Like a hunter*
> *Stalking the scent of his prey*
> *Once he has the scent*
> *Hey it's payday."*

> *"Another metal coffin*
> *It happens too often*
> *Or a plain pine box*
> *Another series*
> *Of locks and blocks*
> *Jump on the beat*
> *Yeah it's the heat*
> *Bullets with no names*
> *Danger without shame*
> *Friction."*

The crowd was straight up jamming. They were caught up in the beats of the music that flowed like butter. Low-riding cars raced their motors in excitement, bouncing the cars up and down in the park although there were signs strictly forbidding low riding.

Security was on high alert as the crowd got even more hyped. A lot of police hated rap concerts because of all the hyped-up behavior they produced in their audiences. Not to mention straight up belligerence.

The concerts were like a religion to a lot of the kids who attended them. A lot of the rap groups had a cultlike following.

Police helicopters appeared over the park, circling low, caught up in the vibe of the crowd.

Lyrical was pumped by the size and excitement of the crowd. He could see himself on the monitors. He was psyched. After all, he was in L.A.

He shouted his lyrics with a depth of feeling that was hypnotic in its effect on the crowd. His delivery was transmitted with the speed of a silver bullet:

> *"Quest for power*
> *Thirst by the hour*
> *Hunger for control*
> *Trying to get you told*
> *As I rap*
> *another tragedy unfolds*
> *quicker than I*
> *can pull the trigger on my Uzi*
> *A drive-by*
> *another shooting*
> *A few days later*
> *dirt and flowers*
> *Didn't I tell you*
> *it's thirst by the hour."*

The crowd veered out of control, jumping in the air.

*   *   *

After the concert, Q drove Brandi's car down Crenshaw Boulevard in an elevated state of excitement, still feeling the adrenaline from the concert.

He raised the car up and down as everyone had been doing in the park.

Brandi changed a stack of CDs. They were pumped from all the action. The X-Masters boomed out of the stereo speakers and Brandi felt just as if they were back at the concert.

The base from the music was booming so loud and hard the speakers were pumping like the beat of a heart.

"These niggas ain't taking no shorts on the stage. Holla if you hear me!" Brandi said.

Tangie high-fived her from the backseat of the car.

Q reached under the seat.

He pulled out a bottle of beer. He swigged from the bottle. "You better be straight up glad that I put some hydraulics on this heap for you, Brandi. You ain't had no power before that. I don't know how you drove this thing."

Brandi forgot that Q was driving. She pushed him. Tangie sat forward, laughing from the backseat. She pushed Q's head from the back, causing beer to spill all over him.

At that precise moment, they heard the sirens. In the same instant they saw the police cruiser flashing the lights for them to pull over.

Q decided in the flash of a second to try to outrun them. He pushed his foot to the gas pedal, hitting the floor. The car jerked forward. It shot a car's length out in front of the police.

Total chaos broke out in the car.

Brandi and Tangie yelled at the top of their lungs in unison. What the hell was wrong with Q? Why the hell was he running from the police?

They asked him this question as though they were twins in

a psychic link. Q was so caught up in the chase that he didn't answer.

Adrenaline pumped through his veins. A false sense of power soared through his body. He mashed the gas pedal to the floor once again.

He pushed the car to its maximum speed, generating theatrics that might have made NASCAR fans smile, but only pissed off the police.

When he had gone a few blocks, making everybody mad as hell because of the chase, a different set of cruisers flew out of an alleyway. They crisscrossed from out of another boulevard.

They pulled in front of the car Q was driving, causing it to crash into the side of one of the police cruisers. Come hell or high water they meant for him to stop. That maneuver brought the car Q was driving to a screeching halt. The police jumped out of their cruisers.

The backup team, SWAT, and the snipers, positioned their weapons, drawing down on the car. There was a sea of cops covering the area.

The police bore down on the car with their guns drawn and nightsticks positioned. They yanked open the driver's door and pulled Q from the vehicle without hesitation, then ordered Brandi and Tangie to get out of the car.

Brandi and Tangie screamed, fought, struggled, and yelled for them to leave Q alone, especially Brandi, but some of the other officers physically subdued them. Their screams were in vain.

The heat of the situation was out of control, on its way to escalating out of order.

"Yo, get the hell off of me, you pig!" Q yelled out as he kneed one of the officers in the groin with all his might. The officer doubled over in pain; that single stroke kicked off major chaos. That was all she wrote.

The cops beat Q. He was vastly outnumbered. Brandi and

Tangie screamed. They both struggled valiantly to get free so they could help their friend, but it was no use.

The streets filled up with angry mobs of people. The crowd got out of hand. They were mad as hell.

They started to throw rocks, bottles, and whatever else they could get their hands on.

The helicopters swung low as the police struggled to get the crowd under control.

By this time, Q was lying on the ground unmoving. Because of the size of the crowd that had gathered on the street, along with the madness and chaos that was swirling around, no one knew who did exactly what.

Even those with the wherewithal to pull out their cell phone camcorders and record, due to the crowded conditions and chaos, they couldn't totally capture the truth.

An ambulance skidded to a stop, pulling up next to Q after struggling to get through the crowd. In an effort to help bring control the EMTs quickly did their job to medically assist Q.

This was no easy feat, considering the circumstances. They loaded him into the ambulance on a gurney in hopes of diffusing the situation by removing him from the scene.

By the time Brandi and Tangie arrived at the hospital Q was being treated in intensive care.

Tangie huddled in the corner with her legs pulled up to her chin. Brandi paced the waiting room area with a dangerous glint in her eyes.

The look in her friend's eyes frightened Tangie. And Tangie had seen a lot in her time, she didn't scare all that easily. After all, her brother was the leader of one of the most notorious male gangs in Los Angeles.

However, Brandi's look bordered on the edge of insanity as though she were teetering on the very edge of her own locked-in reality.

Tangie had never in her life seen Brandi look like that. In

fact she wasn't sure if she had ever in her life seen anyone look like that.

Brandi's face was actually twisted in rage. Her eyes had a cold, calculated eeriness about them. And perhaps the worst thing about Brandi was her total calm. It was painted on her like a veneer.

With the exception of her pacing she was being held in tight control, like a live electrical wire about to spring loose, waiting for just the right moment.

Even her pacing seemed calculated upon closer observation.

All in all it had been another record night in South Central Los Angeles. Unfortunately it wasn't that different from many other nights.

Finally, approaching with a weary look on his face was Q's doctor. He pensively entered the waiting room area. Brandi rushed up to him before he could speak.

Somewhat subdued but anxious, she asked, "How's Q? Is he going to be all right?"

The doctor consulted his chart. "Are you asking about Robert Mounds?" he asked, to ensure they were talking about the same patient. His ID had identified him as Robert Mounds. Naturally the doctor wasn't familiar with Robert's nickname of Bobby Q, or just Q, as most people in the hood called him.

"Yes," Brandi stated impatiently.

They had had no idea what Q's condition was under the circumstances. They hadn't been able to learn a thing while they were waiting, either. Brandi was tired of all the damn waiting, and now these stupid questions regarding Q's name. That exasperation and impatience had reflected in her voice.

The doctor looked down at his feet because he sensed Brandi's tightly controlled rage.

His gaze strayed to the corner where Tangie was sitting. Brandi suddenly had a bad feeling in the pit of her stomach. She didn't like the doctor's evasiveness.

And it was taking everything she had for her not to slap his face. He'd better tell her about Q before she lost her grip on the tight rein she was holding herself under.

Finally, after what seemed like an eternity, he looked at Brandi. "Are you his next of kin?"

Brandi lied swiftly. "Yeah. Robert Mounds is my brother. My mother is on her way."

"How old is Robert?"

"Seventeen," Brandi replied without hesitation.

The doctor aged before her eyes. He looked old, tired, and sad. He ran a hand through his hair before looking pointedly at Brandi. "Your brother is paralyzed. He's never going to walk again."

Brandi's hand flew to her mouth.

The doctor's words echoed in her ears as though a storm had started to brew in her head. She could actually hear the roar of the ocean.

She looked over at Tangie, who was huddled in shock in the corner watching her and the doctor intently.

"Oh my God! Never?"

"Never," the doctor said, shaking his head before slowly walking away.

His words evoked the calm in Brandi before the gathering of the storm.

Q lay unmoving, hooked up to monitors, machines, and IV drips. A mere skeleton of the young, vibrant boy he had been only hours before.

The doctor's words echoed in Brandi's ears, as though someone were blasting them through a loudspeaker. Her mind flashed as though she were watching high-definition TV on a sixty-inch screen.

She saw Q hugging her.

She saw Q ringing her front doorbell.

She saw Q racing her on the schoolyard.

She saw him lying with his feet propped up on her wall, joking with her.

She saw him eating with her.

She saw him listening to music with her.

She saw him fighting side by side with her when the school bullies picked fights with her when they were in elementary school.

She saw him as he was. Not as the vegetable he had become.

They were all memories. They were memories of a distant past. The irony of it was they weren't even old enough yet to have a past.

The doctor's words echoed through the chambers of her mind as though someone had permanently programmed them there.

"Your brother is paralyzed. He's never going to walk again. Never."

It couldn't be true. But it was.

Chapter 2

Brandi's hatred built like slow-gathering lava after a volcanic eruption. She kept replaying the disastrous scene that had led up to Q's paralysis. It was similar to watching an unwanted DVD that would not go off. Those scenes filled every channel in her mind, and on every station it was the same scene.

Inside she felt an ache that she could not describe. She ached and felt dead at the same time. There was no way she could ever have explained that feeling of pain, coupled with the numbness of death, to anybody.

All she knew was that that was what she felt. It hurt like an open wound at times. At other times it just felt like a hole was in her heart. Where her heart should have been beating, it instead felt like flowing ice water.

The room was clean, but everything in it reflected the run-down, poor conditions she had grown up in. Her walls were plastered with posters of rappers and R&B singers that she liked.

Brandi had a nice computer, though. She had done chores that she hated for two months in order to entice her father to buy it for her. He was still making the payments. By the time he finally finished, a newer, faster model would probably be on the market. But the computer was Brandi's pride and joy.

Her dad had been happy he could buy it for her when he saw the smile that lit up her face.

Brandi's stereo blasted the kind of noise that only teenagers considered music. The bass was deafeningly loud, shaking the whole house. But she was oblivious to that as she lay with her head propped up on pillows with her feet on the wall, and a blank expression reflected in her eyes. It was as though her body was alive but without emotion. She looked like she did not give a damn.

She was consumed by only one thought: her best friend would never walk or run again. Period.

She hated herself for thinking that maybe Q would have been better off dead. As it stood now, he was condemned to a life of not being able to use his body. He had been handed a life sentence in a split second of timing.

To make matters worse—if that was at all possible—he now had to live in a useless body that he had once been so very proud of. He had liked to run and pump iron. He had showed off the results of his physical prowess at every opportunity prior to this tragedy.

Brandi's dad, Charles Hutchinson, was in his late thirties. He was a soft-spoken, slight of build, hardworking man, who had become a slave to economic conditions he would never overcome, although he worked practically day and night to keep a roof over his family's head and food on the table.

Though most of the time he was mild-mannered, his wayward, headstrong daughter had pushed him to his breaking point with the noise that she called music. He tried to read the newspaper in his den, but he could not concentrate because of the loud noise that made the house shake.

He wondered why he bothered reading the newspaper at all, considering all the bad news that was always in it. But it was a habit he found hard to break.

Charles stormed his way to Brandi's room, unable to stand the noise any longer. He opened her bedroom door without bothering to knock.

This wasn't something he would normally have done. He respected her right to some privacy most of the time. However, the noise was so deafening she wouldn't have heard him anyway.

By the time he reached her, he was darn near livid because the level of the noise had increased as he made his way closer to her room.

He yelled over the music, "Brandi! Shut that noise down! This instant! I mean it!"

Brandi didn't even acknowledge him. He could have been invisible as far as she was concerned. She was wrapped in a cocoon beyond his reach.

Charles wasn't having that nonsense. No child he had brought into this world was going to ignore him as though he hadn't spoken or didn't exist.

He was only thirty-eight years old but still he demanded respect, regardless of the lack of it that went on around them. It didn't and wouldn't go on in his house.

He strode over to the stereo system in a rage. He pulled the plug on it. The music came to a crashing halt. This brought Brandi out of her stupor fast. She swung her feet over the side of her bed. She glared at her father.

How dare he invade my space without being invited in? This is my room. It is the only place where I have any privacy.

Before she could open her mouth, Charles started in on her. "I've told you a thousand and one times to keep that noise down."

"It ain't noise. It's rap music," Brandi stated belligerently, defending her generation's music of choice.

Charles did his best to rein in his anger, but it wasn't working because of Brandi's nasty attitude. "It's noise, like I said. If I say it's noise, then it's noise. Now keep it the hell down."

He looked around the room in disgust. "Why don't you do something with yourself instead of pumping that garbage into your ears all day long?"

His question went unanswered.

He couldn't believe how sorry this generation of kids was. It seemed to him that all they did was lie around doing nothing all day long. They listened to music. They talked on the phone to their friends, or played war games—or whatever the hell it was they engaged in on those lethal PlayStation boxes and on the computer that kept them entranced and sounded like a war had been started.

That was about all they ever did as far as he could see.

Hell, he'd even heard on the news about some fool kid shooting an innocent man for his place in line to buy one of those stupid game boxes on the day the latest version of the game was released, which the manufacturers treated as if it were the day of the Second Coming.

"Do something with yourself," Charles stated again in clipped tones. He was so angry he was biting the inside of his jaw.

Brandi was beside herself with indignant anger. She wasn't the type who deliberately disrespected her father or got up in his face. But at that moment, loathing surged through her body—a loathing that she had no idea how to control.

"What do you want me to do?" she yelled. "It's summer. I don't have nothing to do."

Charles threw his arms in the air. He rolled his eyes at the ceiling in total exasperation. "Ever heard of a job? J-O-B." He spelled it out for her as though Brandi herself couldn't spell the word. "You could try one of those. Know what I mean?"

Brandi hit her boiling point. "Oh, yeah," she said nastily.

She took a deep breath before hurling the nastiest of her feelings at him. "And then I could get an apartment like this one, right? And work eighteen hours a day to pay for it. And still not have enough, right? You think this is something I would aspire to? Hell, I'm a straight-A student, and I can't even go to the college I'm entitled to because there isn't enough money to pay for it," she screamed in his face.

Charles drew himself up to his full height. Brandi had struck a blow that wounded him deeply. She jumped off the bed. She grabbed some clothes that were lying on the bed. She walked over to the closet, hanging them up, trying to blow off steam.

She turned her back on her dad while putting away the clothes.

Charles couldn't believe her level of disrespect. It was beyond his comprehension. It was a good thing he would never put his hands on a girl-child because if he hadn't had that particular frame of mind he might have strangled Brandi with his bare hands.

He was beginning to understand why people said never put your hands on a child when you were mad.

He couldn't believe the nerve of her turning her back on him like he was some kid in the street she was dismissing. He was her father, and though he knew he had fallen short of some goals, he'd tried to give her what he could.

Unbeknownst to Brandi, Charles had looked into every possibility to try to get her into one of those fancy colleges. He'd even swallowed his pride and asked for a grant for her from his job. He'd done it because he knew she had MBA potential and was smarter than most of the kids around her. But it always boiled down to the money.

He couldn't afford better than a community college, no matter what he tried. Brandi's smarts were far beyond that, and she wouldn't receive the same respect or pay as she would have if she'd come out of an Ivy League college, where she truly belonged. He was just as bitter about the situation as Brandi was.

Charles stared at the back of Brandi's shiny black hair that hung halfway down her back and quietly said, "I pay the bills. So, here's the deal. You live in my house, you do what I say. And I say keep that noise down that you play, and while you're at it—get a job."

Brandi turned from the closet with a storm in her eyes. Father and daughter stood in a face-off, caught in the eye of a vicious storm.

One that was really not of either of their making, but caught in it they were.

Charles didn't flinch. He was a man. He was going to die being just that, a man. And no sassy-behind little girl was going to take that from him even if she was his daughter. "Those are the rules, Brandi. So you might as well get with the program."

He walked out the door. He slammed it good and hard behind him.

Brandi flew into a rage. She ripped her clothes from their hangers. She flung them to the floor. She stuck her middle finger up at the closed door that her dad had slammed.

She kicked the clothes around on the floor, finally stomping on them to alleviate some of her pressure. She knocked the books off her bookshelves.

Charles heard all of the commotion but kept walking toward the den. If he had gone back to her room, there was no telling what might have happened. In any case she knew better than to turn that noise back on. She could stomp all she wanted to.

"I hate you! And I hate this apartment!" Brandi yelled. "You make me sick! Do you hear me? You make me sick!" She yelled until she felt sick to her stomach and her voice turned hoarse.

Finally, she went over to her bedroom window, leaving her room looking like a cyclone had run through it. She climbed out of the window. The repulsive hatred she was feeling traveled straight out of the window with her. It would not be quelled very easily.

Chapter 3

Brandi decided to try to walk off some of her anger before she did something stupid. While she was walking she saw Lisa, who was from around the way, arguing over a drug deal.

Paging for drugs was a way of life for Lisa, who had a habit she couldn't support. She was always trying to buy drugs on credit while waiting for the checks she received from welfare and disability. One of her sons was mentally disabled.

The disability had occurred as a direct result of her drug abuse because she had continued using drugs during her pregnancy.

Her son had been born addicted to heroin. He had then grown up to have slow mental processes. In any place except the projects they would have taken the child from her, placing him in some type of residential care program.

Chad was twelve years old, yet his mental capabilities resembled those of a three-year-old. You'd think this particular impairment might have given Lisa a reality check. It hadn't.

The dealer she was trying to work a deal with had a major attitude problem. His attitude was the size of every square inch of Los Angeles, and then some.

He was sick of Lisa with her conniving, trifling, begging ways.

He pushed her away from the door. "Lisa, get outta here. You ain't got no ends. Paper, baby, you know what I mean." He rubbed his fingers together indicating a cash payment was needed.

Lisa, as expected, wasn't fazed and didn't move.

"And I ain't your creditor. Understand?" he yelled in her face. "Who the hell do you think I am? Bank of America or Chase Manhattan? No money. No re-mix. Now back the hell up from the door!"

Lisa pushed him, trying to get inside the door. She could smell drugs and almost taste them. But Kenny, or D-Money, as he was known, blocked the door, firmly keeping her out.

He knew Lisa figured if she could get inside, she could maybe do some negotiating. And he wasn't negotiating pound for pound when it came to flesh. Either cash money was produced or there wasn't nothing happening.

Brandi could feel the coldness that rolled off of D-Money like a slick sheen, even from as far away as she was standing.

Lisa was unable to move the dealer or change his mind. He had seen every trick in the book when it came to people copping drugs. He sold to junkies who were masters of the game. Hell, he'd been a part of inventing the game.

And in his time in the game he'd had to fend off some of the most dangerous junkies alive. Niggas that would take your head off of your body for a fix.

Lisa resorted to the age-old antic of begging. Perhaps she could appeal to his soft side. That was if he had one. Most drug dealers didn't.

But sometimes if she pleaded long enough one of them would throw her a bone, even if just to get rid of her. And she was grateful when they did. She didn't care. She had lost her pride long ago, and there wasn't any shame in her game as long as it produced results.

"Come on, man. Please. Just a little taste. I'll pay you when I get my check. You know I'm good for it."

He knew without a doubt she wasn't good for nothing except running to a different dealer when she got that check, and that was word.

Lisa shook. She pulled her hair. She scratched her arms. A heavy sheen of sweat broke out on her skin.

Her eyes had become unfocused and disoriented, glazed over from need.

All she could think of was getting some of that heroin that would make her feel better. It would erase her worries. Heroin transported her to places other than the ones she was in.

It put her in one of those nods where nothing hurt and everything was all right. All she wanted was that feeling one more time.

Brandi watched her. Right then and there she made a decision. She would never be at anybody's mercy. Whatever it took, and whatever the price was, she would rule by any means necessary.

It was as simple as that.

Lisa reached into her pocket. She pulled out a card. It was the last of what she had to buy food for her kids on. She handed it to the dealer.

Disgusted, D-Money slapped the card out of her hand to the ground. Even though he was a dealer, he was pissed off that she was taking the last of what she had to buy food with for her kids to buy drugs instead.

Lisa didn't give a damn as long as she could feed that monster on her back.

He'd seen her kids out on the streets, hungry and begging plenty of times, so she could buy drugs.

As for her son Chad, D-Money could barely stand to see him. He stuffed money in his pockets when he saw him just because life had been so damn cruel to him.

Chad hadn't asked to come here.

And he damn sure hadn't put in a personal request to have Lisa for a mother.

At one time D-Money had been one of those kids himself. His mother had sacrificed him for drugs over and over again during his youth. She'd sold him off as a male prostitute to support her habit.

Once some dealers had even kidnapped him because of a drug debt she owed. The images of his capture still roamed around the recesses of his mind.

That was how he had become a dealer: survival. True that. But even he hadn't yet reached the lowness of taking the last food out of a child's mouth.

He got so mad as the violence of his memories assaulted him that he pushed Lisa off her feet onto the ground.

"Ho, I said come back when you got some real paper. No ends. No paper. No re-mix."

Re-mix was the hottest thing in heroin on the streets. It was fresh on the streets of Los Angeles via Mexico. The demand was high. It was strong, and black like gummy tar, but it was formed in the shape of a rock. The users were bugging.

This heroin was so good you could take a little piece the size of a match head, stick it in a bottle top, and cook it up. Once a junkie did that they were hooked, and hooked but good. They lived for that high.

D-Money was in pocket because he had the supply. If you had the hookup, then you were the man. It was the fastest source of earning money that he'd ever stumbled across.

He picked up the card and threw it at Lisa. "Go to the store and get some food to feed your babies. Stupid black ho."

He slammed the door, shaking his head angrily.

Lisa beat her fists on the ground, sick and in frustration over wanting the re-mix. She was going to have to find a way to get it.

Brandi watched Lisa wallow in her weakness—and knew without a doubt a change was about to come.

Chapter 4

Brandi climbed back through her bedroom window amid all the chaos she had left behind. She flicked on her computer. She sorted through her various CDs for her favorite game of *Street Wars*.

She found the disk, flicked it into the computer drive, and grabbed a pair of headphones so she wouldn't have to deal with her father again. Then she plugged the headphones into the stereo system, clicking to her favorite rap station and immersing herself in the game. She engaged in the street battle it presented with great intensity. Her observation of the game's format was at a high level.

She was in such a rage that when she finished playing the game, everything that had had breath within the sleek computerized death trap was dead, and she was left with a bright sheen of sweat creasing her forehead.

All that was left standing in the game of *Street Wars* was the character on the screen, which represented her as the player.

Brandi's skin glistened from the exertion of the play. Her heart raced as though she had been in the battle of her life.

She had an idea of what Q had felt when that sudden rush of adrenalin hit him on that awful night, the last time he would ever walk.

What she didn't know and what Q hadn't known was how to control it. Neither of them knew how to control an impulse that on the one hand represented a sense of freedom and on the other hand caused destruction.

After disposing of her enemies she flicked to CNN, deciding to watch all of the war coverage. Normally, it was a channel she skipped when she was surfing.

She really didn't care much for the news. But she had suddenly developed an intense interest in war strategies.

She watched one of the country's leading, most revered generals discussing strategic tactics in wars of life and death. She studied his demeanor. She also studied the look in his eyes, and the modulation and tone of his voice as he discussed what it took to win.

"Hmmm," was all she said.

Later that night Brandi stood looking at a crudely drawn blueprint of the projects. She had used different colored tacks and different colored Magic Markers to indicate the territories. She had also staked out the layout of all the buildings.

The projects where she lived were simply called the Square. It had inherited that name because it was built in the shape of a square.

All it was was just one big rectangle when all was said and done.

Though its name was simple it was considered to be the most dangerous set of projects in Los Angeles. The Square was one of the deadliest pieces of real estate to exist in the country, if not the deadliest.

A lot of people like Brandi's parents hadn't moved out simply because they couldn't afford to. The rent was cheap and the size of the apartments for the price was acceptable.

The rent may have been cheap but the cost was high. Many a parent had lost a child or other family member in the name of economics.

If they weren't lost to death, they were lost in the prisons, serving fifty, sixty, and seventy-five years, a good majority of them before they ever hit twenty years old.

Just how does one begin to do fifty years?

It wasn't a subject you ever heard discussed but it was as real as day and night. The cost of it had been tallying up over the years.

The headphones were still blaring in Brandi's ears as she studied the territories. Systematically in her mind she initiated a takeover of each one.

She was pumped.

Crudely, before she fell asleep that night, she drew maps of all the surrounding businesses, too. Loot, she was just discovering, carried its own weight. It was all about the loot. Loot equaled power. Brandi was slowly deciding she wanted to be a power broker, one who didn't take any shorts.

There was little point to living if you didn't have paper. You couldn't even call it living, perhaps existing was a more apt expression for it. The world was divided into the haves and the have-nots.

Brandi didn't want to exist as her parents did, she wanted to live. It was going to take paper. It was going to take major paper, and a lot of it, to do that.

Ever since the night Q had been injured something inside of Brandi had been remolding itself. It was reshaping her thoughts and her mind.

Whereas she used to resist certain thoughts as completely negative she had now started to follow those threads of thoughts that her mind produced, at first at random and then as time went on with more regularity.

The following morning her rap music was blaring once again minus the headphones. The bass was once again shaking up the house. Heck, it was her house, too. She lived there so that should entitle her to some rights.

She woke up to the same attitude she had fallen asleep

with. Only her belligerence had taken total, final control, up-
ping the stakes on her attitude another notch or two.

Brandi's mother, Rita, stood just inside her door, staring at
her with a weary look on her face. She was thirty-five, petite,
and a real looker.

Rita was extraordinarily pretty. She always had been. She
was the kind of woman that turned heads wherever she went.
Brandi had inherited the best part of her looks.

However, whereas Rita was petite, Brandi was tall and
slender, like her dad.

Rita's looks, as extraordinary as they were, had not gotten
her out of the projects. There were days when she wished
they had. Today was one of those days as she played referee
between her husband and her daughter.

Rita sighed. She walked over to Brandi. Gently she tapped
her on her shoulder. Brandi turned to look at her, a bit an-
noyed at once again having her world interrupted at someone
else's whim. "Hi, Ma."

Rita shook her head. She walked over, turning down the
volume on the stereo so they could hear each other.

"Hi, Baby. You know your father is downstairs, throwing
another tantrum about this music. It's too loud. Besides, it is
Sunday, and you know how he likes to listen to his Gospel on
BET on Sunday mornings. He can't hear a word that is being
said in the sermon because this music is so loud."

Brandi bit her lip to keep from telling her mother she'd like
to give her father a sermon all right, but it certainly wasn't
along the lines of the one he was listening to on BET, which,
by the way, she considered an immense waste of good time.

Those preachers were getting paid.

Her dad actually thought that somebody who was getting
real money had something to say to somebody like him who
had none, or cared about anything other than checks for the
CD, tape, or whatever was currently being sold via the coveted sermon.

This time Brandi shook her head at the lack of intelligence on both her parents' part, but she refrained from spouting her feelings aloud. If they wanted to be gullible that was their business, as long as they didn't expect her to be.

Instead she decided to sulk in a manner that would be more understandable to her mother. "Daddy throws a tantrum no matter what I do. It doesn't matter. Everything I do is wrong to him."

Rita rubbed at the tension spot that was starting just at the base of her neck, creeping slowly toward her head to hit migraine level.

She was so doggone tired of the opposition between Brandi and her dad. Each of them attempted to make their point to the other. And each of them fell on the deaf ear of the other since they both wanted to prove a point. That point was that they were each right.

The two of them were more alike than they knew or liked to admit.

Exhausted by both of their antics she said, "I know. But you know how he is, Brandi."

Charles pushed Brandi's door open with a bang, interrupting their conversation. "Rita, you don't need to explain me to no child."

Although the volume was low on the stereo he walked over and turned it off anyway. Very nastily, and with an attitude to match Brandi's, he snatched the plug out of the wall.

"I can do what I want to do because this is my house, and I have a job, which, by the way, pays the bills and pays for all of this wasted electricity she's using," he yelled at the top of his lungs.

Rita rubbed her tension spot more furiously. Brandi's eyes narrowed.

"All Brandi wants to do is pump that garbage in her ears, sit in front of that computer, and roam the streets. She ain't going to be happy until she finds trouble. And you know damn well if you go looking for trouble eventually you will find it!"

Charles took a deep breath he was so angry, and then he huffed, "She ain't going to be satisfied until she winds up like Q. The insurance fixed up your car but it can't fix him. Now, can it, girl?"

That did it.

Brandi was on her feet. Just the sound of Q's name flooded her body with icy fury. She walked straight up to her father and looked him in the eye. How dare he allow Q's name to come out of his mouth in such a disrespectful manner? He didn't know a damn thing about Q.

Pure malice as well as a wild hatred arose in her eyes.

"You're always talking about how this is your house and you pay the bills. Telling me to get a job. Well, for the record"—she made sure there was an extremely nasty emphasis on the word *record* and then repeated it once again so it was nice and clear for him—"for the re-cord I don't want a job. Okay? It doesn't seem to be getting you too far."

She was so angry she couldn't trust herself to speak for a second as an image of the paralyzed Q loomed before her eyes. She turned away.

Finding her voice she raised it barely above a whisper. Finally she managed to say, "You don't know nothing about Q. So, why don't you just shut up."

Rita was shocked.

She couldn't believe her ears. She just knew Brandi hadn't told her daddy to shut up.

What was wrong with her? Maybe she needed some help to deal with Q's crisis. They sure hadn't raised her to be the way she was acting.

Sure, they had their share of problems, as did any family, but she'd never heard Brandi talk like that to either her or her father. Brandi was one of the most polite kids she knew.

And she had definitely never witnessed such a demonic—

yeah, there was no other word for it—such a demonic look on Brandi's face. Her features were twisted in hatred at her dad, and Rita knew for a fact that Brandi loved her daddy dearly. She was crazy about him.

What was going on?

She decided it must be the shock of what had happened to Q. Maybe they should be dealing with that differently. Brandi was obviously harboring some deep-rooted feelings about it that were manifesting themselves in ugly ways.

"Brandi don't—"

Charles pushed Rita out of the way before she could finish her sentence. He couldn't believe his ears. They were ringing with Brandi's last words.

She had told him to shut up. The sound of it was reverberating through his brain as though it were being shouted through a woofer on a stereo system.

"Who the hell do you think you're talking to, Brandi?"

Charles grabbed Brandi by both of her arms and shook her like a rag doll. He shook her so hard that her teeth rattled. Rita tried to pull him away but he had a serious grip on Brandi, and she couldn't loosen it. Though she tried with all her might.

Brandi screamed in his face. "Get off of me! I hate you! I said, get off of me!"

She managed to shake herself loose but only because the shock of her hatred washed over Charles, causing him to loosen his grip on her.

She went into a total rage.

She ripped clothes from the closet. She snatched her high school diploma from out of the little glass frame. She threw the glass part of it on the floor. She tore what she considered just a useless piece of paper into little tiny shreds, dropping them onto the floor like the trash she felt they were.

She stomped on the glass, smashing it before knocking everything from the dresser. Then she went over to the shelves and knocked everything from them, too.

Both Charles and Rita were frozen in place. It was akin to witnessing a cyclone develop before your eyes that you hadn't seen coming.

They were momentarily shocked by such an unusual outburst from Brandi. Her actions had rendered them temporarily incapable of doing a thing about them.

She had always been a bit headstrong. But this display of seething anger and acting out was truly out of character for her.

Finally coming to her senses Rita stepped in to try to calm her down.

Charles just stared at Brandi as though she didn't belong to him. He felt like he had only just seen Brandi for the first time in his entire life.

He was so mesmerized by her actions that he had become incapable of doing anything that he wouldn't come to deeply regret later.

He seriously wanted to slap her face. However, he was deathly afraid to put his hands on her again due to the indignation that was racing through his own body.

He couldn't believe the scene being played out in front of his eyes. Her level of disrespect coupled with her absolute carelessness for their feelings had exported him into a realm of unfamiliar ground.

This child that he had nurtured all of his life had totally flipped out. Brandi was screaming at the top of her lungs. She was screaming so loudly and strongly that her voice was turning hoarse.

Her face was so contorted that if you didn't know what she looked like it would have been difficult to decipher her features.

When she stopped the animal-like screaming long enough to speak she said, "I ain't you!" She directed this sentence straight at her dad, who was still the target of her hit list.

"I ain't going to be like you. I don't know what I'm going to do but I know what I'm *not* going to do, Daddy, and that's become a puppet like you. You're just a poor little puppet. A puppet that goes along with whatever rules have been set forth before them with no questions asked. It's just that 'them is the rules,' as you like to say."

Without even stopping to breathe she said, "And you have nothing to show for it." In pure disgust she looked around the run-down room, waving her hand in total dismissal of the shabby economic conditions they lived under.

"I'm not going to always be pulled by my strings. By other people at that, whenever they feel like it. Oh, nah. Not me. That's giving somebody else too much control, Daddy. You can't hand other people control over your life. Don't you understand that?"

She was so filled with the indignation of what she'd just said, it forced her to take a deep breath this time before she could continue speaking. "I hate you. Do you hear me? I said I hate you. You ain't stand-up, and you never will be! If your generation had stood up, then my generation wouldn't be in this position. I might not be going to college but I've studied the history of mankind, and that, what I just said, Daddy, is clear as a bell. Y'all didn't stand up."

Coldness flashed from Brandi's eyes, the tentacles of which wrapped themselves around her father. "Did y'all think two men could carry the entire ball? Martin Luther King and Malcolm X?"

Charles didn't answer. Rita covered her mouth. She'd never seen this socially angry side of her daughter. Brandi just looked at her father, not surprised that he didn't have an answer.

Her voice a whisper with the pain of what she was thinking, she said, "Two men got killed and everybody else just gave up. Is that it? Two people were expected to carry the ball for generations of people both at the time of and after their deaths?"

A picture of Q lying broken on the ground flashed before

her eyes. If somebody had stood up a hell of a lot earlier maybe this type of thing wouldn't have happened or so easily have been dismissed. What had they all been thinking?

Brandi was so pissed she spat at her father's feet in absolute, consuming disgust.

Charles had had enough. He slapped her face so hard the sound of the slap reverberated throughout the room. Brandi's ears rung. However, she was so numb with her all consuming anger and hatred she barely felt it.

Every word that left Charles's mouth was clipped and to the point. "I've had enough, Brandi. I tried to do what I could for you, but it is never enough. You have your own car; you have a computer, the latest in electronics, enough food and clothes. But that's not enough. Is it? I've practically broken my back to give you the best, worked eighteen- and nineteen-hour days, and that's not stand-up enough for you?"

Her dad didn't bother to let her answer.

"Hell nah, it isn't enough. I may not be Martin or Malcolm but damned if I haven't been here for you. I wouldn't be too proud if I were you, Brandi, because you're going to find out that you aren't running this world."

And here's when Brandi knew she'd really stung him: "And you're going to find out there isn't a person in this world whose strings haven't been pulled at one time or another. We're all puppets, as you like to call it, to some degree. But you know what? Life can teach you better than I can. Now get out!"

His last words snapped Rita awake. She had gone into a kind of trance at the exchange that was taking place between them. She'd had no idea that Brandi's feelings ran that deeply, but now she'd been awakened.

"Charles, no. She's just a child, you can't put her out."

Charles turned his back on her. "I can. I will. And I just did. Get out of my house, Brandi. Now!"

Brandi grabbed a duffel bag. She shoved clothes into it as

fast as she could. He didn't have to tell her twice. Her mother tried to stop her but she pulled away. She was sick of her father's unrelenting attitude, anyway.

"Don't go, Brandi. Your father didn't mean it."

"Don't put words in my mouth, Rita. I meant every word of it. Let her go. She's one of the only kids in this project who has both of her parents, and she doesn't appreciate us. So let her get out there and make it on her own. I brought her here, and I will damn sure take her out if she ever speaks to me like that again, so you'd better let her leave with that smart mouth of hers while you still have a child."

Brandi snatched her duffel bag, zipped it up, and pushed her way out of her bedroom door, racing down the stairs.

Chapter 5

Outside of the apartment Rita chased after Brandi, heart-broken. She shouted for her to come back into the house.

My God, she couldn't believe the level to which the situation had escalated. Brandi jumped into her car and put the key in the ignition, gunning the engine.

An icy calm had swept over her. She had no intention of going back into that house. He wanted her out, he had it. Out she was.

Rita stood at the window of her car as tears swept down her cheeks. She wept. "Brandi. Baby, please don't go."

Brandi felt some of her anger evaporate at the sight of her mother's torrid tears. She still shook her head. She knew it was time to go even though her mother was in denial, trying to hold on.

"Ma, I gotta go. It's time. Believe me, it's time. I can't take any more."

Rita swiped at a falling teardrop. She sniffled, wiping her nose with the back of her hand. Staring out onto the street she contemplated her choices.

Finally reaching a decision—not one she was satisfied with, mind you, but a choice that had to be made neverthe-less—she said, "Then just wait one minute. Okay? Please, Brandi. I just want to give you something before you go. Please. Just give me your word that you'll wait for a minute."

"Word, Ma."

Rita was satisfied. She knew that on the streets word meant bond, and in the hood that was sacred. It meant that Brandi wouldn't go anywhere until she returned.

Rita ran back into the house. Brandi sat gunning the engine. Her bottom lip trembled. She was so mad that her leg shook with the anticipation of pushing on the gas and getting the hell out of there.

She cranked up the CD player rebelliously as loud as it would go. The volume on the base rocked the back of the trunk of the car it pumped so loudly.

Charles glared angrily out of the window at Brandi. The Sunday sermon he had been trying to listen to was all but forgotten. He couldn't believe how upset and disgusted he was with his own daughter.

She was his flesh and blood. She was a daughter who had been his pride and joy. She was a daughter whom he had considered to be smart in many ways.

So much for that fantasy. She was about as dumb as they came today. She was a foolish young girl who had no idea what the world was really made of. But of one thing he was certain, and that was that she would find out.

Up in their bedroom Rita extracted a key from her bosom. She removed the lace covering from an old black trunk. She inserted the key into the lock and pulled out a huge knotted cloth that she didn't bother to open.

Next she pulled out an old, antique-looking Bible.

It was in fact generations old. It had been passed down through many a year. She had been saving it to give to Brandi when the time was right. But today seemed to be about as good a day as any.

She flipped through a few pages, saying a special prayer for her baby girl.

She locked the trunk. She re-covered it with the lace cloth. She raced out of the living room where Charles was back to watching television quietly and in peace now as though nothing had happened.

Brandi's music was blaring outside but not in his house.

Rita couldn't believe him or his nonchalant attitude about the situation. She'd deal with him later. How could he be so casual about the criticalness of the situation?

However, looks could be very deceiving because on the inside Charles's heart was breaking.

The pain was sharp and physical in nature. He could actually feel a lump forming in his chest. And the emotional cost was something he vowed to never speak of, not even to his wife. He had basically lost his daughter, and he knew it.

As well he couldn't believe he'd thrown his only daughter out of the house, but there was no turning back now. Where would she go? What would she do?

When Rita slammed the door behind her on her way out he wiped a tear from his eye.

His choice was a tough one. If he didn't put his foot down now it might cost them all a lot more later. He had no choice but to risk it. Brandi had to know she couldn't walk over them.

In that learning process she would have to grow up and become a real woman. She couldn't go on being a little girl. Not in this cold, cruel world.

He had sheltered her. Now she wanted to run out from that shelter, thinking she knew it all. She would find out.

Charles sighed and prayed to the Lord under his breath that he had made the right decision.

Rita walked up to the car. She handed Brandi the huge knotted cloth. Brandi was shocked upon unwrapping it. She found the cloth filled to the brim with one-hundred-dollar bills. She never would have expected that of her mother for some reason.

She had underestimated her. Stuffed inside of that nondescript cloth was a lot of cash. She stared at her mother in astonishment.

Rita shook her head. "That's only what it is, Brandi. Money. Nothing more and nothing less. Money is the root of all evil. Remember that. Money won't buy you happiness despite what you might think."

It's a hell of a good start, Brandi mused to herself.

Rita looked across at what horizon she could see from the projects.

"The most important thing I have to give you is this." She handed Brandi the Bible.

"This will take you places that neither your father or I can. It will protect you when neither of us can, either. The words in *red* are living life. They are the words of Jesus, the living Christ. You'll just have to trust me on that for now, since you don't know for yourself."

Brandi took the Bible. It held little meaning for her but she didn't want to hurt her mother's feelings. Right then her mind was wrapped around that cash.

"Thanks, Mommy."

Before she could break her resolve to leave her mother, she simply said, "I'll see you around."

She sped away from the curb, careening on two wheels around the corner.

When she was out of sight she pulled the car over to the curb. She picked up the Bible from the front seat, jumped out of the car, and threw it into the trunk, slamming the trunk shut. Out of sight, out of mind.

She couldn't be riding around with a Bible on the front seat of her car, not with what she was thinking.

Rita arrived back in the living room to find the strongest man she'd ever known weeping.

Brandi decided to make her way into the very heart of South Central, the place where she knew the formulation of her plan would be do or die.

And where she knew for a fact that only the strong survived.

Chapter 6

Brandi cruised through the hood watching the activity on the streets, observing the players acting out their reputations. They postured, protecting their status as well as their territories.

She relished the game from the viewpoint of an avid student. She was a student, one who needed to learn—and learn quickly.

She saw the haves and the have-nots.

There were, of course, the wannabes and the ones who had once been or used to wannabe.

They played the game either in their own minds or with each other. It didn't matter, one way or the other the game got played. It went on, and on, and on, and on.

That was level one.

Level two was where the real danger lay. The game was being played with a capital G. And any fool knew it wasn't for the faint of heart.

The more money and affront to the prestige and power of those who played for keeps, the more dangerous and treacherous and deep were the waters, so to speak.

Brandi's limbs were stiff from sitting in the car, planning, and observing. She decided to visit Tata. Her real name was Tatiana.

Tatiana was named after some foreign African princess her mother had learned about long ago. Tata's mother was dead, but the legacy of the name she'd given her lived on.

There weren't that many people who knew about no African princess called Tatiana, if such a person really existed. But Tatiana's mother had claimed she did before she had died.

She'd insisted she could name her child whatever she wanted to name her, as was her right, so she did. But everyone called Tatiana Tata for short.

Tata's mother had always been strong-willed, and she remained that way until her very public death. Tata was a lot like her in this manner.

Tata lived alone. She was a fifth-generation projects girl, and she had "inherited" her apartment.

Tata had been pretty much raising herself and living alone since she was fifteen—since the fatal day of her mama's demise. She had lied, connived, and schemed to stay in the apartment where she and her mother had lived. Only in the last year had she really become old enough.

Brandi had a feeling she felt close to her mother there, and didn't want to leave the last place where her spirit and memories resided.

Tata wasn't known for her feelings, but Brandi suspected this bit of insightful information might be true about her.

Brandi had known Tata Davis for as long as she could remember. Tata was nineteen years old. She hadn't been in a classroom for as long as she could get away with it. The teachers couldn't stand her when she had been in school with all of her mouth, and her I-could-care-less attitude.

Most of the kids, even in various parts of South Central where they had all been reared, were scared to death of her.

She had once beat a girl in a music class down to the ground with a trombone. She beat her into a seizurelike state. That incident alone had solidified her reputation for craziness, erasing any doubts that might have lingered.

That incident, along with a multitude of other unidentified and unprovable injury-related episodes.

Also her skills with a blade were legendary.

Brandi hadn't rolled with her all that much in the past because she had a death-struck attitude that used to annoy the hell out of her.

However, Brandi had always admired as well as respected her heart. No matter what the circumstances were Tata Davis had a reputation for being stand-up.

Her mother had been like that, too. They didn't bow to pressure when the going got tough.

She had a rep for going it alone when things got heated. She'd never ratted out her counterparts in any troubled episode.

And a big plus was that Tata was difficult to scare under any circumstances. Life didn't mean anything to her. She wasn't scared to die. Once the fear of death was taken away from a person, there was very little one could do to hurt them.

Brandi was thinking that attitude Tata had on her just might be extremely useful if channeled properly. She was hard-core to the bone with a heart made of ice. This made her the perfect choice for Brandi's plan.

Brandi stood on Tata's front porch and banged on her door. Her mind was made up.

Tata Davis was an extremely beautiful girl, one who under different life circumstances might have been living in a palace, without a worry in the world, instead of in the hood.

Tata arrived at the door. She rolled her exquisite golden-brown eyes upon seeing Brandi's usually no-show behind.

She observed Brandi from behind a glint of steel. "What's up?"

"Me," Brandi replied, matching steel for steel.

Tata was rather intrigued by this new Brandi standing in front of her, her voice filled with attitude. Ms. MBA and all that. Tata saw that even the way she carried herself and the way she stood were different. She stepped out to Brandi on the porch.

"Yeah?"

Brandi didn't move. "Did I stutter? Yeah."

Tata watched a hydraulic-driven low rider drag down the street. She reflected on the fine specimen behind the wheel. He winked. Tata didn't.

Finally she returned her attention to Brandi. "All right. Let's hear what you've got."

Inside Tata's room Brandi had to step over piles of CDs and clothes that were strewn across the floor. A stereo system was the only item of luxury in the room.

There were two twin beds with shabby covers on them that had not just seen better days but had seen all the days they needed to see.

They should have been in the garbage on their way out to the dump.

Posters of some of the hardest-core gangster rappers in the industry plastered Tata's walls. The rougher the lyrics, the harder the beat, the more respect Tata had for the rapper.

The evidence of that was plastered all over her walls and in the CDs. Rap was a religion to Tata. And if you weren't authentic and hard to the core you were not in her collection.

As well if you hadn't been shot, near dead, or stabbed one hundred times, and lived to tell about it, she didn't want to hear from you. Period.

You couldn't holler at Tata on wax if you were a punk.

She was also an avid basketball fan. She followed all the games. You'd better not even think of bothering her when there were championship games being played.

Tata flopped down on one of the twin beds, indicating the other one for Brandi.

She propped one shiny red brand-new Air Jordan sneaker on top of the other on the wall, laying her head back on a pillow. Her Air Jordans were the only other evidence of a luxury item in the room. The ones propped on her feet were two bills all day long.

Brandi sat on the other bed, determination reflecting from her eyes while icicles formed in her spirit. She knew once she crossed this border there was definitely no turning back.

Everyone reached a crossroad at one point or another in his or her life. This was definitely hers.

It wasn't the one she would have ordinarily chosen, given a decent choice.

The reality was that not everyone received a choice. She hadn't. Being poor and black had certainly not been her choice of existence. But it was a hand she had been dealt nonetheless. Now she would have to play it.

So in light of this revelation she had decided to play it for all it was worth. The only thing she had to lose was her life, which she didn't mind giving up under the circumstances.

Hers was a life of constant struggle and conflict. So were her parents' lives. She decided without a doubt she didn't consider that a life.

Brandi's gaze strayed to the dresser where an automatic gun with a clip in it was prominently displayed. She contemplated it for a brief second before returning her attention to Tata.

Tata watched her every movement like a tiger stalking its prey.

"How many girls can you round up?"

"Plenty. Why?"

"Cuz I asked, that's why."

Tata snatched her Air Jordans from the wall. She sat up on her bed with an expression that said she had little to no tolerance for people who challenged her.

Her eyes strayed to the automatic sitting on her dresser. With coldness lacing every word she asked, "What you say?"

Brandi was as calm as the wind before a storm that attacked with a vengeance. She'd observed Tata's glance at the automatic. If she reached for it Brandi would take her life before she could touch it.

It was as simple as that. One deathblow to her windpipe, and it would be over. She'd walk out of the house leaving her body there.

Brandi had been a student of the marshal arts since she'd learned how to walk, courtesy of her father.

He had never intended for her to use it in the way she was preparing to. He had only wanted her to know how to protect herself in a tough neighborhood. As well he respected the rigid discipline that marshal arts taught a person.

As a result Brandi was well trained in the art of self-defense. The choice of how to use it was hers, and she had made her decision.

The threat that was reflected on Tata's face was no match for the debilitating hatred that resided in Brandi's heart. Against her will a picture of Q, broken and crumpled on the ground, flashed before Brandi's eyes. "You heard what I said, Tata."

Brandi stood up. So did Tata. There was a subtle shift in the room. Brandi made the first move, stepping directly up in Tata's face.

Tata was ready to knock the hell out of her. Nobody got up in her face like that. What the hell was wrong with Brandi?

And this wasn't the Brandi she thought she knew. This Brandi was like some damn machine. She was a stranger residing in Brandi's body. Something wasn't right. And that same something told Tata to hold her peace.

Her adrenalin was racing out of control, though, so Brandi had better make it quick.

"Tata, I didn't come here for a pissing match, or for a battle of the wills, or for a proving contest between us of who is the toughest. I came here because I have a plan. A plan that is going to change a lot of lives. Yours included if you're down."

Brandi paused for effect to give Tata a second to reflect on her words. She wanted what she'd said to sink in.

"Because I have something that you *don't,* that makes me the leader and you second in command. If you aren't with this point now, just let me know and I can be walking out of here. I don't have any time to waste. Straight up."

Tata hesitated.

The sheer audacity of this heifer. She was mad but intrigued. She popped the gum that was in her mouth, rolled her eyes at Brandi, then flopped back down on the bed, again propping her Air Jordans up on the wall.

"All right, MBA, lay it down. Let's see how it sounds. I'm gonna give you something I don't usually give people. That's the benefit of the doubt. Speak."

Brandi walked over to the window and pulled back the curtain, looking at the GMC Jeep parked in Tata's driveway. "That's a smart Jeep."

"You're a smart girl. Let's hear what ya got," Tata said, now anxious to hear this plan that Brandi seemed ready to die for, especially getting up in her face.

Brandi left the window.

"I want to control the income flow in this part of South Central as well as in the Square. By that I mean every dime of it. One way or the other. By whatever means it takes. And that is just for starters. Consider it the appetizer."

Brandi paced the tile floor in Tata's bedroom.

"I also want to pull as many of the sister gangs as possible together to form one gang. They would reside under one leadership. That leader would be me"—and here she paused for emphasis—"and you, Tata."

The sound of her name attached to a top position most definitely had Tata's interest. But she played it cool so she could hear Ms. MBA's entire plan.

"There of course will be some we won't get. Others we don't want. And still others that we will take over their turfs once the plan is in effect.

"There's power in numbers. Each member will take a vow of silence. They will take a vow to protect one another as though each of our lives were their very own. They will take a vow to pursue the highest level of learning possible. I will train them in the art of how to be in control of their minds and in control of their bodies."

Brandi glanced at Tata to make sure that she had her rapt and fascinated attention. Tata hadn't taken her eyes off of Brandi since she'd started speaking.

What she'd listened to so far was the best thing she'd heard since the invention of peanut butter and jelly.

"There will be exercising and more exercising. I'm talking walking, running, jogging, complete physical workouts, as well as complete medical physicals. Every member has to be in tip-top shape. They have to be as lithe and limber, and as dangerous as alley cats. They have to be hand-picked, Tata."

And here is where Brandi added her greatest emphasis. "They can't be afraid to die."

Tata just stared at her, emotionless.

"There will be no drinking of alcohol, no smoking of any kind including cigarettes, no cracking, piping, coking, re-mixing, heroin, sniffing, shooting, breezing, or whatever the hell it is that everybody is doing with that mess. The rule is zero tolerance. Period."

Brandi was absolutely mesmerizing as she laid out her plan to Tata. She had such a draw that she could have been speaking on a street corner or at the United Nations.

It wouldn't have mattered. The girl had the brains, the heart, and the charisma to do this. Though Tata would never admit it as long as she lived, she was stunned.

And the sound of sweet *chi-ching* was definitely ringing in her ears.

"The only thing being done will be making m-o-n-e-y, and plenty of it," Brandi continued.

While she paced Tata listened. The bond needed between

the two young women to solidify this union was forming with every word that was leaving Brandi's mouth.

"We will learn how to use every available weaponry. The most important weapon is the mind. The mind is first and foremost. The second weapon is the body. Everything else comes after that.

"Including those," she said, indicating the automatic lying on the dresser.

"Tata, we are going to lock and grip the drug trades as well as everything else that makes money around here. We're going to provide protection to the businesses in our neighborhoods for a price. This way while everybody is out kicking it on the block we can be getting phat paid at the same time.

"Our names will be ringing. And people will know that we're the generation to bow down to. We ain't taking no shorts like our parents did. We're going to take over, solidify and represent. You know what I mean?"

Tata nodded but didn't speak.

She wasn't sure she could have spoken, such was her shock at the words that were leaving Brandi's mouth. Somebody had created a monster in this girl. It worked for Tata, she was down for getting the bank and being in control.

Brandi strayed for an instant. "One day maybe we'll knock down the projects, and build some real houses and playgrounds around there."

Tata pursed her lips on this statement but that was all. She wasn't big on idealism. She just wanted the cash.

Recovering, Brandi said, "The finances are in place on my part to make the start. Finance and discipline are the new names of the game. The one I'm creating. We need to be controlling things up in here. And this is where it starts."

Finally Tata said, "You'll be stepping on toes."

Brandi gave her a deadly look. "They'd better be worried about stepping on mine. We'll work deals where they have to be made. Everything will be in our total control. As I already said I ain't taking no shorts. We will do what we have to do. That will send a message to everybody else."

Tata sat up on the edge of her bed.

"Start looking for burial ground, Tata. There are bound to be some diehards once we set it off."

Tata's attention riveted on Brandi.

It was a damn good plan, and she knew it. Plus she knew they could do it. With her and Brandi at the helm, the loot and power would be piling up faster than you could spell m-o-n-e-y.

It was too bad she hadn't thought of it herself and didn't have the loot to kick it off because then she could have been the leader.

But the truth being told, she had to admit to herself that Brandi had something that she didn't. And that something was a special draw along with an extreme amount of intelligence.

Brandi was a natural-born leader. And she would run the gangs and the setting up of a criminal empire as though she were building a corporation.

Which was intriguing in itself because Tata knew that in the hood that was not how the game was played. Brandi had come to the game with a leg up already just in how she thought.

Tata knew she would never have come up with the idea for the type of training and discipline Brandi was talking about in readying the gangs and solidifying them as one unit.

That alone was sheer brilliance.

She'd knock down a good portion of the competition with that one single stroke.

Had Tata been in control they would have just started strewing bodies all over the place and immediately taking over.

With the patience and discipline Brandi was talking about,

their people would be more than ready when they hit the streets.

Tata would bring her own brand of brilliance to that kind of war because she knew every crook, cranny, alleyway, and corner of the streets, and then some.

She also knew where most of the bodies were buried.

Which meant she could locate burial ground, if needed, that no one had even thought of yet. A hundred years could pass by, and any body she had been a part of burying wouldn't be found.

What Tata didn't know was that Brandi planned on having Fishbone's backing, which meant seriously minimizing the death roll, if there had to be any. Fishbone's name carried great weight and would back niggas off as though a bomb had hit the area.

Tata was still weighing out Brandi's plan. Hell, with the single move of solidifying the gangs alone Brandi was talking about creating an army, their very own army, right smack in the heart of the hood.

What could be better than that?

Tata couldn't believe her change in luck. A war commander was what she would be because that's exactly what she was. She would be a street general. And, she knew that was why Brandi had sought her out.

That and her reputation for being die-hard loyal. Because what Brandi was proposing meant there would be prison time, maybe even death for some, unless somehow they pulled it all off without a hitch.

Tata was nobody's fool. It wouldn't happen. If you shook hands with the Devil, then you had to expect to pay. But, damn if they couldn't ride the tide as high as it went until that handshake ran out and that payment became due.

Brandi wasn't the only thinker. Tata made up her mind on the spot if it came down to it she would hold court in the streets. She would die representing because that's who she was. It was that simple.

Second in command under these circumstances wouldn't be too bad. She could live with that. Next to Brandi, she'd be making the most money and have the most power.

Tata opened her mouth to speak. Nothing came out so she shut it.

Brandi watched her intently, never saying another word. Allowing her to come to her own decisions. She knew a person's decision to risk their life as well as their freedom should be their own. A decision like that shouldn't be made by anybody except that person.

Finally, Tata said, "If you're planning this I guess I don't have to ask if you made the home break from your daddy or not?"

She knew Brandi's daddy was overprotective.

"No, you don't," Brandi replied sarcastically, hearing a name that had no place in her present thoughts and decided course of action.

Without warning Tata threw a deathblow kick aimed directly at Brandi's throat. If she connected it would take her out.

Brandi moved so fast the speed of her move happened like a blur. Something you thought you saw but that happened so fast you couldn't be sure if you'd really seen it or not.

She neatly blocked the kick, holding Tata's foot in a break-lock grip. She wasn't even exerted or phased one way or the other.

Brandi didn't care. She knew her self-defense, plain and simple. And she was ready to die for what she believed in.

Tata nodded her head at Brandi. For the first time she smiled.

"I'm in."

Brandi released the break-lock grip on her foot.

"Good. Let's get to work, then."

Chapter 7

The next recruit in the lineup was Tangie. However, she was an easy decision. It was no contest. She was Brandi's girl. That was just how it was, so that was that. She was also not to be underestimated. Tangie was shrewd in her own right.

As well she would follow wherever Brandi went. That was just how they were with each other. She was a great asset. One because Fishbone was her brother. And two because she was a steadier, older-type personality than both Brandi and Tata. She wasn't quite as flighty as the two of them.

When it came time for the need of a little grounding, Tangie would be the one with the skills and would know how to provide that.

By virtue of Fishbone being her brother she alone had the capability of rounding up the type of street presence on the male side of the fence that even a military commander might have admired.

The importance of this, given the course they had decided to embark upon, could and would not be ignored.

Tangie was loyal to a fault as well, if she cared about you. So that secured her place in the top ranks of the gang because Brandi was like a sister to her, and she loved her as such.

Now, as for Tata, Tangie actually wasn't as crazy about her.

However, under the new game that was going down she understood Tata's value and position in the organization.

As such she admitted to herself it was a good flash of insight on Brandi's part making her second in command.

Tata wouldn't hesitate to do whatever needed to be done to ensure they were always on the winning side. They would be well protected under her command. And she was one down chick when it came to combat.

Also Tata was stand-up. She would give an order and deal with whatever circumstances came to be or whatever the outcome was because of it. Tangie knew that about Tata without a doubt.

That night the three of them snuck back to Brandi's parents' home and through her bedroom window once Brandi determined the coast was clear.

Her parents slept like rocks. As long as they were quiet Brandi knew that her parents wouldn't realize that they were even in the house. This obviously had its good and bad sides. Good in that Brandi could get into the house to do what she needed and be gone without a conflict. Bad in that the wrong people could have gotten into the house as well and done the same thing or worse.

Once inside Brandi's bedroom Tangie and Tata sat on the bed looking around at the disaster of her room. They both decided it must have been one nasty fight she had had with her parents because her room looked like a war zone.

Tata popped her gum while smiling at the disaster they were sitting in. Tangie nudged her to remind her to be quiet. Tata put her hand over her mouth in compliance. In a staged whisper she said, "Looks like my girl went on a rampage up in here."

"Yeah, you're right. At this rate she might turn into a female Fishbone."

Tata smiled at the mere sound of Fishbone's name. He was the one man she wouldn't have minded trying out that true-to-the-game, romanticized, a-woman-is-down-with-her man thing with. She had fantasized about him plenty of times.

"Fishbone is fine as hell, girl. Your brother is the man. Plenty a loot, and he's a world-class leader."

Tangie laughed.

She was used to women drooling over Fishbone, but she definitely wasn't used to Tata daydreaming about no man out loud. This new plan of Brandi's was going to take some getting used to.

Tata laughed, too.

She had her own plans for Fishbone when the time came. Looked like that opportunity might present itself one helluva lot faster than what she had originally thought. Being this close to Tangie meant definite access to Fishbone.

For a hot minute she sweated about the low rider she'd seen earlier while talking to Brandi on her front porch. She immediately decided against that, especially with this new plan off the hook and in effect.

The last thing they needed on their minds were men who could distract them.

Besides she knew Brandi would throw a hissy fit because of all her rules. Which included being at the top of your game and at your top fitness level.

That translated into the reasoning that a whole lot of flesh hitting flesh was going to have to stop, especially in the initial takeover, unless somebody wanted to get killed.

When you were getting ready to get down the way they were planning, a man could be in the way. He could also compromise your position knowingly or unknowingly, and that definitely could not happen.

So hitting it off with them was definitely going to have to be on lock. Some of their takeovers could be in direct conflict.

As it was they were going to have to use some woman to get underneath those who were holding it down. They certainly couldn't be one of those women.

Tata sighed out loud at the thought of foregoing that activity for a while, but she knew Brandi was right.

If they were going to be a team that meant they all had to respect each other and be down as one unit. Otherwise, it would be divide and conquer. Any good general or war commander knew that.

Brandi retrieved her wrinkled plans from where she'd hid them behind the mirror, taped down securely. She spread them out on the bed allowing Tata and Tangie to take in the visual markings while she turned on her computer. She turned off the volume.

Brandi sat down once the game was in place. She played as though the other two girls were not even in the room with her, like she was alone.

The only sound in the room was the sound of Brandi's heavy breathing as she exerted herself in a war to win. Tata and Tangie watched the violent graphics flash in multicolors across the screen as the bodies continuously dropped and piled up at the speed of light.

Firepower lit the screen in constant flashes. Death trailed those on the screen who would challenge it. The same would happen for those off the screen.

On and on Brandi played until finally they all saw the words at the same time:

YOU ARE THE NEW CONQUEROR. YOU WIN.

Brandi turned around from the game to stare each of them in their eyes. "That's our new posse. Welcome to the Conquerors!"

Tangie noticed the same look in Brandi's eyes that she had seen in the eyes of her brother a million times, with one subtle difference. Brandi's eyes were ablaze with fire.

"We will win by securing the area as well as by mental and physical force," Brandi whispered with a fervor found among military forces.

Tata matched her fervor. "Damn straight we will."

Tangie only nodded as they all stacked their hands on top

of one another's with Brandi's on top, vowing that they would die for one another if need be.

It was on now. They had all bought into it.

Together they rolled up the blueprint of Brandi's plan, climbed back out of the window, and went to their new headquarters. It was a headquarters that had already been secured by the very capable Tata Davis.

Chapter 8

Before too much time had passed their warehouse head-quarters was full of young black females.

Brandi wasn't too fond of the word *gang*. To her it made them sound as if they were street hoodlums who didn't know what they were doing.

Gang also had an elementary school sound to it in her opinion. It reminded her of her days on the school playground when she had been trying to avoid bullies.

She much preferred the term *posse*. Yeah. Posse. It had a slicker, sleeker feel to it. She had always been one who liked to go her own way. She was not a crowd follower.

Everybody they needed and wanted on board was. They had all agreed to band together as one unit. They had each vowed they would be like adhesive and stick like glue.

There were a few female gangs still out there, either because they hadn't been chosen or they hadn't chosen to be a part, but so be it, you couldn't have it all.

The Street Laws, the main gang that was still on the streets, had been rejected by Brandi as being too ghetto. Their leader, Left Eye, didn't have the stamina for the type of discipline Brandi wanted to build. So they hadn't even received an invite.

Every female who was a part of Brandi's posse and was in

the house had been personally recruited and scrutinized, their security checked—then medically checked, and determined to be in tip-top physical shape and general health.

They had each accepted all the vows put forth before them without recourse or resistance.

Each one had been determined to have a particular skill. A skill that was useful to the group as a whole. They all possessed one very important trait: each and every one of them cared less than nothing about dying, simply because most of them had never lived. And as the saying goes, you can't miss what you've never really had.

They all had a singular vision. They were united in a single focus as well as devoted to this venture Brandi had put together.

There wasn't one of them who wouldn't do what it took to make the vision a reality. That was why they had been handpicked and chosen.

The warehouse space Tata had secured was huge. It had the perfect accommodations for what they needed, seclusion being at the top of the list.

It was filled to the brim with young black females who had been assembled together for one purpose.

They were all dressed in deep-red spandex leotards with jet-black tights. They all had deep-red silk shirts tied around their waists and jet-black leg warmers.

They were wearing black military boots polished to the highest of shines. The shine was so high on those boots, they would have made the originators of the shoe shine proud.

Each girl had spit-shined her own pair of boots in the same manner as in the days of old. The boots were so shiny you could actually see your reflection in them.

Had it not been for the boots and the expressions on their faces, anybody looking at them could have easily mistaken them for ballerina dancers.

They each had a red scarf tied around their heads in bandanna fashion with black caps covering the scarves. Emblazoned in sterling silver across the front of the caps were the words THE CONQUERORS.

Brandi surveyed the crowd of girls in the warehouse. She was pumped. Her dream was standing in front of her so close she could reach out and touch it.

She had a room full of young, energetic girls. They were all under her command. They were all ready to do what it took to be at the top of the game. Controlling, not being controlled, this was what she had been trying to tell her daddy about.

Each girl that was in the warehouse was ready to undertake developing the mental stamina it took to lead, to take, to be a force to be reckoned with.

Brandi was proud of each and every one of them for this reason. Because she knew they would need all of that and then some.

Respect she knew wasn't something that was easy to come by. She had earned the respect of every individual in the room.

R-E-S-P-E-C-T.

South Central (Watts) was about to find out what it meant, Brandi style.

In addition to all of this she knew she was very fortunate because she had managed to foster in them the need for as well as the importance of respecting each other for their capabilities as well as for themselves. No easy feat regardless of how you looked at it.

"Ladies, you all know why you're here." Brandi stood in front of the room facing them, calculating the strengths and weaknesses of each girl.

The strengths she would capitalize on. The weaknesses she would build into strengths. In turn those same strengths would reach out to others and become collective strengths.

One voice. They would become one for all and all for one. If you took one of them down you'd have to take them all.

All of the women were focused on Brandi. There wasn't a single, solitary sound in the room save her voice. They stood at rapt attention with military precision, their eyes cast forward as though waiting for God himself to sanction them.

Their shoulders were back, their heads were tilted in a sense of pride.

They waited. They listened intently to Brandi's every word. More than that they listened carefully to the very timbre of her voice the modulation of her words, even the volume at which each syllable was spoken.

Their collective intensity was something rarely seen or heard of as one unit.

So far Brandi had taught them well. She had inspired them into being one unit, into regenerating themselves as a single unit with one goal.

Now the time had come to separate the women from the girls. And this ritual had to be done because, as any gardener worth his garden tools knew, there must always be pruning and weeding of the garden.

Phase 1.

Brandi studied the rhythm of each girl's body. Though there was no movement, she could determine each of their rhythms instinctively as if she herself lived inside each one of them.

"If there is anyone in this room who is having second thoughts, leave now," she stated icily. Her words held absolutely no emotion, it was just a volume of sound rising up from a bottomless well.

No one moved.

Brandi surveyed the women callously, purposely, and coldly. Her gaze stopped on certain individuals in her precise calculation.

"If there is anyone in this room who is scared to die, leave now. Just get out," she said, testing her power with them.

There was absolute and total silence. Not one sigh or

breath could be heard in the room. And not one of the girls in that room made a move to leave.

"If you're worried about your mama, your baby, or your baby's daddy, you shouldn't be here. Leave right now," she said with the sort of nastiness that would test anybody in the hood regarding his or her mama.

Again, not one of them moved.

A small smile played itself across Brandi's lips. "Tata."

Tata left the front row. Brandi held out her hand. Tata placed a straight razor in it. Brandi slashed her wrist, a deep, rushing gash, without the blink of an eye and without any forewarning.

She stood there with her blood dripping on the floor of the warehouse.

Like a wary wolf she watched the girls in the room, gauging their reactions, looking for a sign. There were none. There was absolutely, emphatically no reaction at all on any of their parts.

She could have chosen to bleed to death and not one of them would have moved. They were so resolute she could have poured a glass of water and gotten more of a reaction.

"The blood you see dripping onto the floor is not mine." She paused.

She searched for puzzled looks to her words.

There were none. The girls waited stoically.

"It's yours," she continued in her monotone. "If my blood is spilled so is yours. If your blood is spilled so is mine."

A bomb could have dropped in that warehouse and still not moved those young women. Each of them had seen enough heartache, abuse, and unfairness to last them a lifetime, and not one of them was twenty years old yet.

Nothing would move them, short of their mission.

"Tata," Brandi called again.

Tata emerged yet again. She took the straight razor from Brandi. Then she tied a red silk scarf around Brandi's wound to stem the flow of blood, which was quite a bit at this point.

Brandi herself was so resolute, so intent on making her point, that she wasn't even affected by the loss of so much blood.

Once the tying off of the blood flow was completed Tata took her place in the front row again.

Before the sound of Brandi's voice could be heard again in the warehouse Tata slashed her own wrist—and stood there with the blood dripping.

There was total silence.

In fact the silence was so loud it was almost deafening, as only total silence can be.

After a time Tata laid down the razor on a nearby table. She tied up her wound with a red silk scarf. There was dead silence in the warehouse as the young women continued to observe these procedures.

Finally, they were thinking, *someone felt their pain and was taking them seriously.* As far as they were concerned it had been a long time in coming.

Tangie, who was also in the front row, averted her eyes for a minute after glancing at Brandi and Tata's pools of blood rapidly staining the warehouse floor.

As though there hadn't been any blood spilled at all and this was the least of what would be spilled, Brandi said, "It is a pleasure to see that all of you ladies are on time. I detest tardiness for any reason. If you're not dead, then you need to be here on time. If you are dead, then someone needs to bring your body so we can see that."

Brandi started her ritual pacing. This was her serious think mode. She always got it on when she was about to say something that was of the utmost importance to her.

"When you serve in *my* world, tardiness can cost you your life. A split second of wrong timing on the streets, and you are no more. It is as simple as that. Got it?"

The girls all nodded their heads collectively as one unit.

"I intend to train you in the art of real discipline so that one of those split seconds I was just talking about never happens to you."

"Timing, rigid control, and discipline will be our saving grace. So every single day you need to be here at the crack of dawn. As I said, even death won't be an excuse. If you're dead find somebody to drop off your body. Be ready to roll once you arrive."

Brandi stopped pacing to stare at them. She was a long-time student of the effects of yoga, fasting, proper diet, mind control, and world-class leadership during different centuries—not to mention war tactics, and not just the ones she played on her computer.

Now it was all going to pay off.

"There are no exceptions to this rule. Let the workouts begin."

At Brandi's words the warehouse suddenly came to life as though a bunch of mannequins had suddenly had their ON buttons pushed and could now move.

They gathered in formation with Tata and Tangie in the lead, running around the vast warehouse in unison. Their boots slapped the cement floor in time and rhythm just as they had been instructed. They ran like a well-trained drill team.

Brandi watched them all with a keen sharp eye. She judged their wind and distance. She timed them. She ascertained who would be good on the sprint for speed, and who would be best for going the distance, for wind control.

She called out to them, pushing, urging them on, and building their stamina. She pushed them toward their absolute limit of physical endurance.

She knew they were made of more than what they credited themselves for.

She had nutritional menus that would be passed out to each of them to follow religiously, and these, too, would assist in building them to where they needed to be for their undertaking.

They worked the bars, the mats, the treadmills, the weights, and all of the other equipment that had been secured for their workouts, well-being, and overall health.

Private, very well-paid, hand-selected trainers had been brought in for martial arts training, and for training in weaponry and artillery.

This would continue until they were honed into the machines that were needed for this kind of a task.

Finally Brandi took her attention off of the formation. Her mind flitted to another issue at hand. She called out to Tangie. "Tangie, I need to see you for a minute."

Tangie left the lineup. She walked over to Brandi.

"Set up a meeting with Fishbone, okay? I need to make sure him and his people get their share, and that none of his people get hit. We've got to keep the heat off."

Tangie hugged Brandi. Then she walked over to the table where Tata had placed the razor. She slashed her own wrist. She stood with the blood dripping, looking at Brandi.

Brandi unwrapped the silk scarf from her own wrist, tying it around Tangie's. "Word, girlfriend. Word."

Brandi knew in that instant Tangie would die for her no matter what the cause was.

Chapter 9

After all the brutal mechanics of the strictest of discipline they'd had to endure, including a trip to the mountains where they had been tested to the absolute ends of their physical endurance and survival skills, they were finally ready to tackle the giant looming in front of them.

And when ready was ready it was ready.

Brandi had left no stone unturned. She'd had an extremely successful meeting with Fishbone. She'd been given the green light for her selected territories.

Her posse was raking in the cash like the smoothness of rich butter, like cream that was made to flow, splashing its thick, velvety richness from a carton with no end in sight.

The money machines were churning.

She couldn't believe how easy it had been. Well, it had almost been easy. Looked at from a different perspective it might almost have seemed too easy, but Brandi was psyched from finally toppling an obstacle instead of an obstacle toppling her, so all she could see were the bright lights ahead.

Props had been paid. Respect had been given where due. And payoffs that were a must and that needed to be in place were.

Collections from a number and variety of businesses were a steady stream of revenue for the posse. As Brandi sat at her computer night after night contemplating the numbers, it was like watching the Dow Jones rise, and rise, as though it could never fall.

She was in effect Ms. Wall Street herself.

She was so high on the smell of the money she had made an Excel pie chart to reflect the influx of cash flow, and it was astonishing at the rate it was flowing in. Her girls were the absolute bomb. They were South Central's newest divas.

And everyone wanted to be in bed with the slickest crew this side of the Santa Monica Pier, in a manner of speaking. All those who could be, were.

The Generation was in effect. Bow down.

Brandi was ecstatic. She made personal visits into some of the neighborhoods at collection time just so she could feel the adrenalin and see the looks of pride from her own people for herself.

Of course, not everyone was happy. But, then again, you couldn't please everyone. Could you?

On one particular day a middle-aged southern woman, who went by the name of Frenchie, had greeted her. She beckoned the smartly dressed Brandi over to her counter with a smile on her face.

Brandi was dressed as though she'd just left the penthouse suite of one of Los Angeles's top corporations. She had a sleek leather carrying pouch to touch off the effect of her total look.

The most elite of corporate America residing on Wilshire Boulevard didn't have anything on her.

Just because her business was primarily run in the hood didn't mean she had to run around looking like a hood rat. No. Business was business, and business begat more business if you knew how to work it.

Respect.

She made people feel as if they were dealing with a legitimate entity, not an illegal one, because of the way she carried herself. Mind control. You were what you thought you were. And people thought you were what you projected. Image.

To Brandi the image you put forth was a big part of winning. And now was her time to shine. So in effect she was all that and then some.

She had achieved the domino effect. It was one of the most impressive strategies she had ever seen. It was the ultimate in waging a war. She had learned that the cascade effect was absolute. And she wasn't even twenty years old yet.

You built up the dominos, toppled over the first one, and all the rest of them followed, falling into place. Bingo.

She was extremely well put together from head to toe, and she generated a sense of both class and style. It was inbred in her. It was simply in her genes.

Her crystal nail tips shone with the brilliance of color and design as though she were the only thing on anyone's mind.

Word on the street was that Brandi was the mastermind behind a whole lot of new things that were going down in their hood. It was like a new sheriff had come to town, as Frenchie had started to think of Brandi.

She liked Brandi's spunk. Secretly, she wished she had her heart. But more than that she admired her mind. She was young, and you could see that her mind worked with precision-like calculation.

She knew exactly what she wanted. She had made up her mind to get it by any means available. Using the word *necessary* was too old a cliché for Brandi.

In addition to all of this, to Frenchie she was an extremely beautiful young lady, one that it was hard to take your eyes off of.

She had that something that was hard to define but was very definitely there, nevertheless.

Brandi had a special air about her that invited you into her domain, yet kept you at the appropriate distance.

She was tall, flawless, and in total command. A position that people twice and even thrice her age hadn't reached.

In her way of southern hospitality and out of loyalty, Frenchie glanced at the door to watch Brandi's back. Then she smiled before she beckoned Brandi over.

She needn't have bothered watching Brandi's back because that was already in place and in effect outside and inside the store.

Frenchie would have been surprised to know that some of the customers in her store at that moment were trained young killers. They were without any doubt young female gangsters without a thing to lose.

In an instant they would have launched an attack that would have left nothing breathing in the store, including the dog watching them laconically from his corner, if Brandi was threatened in any way.

Brandi had not only managed to inspire loyalty but also a certain bonded type of love in her following.

The entire area was on lockdown when Brandi entered, and undercover snipers covered the area. One nod of Brandi's head and a person wouldn't be able to get in or out of that area.

Brandi was a formidable opponent even to men. And to that effect she had two very special gems on her side. She was young, and she knew her own mind. It was not to be messed with.

In her strong, southern-accented stage whisper, so as not to be overheard, Frenchie said, "Child, I'm sure glad we ain't got to worry no more since you came around to protect us. There ain't been no robberies in this area since you did. Shoot, I can count my money at night without even locking my door since BB."

Brandi frowned, not understanding what she was talking about. What the heck was BB?

Frenchie grinned. "That means since *Before Brandi*." In

Frenchie's world among her peers this was the highest form of respect, as Brandi well knew.

Brandi shook her head modestly, though she was disturbed by the reference more than she would have liked to be. However, she could never let that on.

She had left that life, as well as any teachings of the Gospel, far behind the moment she left her parents' house and put a gun in her hand, taking a stand against everything good she had ever been taught.

It didn't matter, Frenchie was oblivious, anyway. She would never have noticed the slight uncomfortable twinge Brandi had given off.

"A godsend. Yep, girl, that is what you are, I've decided. A godsend."

She handed Brandi an envelope stuffed to the brim with cash. "I'll see you next week or whoever you send, child. You just keep on doing what you're doing."

After Brandi left Frenchie hummed a tune. She was happy she no longer had to deal with crackheads, stickup boys, and whoever else felt like robbing her of her hard work and livelihood whenever they were in the mood for easy money.

In the back of the store an old woman named Pearl stared bitterly at Frenchie from her worn recliner that had definitely seen better days.

She pulled her shawl closer around her shoulders to ward off the chill, though it was close to eighty degrees in Los Angeles already, and it wasn't even 11 AM yet.

Pearl cleared the frog from her throat while continuing to stare at Frenchie as though she'd lost her damn mind as well as somebody else's.

Every time that girl came in the store Frenchie worshipped her like she was kneeling at the altar of God, and Pearl was good and sick of it.

She was so disgusted that she was having a hard time believing Frenchie was her daughter and that she had raised her. She'd done told her time and time again that God is a jealous god. You don't put nothing before him and nothing after him.

What the hell was it going to take to get that through that thick head of hers?

Frenchie, knowing what was coming once she heard her mother clearing her throat in that nasty, determined way, had decided to just kick it off and get it over with.

She knew how her mama felt. But like she'd said, she hadn't been robbed not once since that girl had taken up some neighborhood initiatives, and she for one was grateful.

Hell, they had politicians strutting around year in and year out who hadn't done one tenth of what a mere child had accomplished.

Frenchie looked at her mother and saw the scorn and malice in her eyes. "What, Mama? What is it now? What are you looking at like that?"

Pearl spat on the floor she was so angry. She couldn't help herself. She was starting to wish Frenchie would just keep God's name out of her mouth. What she'd said to that girl was darn near blasphemous.

"I'm looking at the biggest fool God ever sent here, that's what I'm looking at. Why you calling that girl a godsend? God ain't never sent nobody to right one wrong with another, and don't you ever forget it," Pearl huffed.

Frenchie knew she couldn't win this argument so she just shook her head, muttering under her breath while dusting off the countertop. "Mama, I'm just doing what I have to do."

Pearl might have been old but deaf she wasn't.

"Like I said, Frenchie, God ain't never sent nobody to right one wrong with another. And only a fool would believe that he did. Now in L.A. there needs to be plenty of bowing and scraping going on with the things that I see. But there is only one power that needs to be bowed to, and that power ain't Brandi Hutchinson."

She pointed a shaky, wobbly old finger in Frenchie's direction. The tone in her voice made Frenchie completely stop what she was doing. The hairs stood straight up on her arms. She turned to face her mother. Pure fire was raging in the eyes of the old woman.

"You mark my words, and you mark them well, you hear, girl?" Though Frenchie was middle-aged, in Pearl's mind she would always be a girl, especially when she acted stupid like one.

"When that girl's fall comes, great will be the fall of it and all who follow."

Frenchie couldn't ever in her life remember seeing the look she saw on her mother's face that day regarding the one and only Brandi Hutchinson.

Chapter 10

"Dear Mary Mother of Jesus," Q's mother uttered every time she considered her son's condition. It seemed like she'd been uttering those same words since the night she had received the terrible phone call regarding Q being injured.

She had not been prepared for what had awaited her upon her arrival at the hospital.

She had received the one foreboding phone call that every mother hopes that she will never receive.

Considering the utter pain she'd found herself in since that call regarding her own son, she could only imagine what it must have been like for Christ's mother, watching her son first being condemned and then crucified.

She couldn't describe it if she wanted to. She'd gone from disbelief into semishock, and then back to disbelief, only to swing into horrifying reality when she'd arrived at the hospital to see the embodiment of what once was her precious, vibrant, and handsome son.

It was a mother's worst nightmare. One step removed from death. Lord knew she hated herself for it, but sometimes she wondered if it wasn't worse, because day in and day out she had to watch him suffer with no end in sight.

Renita, Q's mother, was a nurse's aide. She worked in medical situations on a daily basis. For the most part she cleaned, kept people company, and helped to bathe, wash, feed, and turn them, as well as tidy them up. She also performed light medical duties.

Over the years she had worked on numerous cases with people who were ill or disabled in one way or another.

She knew something about caretaking for sick people, she most likely knew more than most people did.

However, she had never even in her wildest dreams imagined she'd ever have to perform these duties for her own son. A son who was so full of life, who hadn't even begun to really live life yet.

The final, absolute verdict was that her son couldn't move. For both him and Renita it was to be a new day.

While Brandi was busy ushering in and creating a new day as well on her side of the world, Q had been suffering inside a body that refused any type of mobility from the neck down.

He drooled constantly. As well, one of his arms dangled at an odd angle, and there wasn't anything the doctors could do about it. They had done what they could. Unfortunately L.A. wasn't the Land of Oz where you could go to see the wizard for magical cures.

Brandi visited him on a regular basis regardless of what was happening in her day. And since she'd started raking in the bank, her boy Q lacked for none of the amenities it took to make a paralyzed confinement comfortable.

Regardless of what she spent on Q, she couldn't buy back his health or his past before this had happened. She also couldn't purchase for him a new future.

Q's mother was single and very underemployed, so Brandi's financial assistance was a source of relief both for Q and his mother.

Although Q's body no longer worked, his mind functioned as well if not more sharply than it ever had. Q knew the effect of the burden he had created on his already-overworked mother.

Now, in addition to caring for other people, she had to come home and take care of him as well. For her there was no escaping the constant, round-the-clock care of other people, not even in her own home.

And no matter how many times Brandi offered, Renita refused to let anybody else near Q with the exception of herself and Brandi and a few others for his care.

People had already done enough to hurt her son. How did she know they wouldn't send someone to finish him off? She knew she was being paranoid but that was the way it was.

She was completely traumatized by his condition. She accepted the fact that it had made her paranoid regarding him as well.

She allowed only those select people whom she considered his friends in the house. That occurred only so Q would have some company and not be completely isolated with only her for companionship. He was too young for that.

She let in only his trusted friends who had been friends with him since childhood, before the accident.

This behavior and attitude of Renita's contributed in great part to Q's suffering, unbeknownst to her.

Q had a bright mind in a body he couldn't control. He couldn't move but he understood what was going on around him.

He definitely understood the fact that without a doubt he had caused his mother additional pain, pain that she didn't deserve.

It was a pain that had damn near crippled her emotionally when she saw him for the first time after the incident. He knew the emotional baggage of it had been growing by the day.

Nonetheless, it was a situation that had to be dealt with. In light of this Q was grateful for Brandi's help.

He had been over that night a thousand and one times in his mind. It played like a CD that was programmed on constant REPLAY or like a film reel that had gotten stuck on the same scene while the man who controlled the tape went on break or something.

Though he would never admit it in this lifetime, actually, he couldn't admit it, even if he wanted to, at least not out loud, since he couldn't speak, either, his voice box had been injured from a choke hold on that night. He hadn't spoken one word since.

However, the truth of the matter was he had wished more than once, well, on numerous occasions, actually, okay, maybe all the time, that he had handled things a bit differently that night for all of their sakes, particularly for his mom's.

He could hardly bear to see the pain in her eyes or the non-stop, crippling pressure she felt from her inability to change his circumstances. At night he heard her crying, muffled and softly in her room.

And he had never heard the name of Jesus' mother so many times in his life. Mumbling softly even in her sleep she constantly repeated the words *Dear Mary Mother of Jesus, Dear Mary Mother of Jesus.*

Q didn't know or understand why she kept doing that, but he did know something about pain, pain that stifled one's life, and that was what he had done to his mother.

She had consulted every available medical resource she had, and the prognosis never changed.

Q was and would always be exactly what he was right then. Nothing they could or would do could change that.

His intellect as well as his brightness shone clearly from his eyes but these things were trapped in a nonfunctional body.

It was like seeing a brilliantly sparkling, valuable diamond that you couldn't touch or get to because the obstacles in front of it couldn't be overcome.

Then there was Brandi.

Though Q was ever grateful for all of the comforts she threw him and his mother's way, as well as for all of the personal time, devotion, loyalty, and care that she had lavished upon him, he was frightened for who she had become, and for who she continued to emerge as on a daily basis.

Though he had run from the cops that night, pumped up and thinking it was cool, Brandi was on some extra, extra special something.

She was on a level far removed from what Q had done that night.

He had pulled a childish antic that had cost him the quality of his life.

But Brandi was creating waters that were dangerous and filled with the kind of poison that was almost always fatal, and that was hate. She was fueled by it as well as blinded by it.

Q, despite his disability, was still wired into the streets. He hardly recognized his best friend in the reports that were filtering back to him.

She wasn't the Brandi that he knew at all. She still looked exactly like that Brandi, but there was a difference, subtle, but there nonetheless.

She had created a distance about her; there was a coldness, something that was untouchable even to him.

This was something that had never existed before. In the past they had shared everything. They had been closer than most brothers and sisters.

It was as though she'd locked herself in some kind of prison and given herself a life sentence that only she could see.

As well she was determined to suffer out the entire self-imposed sentence because somehow she had gotten it into her mind that this was her way of making a difference.

And Q was living with the guilt of it because he knew in part his actions had contributed to it as well as kicked it off. His plight had basically sealed Brandi's deal with the Devil.

Instinctively he knew this was the truth. It was a harsh truth of a reality he was going to have to learn to live with.

Though Brandi talked to him about everything else under

the sun while he gurgled in response, this was an area they never ventured into. And Q could see in her eyes that she never wanted to go down this road with him.

Though he was trapped in a body with little mobility, he had learned to convey his feelings to Brandi through his eyes.

She spoke to him often, sometimes through the eyes only. But most times out loud while he listened.

Through his eyes he always answered her, but these were grounds she didn't allow even him to tread on.

He also noticed that when she smiled, it never, not once reached her eyes.

Watching her was like looking at a beautiful magazine, all glossy, fine, and slick on the cover, with nothing but page after empty page on the inside. Every page was blank. There was no content, not on a single page.

Her innocence was all but lost and so was his.

In a single night they had gone from childhood to the harsh realities of adulthood, and neither of them would ever be able to turn back the hands of time. The clock had run out on them, and they hadn't even been aware that it was ticking.

Q knew that he had stumbled upon the most tragic part of it all. Something even more tragic than the paralysis he lived with on a daily basis.

He had stumbled upon the knowledge of the theft of their childhood—the laughter, the good times, the innocence, and the loss of all of their beliefs in anything that was good.

And with that loss their hope had been diminished. The one and only gift they had received being born black and poor. Hope.

It had all died on a childish whim in a foolish moment, and in the single swing of a nightstick.

Hope as it was born in every child's heart, regardless of the circumstances, a natural gift of life.

Q gurgled at the thought.

It was a sound that no one should ever have to hear, like a

wounded animal suffering unjustly in a pain that couldn't be squelched.

Outside of his room his mother slid down the wall and to the floor in a silent river of tears after hearing that particular gurgle emanating from her son.

She had learned to tell what each gurgle releasing from him meant.

Q took a swallow from the water bottle that was attached to the straw, and always at his side whether he was in his chair or in bed.

It was the one and only thing that he could do for himself as long as the straw was near enough to his mouth for him to move his head.

It was tragic beyond belief. And it was final.

Chapter 11

The factory Brandi had built was exactly that. Its machinery churned out and packaged drugs, but this was no licensed pharmaceutical laboratory creating medicinal miracles.

The drugs being produced created the miracle of a shelter. They created a magical existence of escape from realities that either couldn't or wouldn't be dealt with. From pain, heartache, economic suffering, lack of love, hate, jealousy, reproach, self-loathing.

Or from realities that were better off left alone, especially if you didn't have an answer for them.

For every mother's mind or womb that was poisoned, for every father's faltered steps, for every junkie that overdosed, for every child that put his foot on this path, and for every crackhead that lost his way, pride, or dignity, there was no thought. There was no thought whatsoever.

Cocaine, crack, and heroin had no feelings. They were merely substances and tools. Therefore, they had no regard for their effect on human lives.

The job of the drugs was simply to rule, and rule supreme, to be worshipped, adored, and obtained, regardless of the cost.

The drugs were only part of a machine, and that machine pumped out money, pure and simple. Money made on the greatest of pain and human suffering.

Money and lots of it was made on the backs of the weak. The predator was stalking its prey. The almighty dollar was all that mattered. Beemers, Benzes, gold, and jewels.

There was and always has been a fascination with money. There is a fascination with the making of money, the actual touch of it, the smell of it, and more than that, the power and effect of it.

There's an ease of controlling other people with it. There's a certain empowering effect over one's own circumstances. Money is the most intoxicating drug known to man.

Money's effect as well as its very illusive power rule a lot of people. Brandi was young and impressionable, and she became no different.

Money is the root of all evil, or so it has been said again and again. It is a root that seeks no water, yet manages to find moisture and even grows where there is no moisture. Being the root means it is the underlying cause, the very foundation from which evil springs.

As such it is very dangerous. There are many cases where the fruit cannot be disentangled from its root.

In this case, as in so many cases, there was absolutely no thought for the evils, heartaches, pain, or losses, or for how incalculable they were and what the drugs actually represented.

In fact Brandi really thought that the making of the money was putting her above the power of evil, removing her from being its victim.

Instead it was moving her toward dark forces. It was putting her directly in the path, and clutches of the evil she thought she was escaping, but this evil was much deeper, and at a higher level.

It was not a game for the faint of heart.

There was preparation for every stage of every process in Brandi's new regime except against these forces. But really, there could be no preparation to level the playing field she had stepped on.

Front and center was one thought and one thought only: *chi-ching.*

Brandi oversaw every single aspect of the operation. Security was impenetrable, from inside the factory to the basement, from the roofs, to the alleys, and even blocks away it had all been personally selected, and scrutinized and then put into effect by those closest to her.

Soon after the drug manufacturing was up and running, an overpowering stench began permeating the building and even leaking outside through the crevices. it was like Chemistry 101 in the place.

Brandi went into action.

She hired consultants who discovered a sealant that could be used to plug all the holes, and leaks. She bought special masks for everyone inside the factory as well as those in close proximity so they wouldn't constantly be inhaling the dangerous fumes.

The factory ran day and night.

It was never closed. There was never a time when there wasn't a shift on board bringing in the drugs, sifting them, taking them through the various processes, down to the packaging.

At that point they went through another stage, which led finally to delivery and distribution on the street, resulting in cash, mountains of it that had to be counted, cleaned, filtered, laundered, spread out, paid off, as well as accounted for.

Sometimes Brandi thought back to the day she had seen Lisa ready to sell the food from her kids' mouths to get her hands on the re-mix.

That day had sealed her fate in a way similar to Q's fate kicking it off.

These were memories she didn't allow herself to dwell on. Especially Lisa's predicament, because Brandi had become worse than D-Money whom she had scorned in her heart when she had witnessed his brutal treatment of Lisa.

She had decided right then and there she would never deal with making money at that low of a level. She had to be in control, in the driver's seat, moving it from the top down or not at all.

This was her justification.

It made her feel like she wasn't stooping to the low level of taking food from anybody's mouth because she was dealing with real players at a whole other level.

The same dealer she had watched that day was many layers removed from her position, but still the irony was that he bought and sold from her people's people's people, and so on and so forth.

So the pendulum continued to swing.

What Brandi didn't know was that the pendulum always swung back to the direction in which it was started.

She figured she was insulated and many layers removed. She had it on lock, at least for the time being. She and those she had crowned and paid along the way. Nothing moved in the area if she didn't move it or give the word on it.

So far, everything was as it always was when people were getting phat paid. She was top dog, and she knew it. So did everybody else.

Even the male gangs were now buying from her suppliers, so she was making money hand over fist, and from each end of the deal.

She could roll over in her plush penthouse apartment, never make a phone call, and never leave her bed for the day, and earn an amount of money that most people only dreamed of making.

If they were black people they could work all their lives and not come into contact with what she could make.

She started making so much money she was having difficulty counting it all.

Fishbone was also making a truckload of cash because she had his backing from day one, before she ever made one move on the street. He was making so much money he had trouble figuring out how to store all of it.

He had gotten phat paid merely from saying yes to her plan. He had put his power and backing behind her. He had tipped off and paid off the right people.

Having Fishbone's backing was akin to having the backing of an attorney general from where she came from, and it had given her carte blanche to do whatever she wanted, with minimal repercussions.

Fishbone was not only heading the largest, most dangerous male gang in the city, he was now one of the highest-paid men in it.

He had nothing but respect and love for Brandi because she had come up with a plan that basically could have enabled them as well as their family members to retire at any time. She had created power in the raw. And everyone loved a good racehorse. She was considered to be power in effect.

In the hood being *in effect* meant you were the man—well, she was a woman, but it was all the same, and all in the game.

The plan was running on smooth. And Brandi Hutchinson was the new, the one, and the only Queen of Cash.

Her name was ringing, as the saying goes. But as with any bell that rings too loudly, at some point you can lose control of exactly who hears it ringing.

Chapter 12

Brandi tapped in an automatic code on her pager, sending Tata to finish the collections for the day while she headed over to L.A.'s most elite African-American full-service salon to receive her weekly facial, body massage, eyebrow waxing, hairstyle, manicure, and pedicure.

This was a ritual she rarely ever missed.

Instantly, upon stepping one of her elegant, designer-clad, Prada-wearing feet into the shop, she was swarmed with attention because she was the highest tipper they had ever had the privilege of coming into contact with. And they were used to customers with loot.

However, Brandi was of a different order and league. When she stepped into a place all you saw was green.

Word got around when cash was being spent, especially when there was plenty of it. Everyone from the hair-wash girl to the manicurist to the stylist wanted Brandi's business.

For the most part she had regulars, but every now and again someone new popped up.

However, she was starting to become aware of the danger in new faces, so while she was there she planned to select every single person, down to the girl who waxed her eyebrows, who would work on her beauty regime whenever she came in.

No changes in personnel would be tolerated unless approved of by her or Tata in advance.

Tata would pull the files on those selected. She'd run them through a vigorous security check. When she was done they would know everything about the person, down to the date, time, hour, and minute of when—as well as where—they'd been born.

Brandi paid quite a pretty penny for obtaining this type of access to people's personal information.

However, it was worth it because if anybody tried to slide in to get under her, they would be easier to detect. She wasn't buying into any camouflages. And she wasn't stupid enough to believe that they didn't exist.

She was no fool, she knew if you played the game, then there were certain rules that went along with it. She considered proper preparation the key to her survival.

If somebody came up dirty, then she'd know in an instant. They would no longer be in the lineup nor be employed in any of the places Brandi frequented.

Every place that she stepped her foot in was checked out in advance. And her ego was growing in direct proportion to her reputation.

Her beauty treatment was one of the highlights of her week because this was what she thought of as her downtime. This was a place where she did her thinking, and where some of her new plans, ideas, and brainstorms were formulated.

She knew at some point she would have to try to go totally legit. She was always thinking on what she would do as well as how she would do it.

The time that she spent with cucumbers covering her eyes, in her facial mask with her head wrapped in a warm towel— while a battalion of young women swarmed around her, providing her with every comfort—was a life far removed from the struggling apartment in the projects she'd been raised in.

She enjoyed every minute of calling her own shots and

being her own person, yet she remained in a state of high alert. It was a position where you had to always be guarded.

A leader could never afford to underestimate either their friends or their enemies. That couldn't happen, not for a second.

If she wanted to continue in her current capacity she'd have to keep coming up with new ways to stay one step ahead of the enemy.

The enemy that she could see or anticipate, anyway.

It was the one that she couldn't see that would pose a different type of problem. Checking on things was fine as long as you knew what to check on. It was those things that you didn't think you needed to check on that slipped between the cracks.

In between the cracks was where most evil lived—the place where most people failed to look, even the high-powered Ms. Brandi Hutchinson.

Chapter 13

A man by the name of Chase owned the salon Brandi frequented and was so in love with. His full name was Chase Ajani. *Ajani* meant victor in Africa. He was six foot five, slim, with baby-smooth skin the color of a black diamond, and eyes that were so light a brown they were nearly gold.

Although he had given himself an African last name, as close as he actually came to being African was being an African-American.

He had never even been to Africa. However, he was an avid student of African Studies, which is how he had come up with the name Ajani.

He liked the name Ajani. He aspired to it veritably. Victory had always been in his blood. It ran through his veins like a streaming river.

Chase was also a man who had had to resort to re-creating himself from the ashes of a life that was well hidden as well as better off left behind.

Few knew he was the real owner of the salon, such were his layers of insulation.

As well he owned numerous salons, not only in Los Angeles but also around the country, in depressed areas where young black females spent tons of money to pamper themselves and to groom their images in pursuit of the art of feeling important.

He well knew it was an art to project a created image. He had a feeling the very stunning Ms. Brandi Hutchinson knew that as well.

All of his salons were owned under a variety of names, buried in mounds of paperwork as well as fake DBAs.

At the salon he was thought to be only a high-level, hands-on executive of a business owned by someone else.

He was well respected and revered for his management as well as in his personal running of the salon. His word was the last one they all heard.

Instinctively, people knew Ajani was not a man to cross, without him ever having to utter a word about it. He carried an air that was regal, alluring, and seductive, yet dark and dangerous.

These attributes were just simply built into his carriage. They were built into the very structure and creation of who he was.

The salons were only the front side of his business. In truth he was a courier. One that moved in the shadows of darkness and was hired by people whose names were such a hallmark as to only be whispered in certain circles.

At twenty-five years old he had died many deaths and had been reborn many times, in a manner of speaking. Chase Ajani was currently who he was.

And without doubt or hesitation, he had his eye on the very beautiful Brandi in a major way. There had never been anything in his life that he had wanted that he hadn't gotten.

He decided that Brandi wouldn't be an exception. He desired her in a way that he had never felt before. She intrigued him.

As young as she was, she was one of the most fascinating, exciting females he had ever laid eyes on.

There was an aura surrounding her.

That particular aura included a stamp of beauty, confidence, aloofness, and intrigue.

There was something else he couldn't quite put his finger on, but he could feel this woman without even touching her. She was a keeper. He wanted her for his own in the worst way. However, instinctively he knew he would have to tread carefully.

Infiltration into her world would have to be cultivated. It would have to be as smooth as silk.

She would have to be completely knocked off her feet without knowing what had hit her. He smiled a little at this thought—knocking her off her feet wasn't at all beyond his capabilities.

Most women salivated at the mere sight of him. Once he flashed the depths of his brownish gold eyes at them, letting just the slightest hint of a smile tug at the corners of his mouth, they were captive as well as putty in his hands.

He had always had the ability to put in something that most men neglected and overlooked in their pursuit of women, and that was the time to study their deepest, darkest wants and desires.

He had a knack for tapping into their most vulnerable spots, and for making that particular woman feel as though she were the only woman in his life that mattered. He made her feel like she was a queen.

Once he knew her vulnerabilities, then he would step into her life as a mirror that reflected all her deepest needs and cravings, and then some, allowing her to see as well as live out her best fantasies.

It came so naturally to him—attracting females and getting inside their skin. Brandi he knew without a doubt was worth going the extra mile for.

As well he decided that underestimating her would be a grave mistake on his part because he had already detected battlelike instincts in her. She would not be as easy as most of the women who had crossed his path.

In fact he knew she would prove to be his most difficult conquest.

And here was the good part: for all of her outward worldliness she was pure. Try finding that in an eighteen-year-old anywhere in the country, never mind in the heart of Los Angeles.

However, this was truth and he knew it for a fact because he had checked. The very elegant Brandi wasn't the only one who could unearth people's secrets.

Surprise, surprise, he thought as he smiled. With all that glamour she exuded, most niggas would have been surprised to know that she didn't have the scent of a man on her yet.

A great deal of patience would be required, but he possessed that in abundance. He wondered why and for whom she'd been saving herself. Then he smiled as the obvious answer appeared to him.

Apparently she thought quite highly of herself to have kept her spectacular gem of virginity protected in this day and time.

With all of that attitude she projected this wasn't something one would have expected her to still be in possession of.

He thought about security once again. He had laid out a plan to obstruct her security checks to ensure she found only what he wanted found. He had known she would check even before she had decided to.

Chase crossed one of his thousand-dollar pants legs over the other one. He watched her. He smiled. He contemplated. He was so taken with her it radiated from his very pores. He had never in his life been so captivated by a woman.

Right now he could feel Brandi as though he was touching her, although he was behind a plate glass window, far removed from the area of the salon she was in.

He licked the tip of one of his fingers and stuck it to the glass as though she could see him.

In that instant a shiver raced through Brandi's body.

"Cristal," she said to one of the girls, "can you turn the air-conditioning down in here? It's a bit cold."

Cristal threw the answer over her shoulder. "You got it, Brandi."

Cristal's mother was only fourteen years older than her, and she had been naive enough to name Cristal after the expensive champagne that had opened her up to a night of getting pregnant by a nigga she never saw again after that one night of passion.

Chase laughed out loud upon hearing Brandi's words to Cristal through his listening device.

"It's not as cold as it's going to get, Ms. Brandi Hutchinson," he said aloud, though he was the only one in the room.

He stood up, watching her intensely through the glass. "You can rest assured it is not as cold as it is going to get," he repeated once again. Then he thought about it.

"Or perhaps I should say as hot as it's going to get." He laughed out loud at his own joke.

Chapter 14

Tata lived exactly as she had on the day Brandi had visited her. With all the loot they were making she could have easily afforded to move out, but she didn't. She had chosen to stay. She had her reasons.

Brandi had moved, of course, but that had been expected under the circumstances. For Tata the hood was home. She was never going to leave the apartment in the projects where she had once lived with her mom.

Tata, Brandi, and Tangie were the only members of the Conqueror's posse for whom no security checks had been run, and whose background information had not been sifted and filtered through.

They had all agreed to come together on word, bond, and trust. Those three words—*word, bond, and trust*—were the equivalent of a religious sacrament in the neighborhood.

They had worked out their positions on a handshake, so to speak, and that worked just fine for Tata. But she couldn't even let Brandi and Tangie know that she was visiting her mother once a month who was long since thought to have been dead.

She shook her head as she was assaulted with the memory of the day they had shot her mother in the streets. She could still see the smoke from the guns.

*   *   *

Once all of the day's business was over, and the receipts had been collected and accounted for, Tata prepared for a trip she took once a month religiously.

This trip required a host of decoys, including travel schedules and arrangements for several methods of transportation, before the destination was finally reached.

As Tata rode the shaky cell that they called an elevator—standing between two armed, unidentifiable men, each with a gun to the side of her head pointing directly at her temple—she stared straight ahead just as she always did . . . waiting for the series of locks, jangles, keys, more locks, and then the rattling of chains that always accompanied her visits to the woman now known only as Prisoner X.

Most people weren't aware of the underground prison system, where numbers were not assigned to names of the persons who resided there as they were in normal prison systems.

The prisoners who resided here had had their names erased completely as though they had never been in existence.

As it was there were very few people who resided in these dark dungeons. That was how Tata thought of them every time she rode that shaky cell.

They were definitely dungeons, and try as she might she'd never been able to come up with another word for them.

And lockdown was a 24/7 experience.

Prisoner X came out once a month for her visit and that was it. Which really only meant she was transported from her 24/7 cell to the cell in which she visited, and then back to the cell where she always resided once the visit was over.

Stepping out of the elevator Tata was momentarily blinded by total blackness, blacker even than the band that had been tied over her eyes, which allowed her only shadows of light.

The area they had taken her to was also pitch-black so even the silhouettes and shadows had disappeared momentarily.

Finally, as was standard procedure, the band was removed

from her eyes as she stood in front of the thick plate glass bulletproof window.

She was searched yet again for what felt like the umpteenth time, and then finally her two escorts disappeared into the shadows.

It was always the same drill, except the guards were always different. For as long as she had been going there she had never once had the same two guards for escorts.

Though she couldn't see them, she knew this because she could smell the difference in their body scents.

They weren't allowed to wear cologne, body lotions, or anything that would give off scents, yet Tata could still smell them, and because of the insanity of the setup her sense of smell had been honed over time.

Her night vision had increased in strength as well.

The only people she ever came into direct contact with were the two escorts and the person assigned to let her in, but she was also aware that in the shadows there was a group of armed guards standing with guns pointed at her head and her heart.

The weapons they carried sported red laser dots that were in sync with her heartbeat. They, of course, had the ability to stop the beating of her heart in a fraction of a second.

One wrong move and they would kill her in a hail of bullets. She would never be seen or heard from again, and she knew it.

Yet even though the circumstances were difficult she always waited with bated breath until the shadow entered and appeared on the other side of the glass.

The person whom they'd coded as Prisoner X was her mother, the woman who represented the only softness that Tata possessed.

The woman who'd named her Tatiana after an African princess because she'd thought she was special from the day she was born.

That woman whom the world had written off and thought

was dead, but instead still lived under the cover of great darkness under circumstances that very few people in the world even knew existed.

The deal Prisoner X had made had bought her two important things. One was her daughter's life. The other was that it had preserved hers, even though under harsh conditions.

The only reason she had been allowed to make the deal was because they couldn't be sure whether or not she still had something they might one day need.

Tata was the only other human being outside of the guards employed there that she ever saw—if you could call seeing a shadow *seeing* (all she ever viewed of Tata was her profile).

That suited her fine as long as she saw her precious baby so she'd know for herself that she was alive and well.

What they didn't know but what she knew was that if Tata ever missed a visit or if they ever did anything to her, there would be grave consequences.

They weren't the only ones who could play hardball, and she wasn't in a situation like that without reason. If they took from her she'd take from them.

A life for a life, and even under those circumstances she was more than prepared. She'd turn them into ash if anything happened to her baby, taking herself right along with them.

It wouldn't matter because without Tata she'd have no reason to live, anyway. Being with Tata was all she longed for and looked forward to on each visit.

Tata had never missed a visit, and she had never once been late.

The conditions imposed upon Tata were not difficult, considering the circumstances. She would be allowed these visits only if she kept her mouth shut as well as followed the plan.

The threat of breaking the rules wasn't an option, either. If she ever spoke about it or broke the plan her mother would die, plain and simple. She'd be dead before Tata ever reached her.

In fact the prison would never be proved to have ever been in existence if Tata violated any of the rules.

So not only would her mother be dead for real but also all that would be discovered of where she'd been kept would be land in the desert.

That sealed the deal.

The world thought her mother was dead, anyway. There were a great many people who even felt, thought, and swore they had witnessed her death.

That was the end of the story, or so everyone thought.

Tata vaguely saw the shadow move on the other side of the glass and heard a slight movement. Before she knew it she felt the cool breath of Prisoner X blow through the ventilated pinholes in the glass.

"Hey, baby, how are you?"

Tata closed her eyes against the small breath she felt brush against her cheek. The only physical contact she ever had with her mother.

"I'm fine, Ma. How are you?"

A small laugh generated from the other side of the glass, floated into Tata's ear. "Good as gold, Tatiana."

Prisoner X never called her anything other than Tatiana. She had named her after an African princess for a reason, and she refused to lose the privilege of calling her that by cutting her name short.

Tata looked down, battling to restrain the tears in her heart from floating out through her eyes. The place where they kept her mother was a dangerous place, and there was no room for weakness.

She lifted her head, letting the appropriate edge slip into her voice. "I left you some cash."

Prisoner X nodded, then remembered her daughter couldn't really see her well enough to be sure she'd done that, and so finally released a sprawling "yes," through the pinholes.

She knew Tatiana always left her cash. Lately the amounts

had been increasing. There was nothing she wanted for materially that she couldn't buy.

The only thing she wanted that couldn't be purchased was a breath of fresh air—unless they had that in heaven and by some miracle she arrived there—but she knew she'd never again breathe it on earth.

They continued their visit in the same manner in which they always did, discussing things of no real importance, just feeling close to each other and in each other's proximity for the time that they had.

Chapter 15

Tangie picked up her dry cleaning before heading over to Sepulveda Boulevard. She'd been feeling like she was on top of the world ever since the Conquerors had been created. She tossed her linen-thick hair over her shoulder, putting her face to the wind.

That hair that she tossed so casually made hair salons hate to see her coming. Her hair was waist length and as thick as a Rastafarian princess'. They practically charged extra before she even stepped foot into their salon, since getting her hair to reach a sleek, silky sheen was serious work.

The posse had given Tangie a new lease on life. It gave her something of her own to have and to look forward to. Most of all it gave her a feeling of belonging, a feeling of someone needing her. It was something she could be a real part of.

She'd never really felt a part of anything since her mother died.

She was used to the world of gang life, as well as the mechanics of how it operated, because Fishbone had been a part of it for as long as she could remember.

Her brother had started out by being jumped in back in the day, and from there he had gone through a series of initiations until he had became a bona fide member.

All of these initiations had been clandestine, of course.

Over the years Fishbone had jumped ranks until he was no

longer a part of the ranks but the leader of them. He'd built a legacy of fear, trust, and loyalty in the streets as well as among different factions of the gangs.

She knew for a fact that Fishbone had been the brainchild behind the codes that had been created as a way for the gangs to speak to each other without people knowing the language.

Across the country young kids sported those same codes on T-shirts, usually handwritten—or at least in their humble beginnings the codes had been handwritten.

Those T-shirts and hoodies marked with the hidden, coded meanings were starting to be copied by clothing manufacturers. They were popping up as fashion statements in urban stores around the country.

If Fish could have foreseen that when he created the language, and patented it, he could have retired for life. Many of the gangs used the symbols and letters as a regular part of their very existence.

It was a way to say something without saying it. And only those privy to the language knew what it meant.

In any case, Tangie, being the youngest of three siblings—she had an older sister, too, named Jackie—was always shielded from any real action as well as any real knowledge of anything worthwhile that was going on.

She had the connection and prestige of being Fishbone's baby sister but that was all. That was where it started as well as where it ended.

She didn't have anything in her own right, or at least she didn't before Brandi had come up with the absolutely brilliant idea of building a girl empire that was their own and that they controlled.

Now, she was a part of something real, a part of the cause as well as a part of the effect and the final outcome of things. She belonged, and she was privy to things at the top level.

Fishbone being her brother hadn't hurt matters, that was for sure. In fact it had given her a leg up, although since Brandi was her best friend she would have been in, anyway.

Her connection to Fish was R-E-S-P-E-C-T in a major way, just like Aretha used to sing it. She secretly listened to old, old-school music, though she would never admit that to her hip-hopping, blinging friends.

Tangie was also addicted to shopping in a major way with a capital *S*. She loved to shop.

Prior to Brandi's plan she had purchased her labels from every booster in the vicinity of South Central. She loved clothes. She piled them up from every designer that caught her eye.

Unlike many others in the projects, there was always income for her, due to Fish's activities. Her older sister worked an underpaid job, and she gave her money as well, but it was Fish's loot that had really kept her name in lights on the list of label whores and shopping thieves.

However, now she could afford to just walk into the boutiques and the fancy clothing stores, purchasing whatever she liked.

Shopping soothed something inside of her. It filled a void for her that she couldn't explain. It was her tension reliever.

Though she hated to admit it, the other side of the coin was that with this new venture they were all in, there was a lot of tension despite the regimen of disciplined diets and workouts they all adhered to.

Tangie strolled over to Baby Gap, one of her all-time favorite stores. She had a ball buying clothes for her godson.

Her godson's mother was a close school friend of hers, and at the ripe old age of seventeen years old already had three kids, all courtesy of different daddies.

The Li'l Stair Steps, as others in the hood sometimes called them, were the cutest little things you'd ever want to see.

Anyway, the youngest, Anthony, who was eight months old, was Tangie's godchild, and so she visited Tamika on the regular, bringing clothes for him as well as for the other children.

She also brought food, medical supplies, and other necessities.

Tamika was on public assistance, aka welfare, so she was always struggling to make ends meet. With each baby she dropped, making ends meet was proving to be more and more difficult.

It was funny, though many things had changed in the neighborhoods over time, one thing that remained constant was the existence of welfare, along with people's dependency on it.

Sometimes there were four or more generations that had subsisted on it in one family.

It was the equivalent of tying a heavy rock around one's neck and throwing it into the water, knowing it would pull your body down to the bottom and that you would drown.

Even knowing this, it still never stopped the person from tying that knot around their neck. And the beat goes on.

For Tamika life had gotten a bit more comfortable lately since Tangie's monetary contributions as well as her contributions of food, medical supplies, and clothes had greatly increased.

Tangie arrived at Tamika's apartment, once again arms laden with overflowing Baby Gap bags. The latest in baby styles stuffed inside.

Then she went back downstairs to the taxi to retrieve more bags, and finally grocery bags that she hauled up to Tamika's third-floor apartment.

It was times like this that Tangie became really impressed as well as thankful for Brandi's insane training, because without it she definitely wouldn't have been in the kind of shape required to run heavy bags from the taxi up and down three flights of stairs.

Tamika couldn't help because the kids couldn't be left unattended.

Once all of the bags were in the house Tangie seated herself at Tamika's wobbly kitchen table. That was next on her list of replacements for Tamika. She absolutely couldn't stand that table much longer.

Anthony crawled over to her, gurgling. He placed one chubby hand on her leg while looking up at her, drooling.

Tangie picked up phat boy, as she thought of him, chucking him under the chin and kissing his fat cheek, wiping drool from his mouth while Tamika put away the groceries and peeked into the Baby Gap bags.

"Tangie, you've got to stop spoiling these kids with this stuff," she said, though secretly she was happy to have Tangie's help.

"Girl, you telling me how to spend my money now?" Tangie asked, glancing over the baby's head.

Tamika smiled. "No," she hesitated.

But then, because she loved Tangie like a sister, she decided to plunge ahead into dangerous waters.

"But I would like to warn you to be careful about how you're getting it."

Tangie lowered the baby. "What's that supposed to mean, Tamika?"

"Nothing. But, you're down with Brandi and she's on some self-destruct—"

Tamika looked around, saw her three-year-old daughter watching her, and decided to change her choice of words. "She's on some self-destruct B.S.," she finished lamely. "You know what I mean. You can see it if you know what to look for. I just don't want you to get hit with any of it."

Tamika didn't like Brandi, as Tangie well knew. "Didn't like" might be too light of a phrase for what Tamika really felt about Brandi, but it would suffice for the time being. She actually couldn't stand the sight of Brandi, and never could.

Tangie knew that since Brandi was her best friend, there had always been some jealousy on Tamika's part because she wanted the top spot with her. But she and Brandi were just bonded that way, and Tamika needed to understand that.

Tangie remembered the wrist-cutting and blood-dripping

ritual that had made her cringe. She'd had to avert her eyes because secretly she couldn't stand the sight of blood.

However, she could never let on how she felt inside. She didn't have the privilege or the luxury of showing weakness.

The way she came up, a display of weakness could cost you your life.

As well she was Fishbone's sister, and he was heading up L.A.'s biggest male gang. And now her best friend, Brandi, was heading up the fiercest female gang ever constructed, and she was third in command, so her personal feelings could never be revealed, not ever.

That was just a fact of life.

She was caught in a web that she'd have to see out until the end. She loved Fishbone and Brandi, and so there was no choice. There was no choice at all except to keep pretending she was one of them. Fish was her own blood, and Brandi was the next thing to it.

Softly Tangie's gaze met Tamika's unflinching stare. "I won't. Don't worry."

Tamika huffed unbelievingly as she turned back to putting some food into the refrigerator. She slammed the door in frustration.

Brandi was a selfish hussy as far as she was concerned. Because if she was a real friend it would be easy enough to see that Tangie wasn't made of the stuff gangs and violence were made of.

Any fool with a blindfold on could see that.

The only reason Brandi couldn't see it was because she was blinded by her own selfish ambitions, and Tamika knew it.

What Tamika didn't know was how to get Tangie out before something bad happened, because just as sure as she was standing there with what felt like a pit sitting in the bottom of her stomach, eventually something bad would happen, and Tangie would be smack dead in the middle of it.

Tamika couldn't stomach the idea of the possibility of Tangie becoming another casualty of war.

Chapter 16

That night Brandi, Tata, and Tangie lay sprawled out in Brandi's living room feasting on steamed shrimp along with garden salad topped only with balsamic vinegar. It was one of Brandi's favorite meals.

Tata and Tangie had both had to acquire a taste for Brandi's nutritional meals, but they were surviving. This was huge for Tangie, who used to spend a great deal of her time in Mc-Donald's. However, Ronald McDonald hadn't seen her lately.

It used to be that she ate in McDonald's so much she should have owned some stock in the place. The pounds were melting off her so fast since she was staying away from those double cheeseburgers and fries, one would have thought she was on a permanent fast.

It had been difficult for Tata and Tangie, but they were finally in the swing of things.

There was a certain excitement in creating a new life for oneself. There was also a sense of accomplishment in the remaking and remolding of one's old habits into new and more beneficial ones.

They knew their days of pizza, French fries, burritos, tacos, and anything remotely connected to calories and carbs was a thing of the past.

However, that didn't stop them from daydreaming. Both Tata and Tangie were having visions of chili cheeseburgers loaded with everything, with cheese fries on the side, as they demurely dug into their steamed shrimp and salad.

But neither of them would ever admit their food dreams of grandeur to Brandi, who was a fanatic when it came to this stuff. Brandi believed in doing whatever it took to be on top. If something had to be changed she would change it on a dime without a second thought.

Take salt, for instance. They'd been eating it for all their lives. Their families had been eating it for all their lives. Under Brandi's new diet no salt was allowed. She insisted that salt caused water retention in the body, and eventually led to things like high blood pressure and heart disease.

This information and new set of rules was from the same girl who used to pour salt on her food before even tasting it. Tangie could remember when the girl used to put salt on a hotdog.

In any case, Brandi stopped using it as though she'd never heard of salt, and that was that. It was the total end of her days of using salt. She also coerced every member of her posse to drop it as well. Each and every one of them did, as if salt were a hot potato.

The sale of salt in Los Angeles in the hood was at an all-time low, thanks to the very new and in control Ms. Brandi Hutchinson.

Brandi loved what she thought of as the new and improved them. They were shining examples of how, with the right strength and determination, they could make themselves over into whatever they wanted to be.

They had proven that you could resist temptation of any sort simply by making up your mind.

Tata had the additional burden of withdrawing from her usual sexual exploits. That had been one heck of a temptation for her. She had been working out doubly hard to burn off all that excess energy she wasn't using. Sex had been like a sport for her.

And she had to admit to herself she was growing stronger

and more focused, and her pride was growing with each measure of discipline she attained.

Once they were finished lounging, Brandi stood up. "I think we should expand the operations into the San Gabriel Valley."

Tata nodded. She was down with whatever. "Yeah, more territory, more loot."

Tangie was quiet.

Brandi looked at her. "Well. What do you think, Tangie?"

"About what?" Tangie answered absentmindedly.

"About expanding into the valley?" Brandi was patient.

"Oh, yeah. That sounds fine to me. Everything is in place, right?"

"Yeah, as long as the three of us agree."

"Then let's do it," Tata and Tangie replied in unison.

"I already, of course, spoke to Fish, and his people are in place. The expansion should increase our income share by 33 percent."

Tata laughed. "That's what I'm talking about, bringing in the bank, baby!"

They all high-fived each other. They looked at each other, laughing.

Brandi closed her eyes. This is how we do it.

Chapter 17

Not long after the girls' night out at Brandi's house, some of the Conquerors and Fishbone's gang, the L.A. Troops, were hanging out on Crenshaw Boulevard.

Porsches, Cadillacs, Jeeps, motorcycles, and various souped-up low-riding Chevys and other hydraulic-driven vehicles covered the parking lot.

Sometimes they hung out in front of the McDonald's on Crenshaw. When they chose to do this, there wasn't an inch of space in the McDonald's parking lot or inside of the restaurant that wasn't covered with their members.

Little did most people know that hanging out at this McDonald's was just a smoke screen that Fishbone had devised. It was a clever disguise.

If occasionally they hung out on the streets like low-level gang members it gave the appearance that that was all they were.

In fact this was far from the truth when you considered the type of operations they dealt in and the humungous cash flow that was generated from those operations.

They kept a low profile for the most part, but occasionally it was necessary to project the image as well as the illusion. The importance of this concept was never lost on Fishbone. He knew that people who were shortsighted were easier to take down.

There were plenty of hands that exchanged the money to keep it all flowing smoothly, but that was his business. It was better for him to be underestimated. That was what had always given him his edge.

One of the things Fishbone had learned early on in the game was that most people believed what they saw. And if they saw what they thought was nothing other than a neighborhood gang, then that is what they would be thought of: as the area hood rats.

For the most part his peeps still maintained places in the projects. This was one of the smarter moves they'd ever maneuvered and kept.

Flashing around lots of cash was a quick way to sacrifice your freedom as well as set yourself up as a target for a whole lot of other things.

So even though he and his boys kept a low profile, from time to time they put in what he thought of as their very necessary appearances in visible places, mimicking the antics of what was considered to be a true gangbanger. Yet in reality they were pretty far removed from this life since Fish's leadership.

In fact he had suggested to Brandi that some of her posse, as she liked to call them, do the same thing. She had obliged. He had told her not to let them be flashing and rising like cream in the hood. That was a quick way to draw the wrong kinds of attention.

The only people aware of the serious alliance—in terms of the underlying deals—between the male and female gang factions were Fishbone and Brandi.

As leaders they both understood that the fewer people who knew something, the better, even within their own ranks. You never let your left hand know what your right hand was doing.

People were driving by Crenshaw who would have loved to pull into McDonald's to take advantage of the dollar menu.

However, they quickly decided to keep going when they saw all the gang members sprawled out as though the land at McDonald's was their personal property and they had come to collect their forty acres and a mule.

The truth was that for that night, as well as for any other night they arrived there, the place belonged to them—bought and paid for, in a manner of speaking.

An African man who owned this McDonald's was paid very well for the gangs to be his only customers inside as well as outside of the restaurant.

He figured that for the prices they paid, they could roll wherever they wanted. Not obliging was simply not a smart option, so he had chosen the wiser course of action to accept the cash and turn his head the other way.

The African dude was never one to be known for *not* being smart. In fact he was the poster child for smart, especially when it came to his life and his health insurance policies.

That was just how business was done in this world. So on that night the gangs were out in full force. They were wreck in effect, and everybody knew it.

They laughed as they saw people driving by, wanting to come in but afraid to. They were also trying to avoid eye contact with them at all costs.

That was exactly why some of them were gang members. They didn't want to be on the outside looking in. And they didn't want to walk around in fear. It was easier to be a part than to go against.

Few people if any who were alive knew this was one reason that Fishbone had initially become part of the gang system. He had become a part to protect his family. He had also joined so he could roam the streets of the projects without fear.

He had never been one that liked trouble or violence, though anyone who knew him would be hard-pressed to accept this revelation about him.

He had rebuilt himself from a fearful kid into a fearsome leader, all to protect his own.

Given a choice he might have been anything but. However, he hadn't been given a choice. So he had made the best of what his hand had called for.

He had vowed that no one living would ever see that scared, skinny little boy again who had once messed on himself inside a graffiti-ridden, pissy-smelling hallway while being beaten to within an inch of his life.

He had cowered in the corner in fear, trying to cover his face and head as blows rained down on him.

That little boy had died on that day. He was dead and buried. He was never to be seen or heard from again.

Fishbone sat on top of his Porsche, far removed from that dead kid he had been long ago. He knew full well that one day the cords of his sins would strangle him. But that was for then, and this was now.

Tata and Tangie leaned on the hood of his car, kicking it with him. Some of his gang members were hanging around just laughing it up with each other.

He didn't let his baby sister hang out all that much, but since she had become a part of Brandi's group she was feeling herself, so he was trying to cut her a bit of slack. Still, she needed to understand that it wouldn't be too much.

He had allowed her inclusion into Brandi's posse in part because it gave him a direct pipeline into the only other organization in the city that held any real clout or threat, and as well she was highly placed within the organization.

And because it was Brandi who had created the organization. He loved Brandi as if she were his own sister. He knew Tangie and Brandi were thick as thieves. They had been like that with each other since they were kids.

Besides, he was well plugged into Brandi and her operations, so he could keep an eye on what was going on with the both of them.

He had to admit Brandi was much sharper than he had

ever given her credit for. Everyone in the hood had always known she was smart. But what she had pulled off was sheer genius. She had been wise enough to throw a wide net, as well as smart enough to develop the right network of payoffs before she ever stepped one foot on the street. By the time she did, it was a cakewalk for her.

She had actually made it happen without the usual loss of blood and life. That fact in itself deserved major respect as well as props.

Fishbone looked around casually as though he didn't know the answer to the question he was about to ask. "Where's Brandi?"

Tata glanced sideways at Fish. He was one fine nigga. She didn't know why she'd allowed Brandi to talk her into that stupid abstinence vow. She could kick herself sometimes for agreeing to that nonsense even if she could see the benefits of it.

Every time she looked at Fish she regretted that vow. But a vow was a vow so she was stuck with it. "Brandi doesn't hang out these days, Fish, and you know that," Tata said.

Fishbone grunted. "Humph. Maybe she should."

Tata's glance changed to a glare. "Maybe she shouldn't." What the hell was he worried about Brandi for? She was here. Stupid nigga.

Fishbone slid off the roof of his Porsche and reached over to chuck Tata under her chin. He could see her bottom lip hanging like a spoiled child. He held her in the deep of his eyes before he put his arm around his sister Tangie's shoulder.

"Chill, Tata. There's no need for you to unleash the dogs on a brother. Damn, you ladies are getting a little antsy since you've all been united under one leadership. Chill. I like what you're doing in the hoods."

Fishbone stepped to Tata. He took off his cap and traded it for hers. He put his cap on her head tenderly while probing the depths of her bright eyes.

He knew she had a thing for him.

She was pure sexuality when it came to him. But he wasn't going to feed into it. One, she was too young. Two, she was too young. Three, she was his sister's friend. And four, she was number two in charge after Brandi.

Every one of those reasons was legit—and dangerous enough to keep him from crossing the line. She was a beautiful girl, growing into a fine specimen of a woman for someone else, perhaps, but definitely not for him.

He never played close to home. Any man worth his salt in the art of survival knew that was the thing that could be the death of him.

Besides, from what he understood there was to be no playing of this sort in Brandi's posse by any of her girls, anyway. Tangie had confirmed the truth of the vow of abstinence they had all taken.

But he was sure light flirtation couldn't be included as part of the seal because it was ludicrous to think that young, beautiful women wouldn't at the very least flirt with the opposite sex.

Even Brandi, as driven as she was, couldn't be that staunch.

In any case Brandi's standards made him happy because his sister was the number-three person as well as Brandi's best friend, and he'd love to see her womanhood preserved for as long as possible, especially with all the young hotties he saw out on the streets.

They were giving sex a new name as well as a new reputation with their antics, and none of it was good.

He was quite happy not to have his sister tagged as being one of the hotties. He truly didn't relish going around killing niggas just for the heck of it, and especially not on the grounds of a booty call.

But his sister might be a person who could cause him to lower his standards in a given situation. So he gave a silent nod of praise to Brandi in salute for extracting this difficult vow from young women on the prowl and in the height of their growing womanhood.

He noticed that Brandi wasn't stupid about it, though. She had given them plenty of other things to concentrate on to take their minds off the vow.

As well she had devised ways to redistribute their sexual energy. He wondered if she was aware of just how brilliant she was or if it was just something she had just accidentally stumbled on. Whatever the reason, the sheer genius of it was hard to deny.

Fishbone adjusted his cap on Tata's head.

He threw his hands in the air as though he'd been stung from the heat of Tata's evil glare. "You get the props, baby girl. You're all that and a bag of chips. So just chill."

Tata leaned against the car, relaxing. And he'd better know that. Regardless, Fish was her boy. And one day her time would come, and try as he might he wouldn't be able to stop it, either.

She had her ways. She was biding her time.

"Yeah. You just remember that," she said sassily, satisfied with his contriteness for now.

Fishbone's top lieutenant, Maestro, was a huge, heavyset, light-skinned dude known to be a sharp dresser as well as very light on his feet.

He was heavy-handed on the trigger, though, as some of his enemies had well found out. His fame had spread and so had his power, hence his position in Fishbone's organization.

He was also popular with the ladies. Yes, he was big, but he was also a good-looking charmer in his own right despite his size.

He had been leaning in his Cadillac listening to the conversations around him that were taking place. Finally, he got out of his car, winding, doing the latest club dance.

He finished with an elegant bow before the ladies. He smiled at Tangie and Tata, who were both bowled over in fits of giggles at his antics.

He was a big dude to be winding like that, yet he pulled

it off as though he were no more than 110 pounds. Maestro was 420 solid pounds, if he was a pound, seriously.

"Y'all are the bag of chips. You feeling me? We know you got it like that. After all, you are the Conquerors. We get it like a hundred-dollar bill," he said in his slow southern drawl. "Right, Fish?"

"Damn straight," Fishbone replied, backing his lieutenant.

"These some sensitive shorties, my man." Maestro laughed.

"A nigga can't be flicking they buttons. They some down chicks, and they don't mind plugging niggas, I heard."

Fishbone shook his head, laughing, too. He flipped Tata's cap backward on her head, indicating she was all that.

For Fishbone to do that to her singled her out as someone to be highly respected. For him to do that in front of two different gang factions raised her level of respect even amongst them.

Tangie directed her comments to Maestro, who'd always been like a second big brother to her. "Maestro, you know there ain't but one you. You always know exactly when to hand out a line. Oh, and not to mention when to wind. How the hell you learn to do that?"

"That's for me to know and you to find out, little sister," Maestro said as he took a final bow.

Tata decided to change the subject. As second in command her mind was always on business even when she projected the image that it was not.

Fish had pumped her with the flipping back of her cap, reminding her of her true essence, so she said, "Word has it you guys might be expanding turfs."

Fishbone turned deadly serious at Tata's words. "Word is like the wind. It blows in and it blows out."

Tata turned to look him in the eye. "What happens when it stops blowing?"

"Then it settles somewhere," Maestro answered for Fish.

Tata turned to give him a long look. Fishbone sized up Tata, mentally making note of her comment.

A young man sitting in a brand-spanking-new Jeep staring at Tangie had diverted her attention away from the intimate little group.

He was blowing smoke rings in her direction with a cigarette.

The pure air of sullen sultriness he gave off had captured her attention. He definitely had thug persona draped all over him. Tangie was secretly attracted to roughnecks.

She knew better than to even cast a second glance at anyone associated with her brother, though. However, she had momentarily lapsed into amnesia.

Fishbone became aware that they no longer had his sister's full attention. He turned to assess the situation, definitely not liking what he was sensing.

Maestro frowned.

Seeing the interested curiosity in Tangie's eyes, Fish quickly went into big-brother mode. "Yo, man, get your eyes off of my sister. Nigga, you know I don't play that."

If it had been anybody other than his sister, Fish would have had one of the others address the little thug nigga.

In this case, since it was his sister, he didn't hesitate to back him off and put him in his place without the décor of rank.

The young man backed off the eye contact immediately. Fish rarely spoke to him, and now he had reprimanded him in front of a crowd of people.

Damn, how could he have been so stupid? He'd known better but something about Tangie had captured his eye so he, too, had had a momentary loss of memory.

However, he wasn't stupid, so he knew it had better not happen again. He also didn't miss Maestro's frown. And he knew people had come up missing for less than the frown he saw on Maestro's face now.

"Fish, no disrespect, man." He quickly began the cleanup job. "I know the rules. I was just drifting, man, that's all. I'm sorry," he apologized profusely.

What the hell had he been thinking? He was going to get

the hell off of that weed, too much of that stuff took a brother's mind down.

However, it was too late. The damage was done.

He had caused Fishbone to cop a major attitude.

That's why Fishbone didn't let the little niggas out to play too long because they didn't know how to get down or act.

Some of them acted like they were losing their damn minds when it came to fine women.

"Man, ride up. We're getting the hell outta here. Now!" Fish ordered.

Tata sighed to herself. The party was definitely over. She hated to see Fish go. She could strangle that young punk with her bare hands.

The young man who had caused the infraction hit the ignition, immediately starting the car. He didn't have to be asked twice.

He'd have to work like a damn demon to get back in Fish's good graces. That was if he lived past midnight.

He'd be kicked out of the prized inner circle he'd worked so hard to get in, that's for damn sure. He'd be down in the ranks trying to work his way back up again, and that would be his punishment if grace was given.

If not, his fate could be much worse. "Damn," he whispered to himself.

Even if he had been looking at the hotly gorgeous Tata his fate would have been much better. Tata was a true vision, no doubt, but there was something elusive, something genuine about Tangie that had captured his attention.

That something had also made him let his guard down.

By his grace Fishbone had already decided to simply lower him in the ranks. He always did his best to minimize any spilling of blood. Yet his face reflected none of his thoughts.

Fishbone looked around at his members. None of them were happy with the face they saw on him. They definitely didn't see anything close to grace, that was for sure.

Life would get to be grueling before it got better.

Fish gave the signal they all knew was coming. Then he snapped his fingers. "Let's get it moving!"

He again traded caps with Tata, giving her back her own cap. Then he quickly kissed his sister on the cheek before jumping into his Porsche.

Maestro moved swiftly to his car. He kicked off the engine. The entire parking lot came to life. Headlights flashed and all engines jumped to life.

Fishbone yelled out of his window. "It's been nice, Conquerors!"

Tata watched him, wishing she were in the front seat next to him.

He shot out of his parking space with a squeal of tires. His was the first vehicle to leave the lot. All of them respectfully waited for him to pull out. They lined up behind him like the soldiers they were.

They left Crenshaw Boulevard. just as quickly as they had come.

The dust from their engines was all that remained.

Chapter 18

It was also a night for some of the other Conquerors, long cooped up, to be out and about for a night in the city.

This little act in itself was quite the rarity, but they had been given orders to be seen in various hot spots around the city, and so they were in complete compliance.

In addition to hanging out on Crenshaw Boulevard, some of them had opted for an after-hours gin-and-juice joint, though all they were drinking was sparkling water.

Just because *they* weren't drinking didn't mean the rest of the house wasn't liquored up as well as high off of whatever recreational drug was the current choice of the evening.

None of the Conquerers wanted to be the source of their own income, since everything in there flowing was flowing back into their own money coffers for distribution throughout the organization.

As well they knew firsthand what becoming your own best customer had done for a lot of people. And the training Brandi was instilling in them had them walking around thinking they were better than everybody else, so they saw drug use as far beneath them.

The music was blasting.

Hot bodies were sweating up the dance floor with the latest dance steps. People were floating around in movement to the beat as though they were levitating.

The levitation act was courtesy of the latest hot ten BET videos. Levitation. Where've you seen that happen before? It was like a damn Linda Blair remake of *The Exorcist* up in there.

For those who didn't have an interest in sweating or levitating they were getting their bling on. They were iced out, making sure everybody else in the house noticed them by prancing, styling, and profiling, as though they were on the runways of a Milan fashion show.

The night was fine, and everyone was in high spirits doing their own thing—that is, until a female gang, who went by the name of the Street Laws, arrived.

They were from a gang faction that hadn't fallen under the leadership of the Conquerors. In fact Brandi had rejected them and so an offer had not been extended for them to join.

The Street Laws had decided to crash the joint.

They were just outside of the turf currently controlled, united, and owned by the Conquerors.

The Street Laws had, of course, heard of the Conquerers. Everybody, it seemed, had heard of them. They were tired of hearing the Conquerors' name ringing all the time, as though they were diva goddesses.

The Street Laws gang was led by a girl known only by the name of Left Eye.

Left Eye was hostile. She didn't appreciate being rejected as well as disrespected in a single stroke by not even being offered an invitation to join the Conquerors by the prissy Ms. Brandi.

She couldn't stand the ground that Brandi was currently prancing on top of, making the rest of them look like common gangbangers.

Brandi treated the Street Laws as though they were beneath the Conquerers and nothing more than common hood rats. No, Left Eye didn't appreciate this attitude at all.

After she received word that the Conquerors would be in

the house at the gin-and-juice joint, she had decided to do a little infiltrating into Brandi's private little world.

Left Eye had been stabbed in her right eye with an ice pick and blinded during a fight she took up with one of her mother's crazy dope-fiend boyfriends.

Since then she always wore a black patch over her right eye. Her strength of sight had grown in her left eye due to the loss of sight in her right one.

Though she had only one good eye she could give a person a look that projected more power than if she'd had two.

On the same night that the Conquerors had decided to let off some steam, so coincidentally had the Street Laws.

Unbeknownst to some of the lower-level Conquerors, Brandi's antics had also been eating into Left Eye's profits. She was losing face fast on the streets and with some of her girls as well.

In fact there were rumors beginning to surface that some of them might be defecting from her gang to join forces with Brandi under her very enticing leadership.

A lot of people who weren't in wanted to be. Brandi had created an aura of desire.

Brandi was considered the bomb. She was being hailed as a woman to know and a force to be reckoned with. This had caused Left Eye to be eaten alive with envy as well as a vicious dose of jealousy.

Left Eye wasn't of the new generation of gangs who were making money, living off the fat of the land, and ruling cash as though it were coming in from legitimate, corporate-built businesses and miniempires.

She was from the code of the street. She was a true projects girl. Gangbanging, knocking niggas down a notch, and taking by force and by any other means necessary were the laws she was raised under.

Stealing a few packages, terrorizing, and making a few dollars—that back in the day frame of mind—was where she was still living. But things had changed.

Brandi was of a new generation. She was of a new frame of mind. Everything with her was timing, allies, and strategic placement.

She had outmaneuvered Left Eye without ever stepping foot onto her territory physically because, one, she was clever, two, she was a big thinker, and three, she initiated the type of action that eventually just swallowed up the little fish who wouldn't play.

Checkmate.

Brandi was dazzling, a magnetic draw, and a person whom people wanted to be in business with, hence her current popularity.

Left Eye couldn't stand her. She had decided she was no longer having it. She would send Ms. Brandi a message about what the real Original SGs (Original Street Gangs) were really about.

Brandi needed a lesson in the very foundation of gang life. She needed to be taught the ground rules of street gangs.

She couldn't just come up in there creating her own game. Left Eye intended to teach her a lesson. One that would send a message reverberating that would prevent any wannabes from trying to come up behind her at a later date.

Left Eye sent some of her hood rat Street Laws directly onto the turf of some of Brandi's lower-level Conquerors.

Once this was accomplished all she had to do was initiate in them the sparks, envy, and hatred it took to make the sparks fly.

Brandi had built a very layered empire, so there were different levels and factions within her posse. Some of them were actually far removed from the upper echelons of her organization, although each and every member received the same treatment and the same level of respect.

This was part of the reason they were so bonded with one another.

In accordance with Left Eye's attack strategy the lower level

Conquerors who were in place at the gin-and-juice joint became the target for the Street Laws.

The plan was simple in a setting of this type, and it was no big deal to kick it off.

One of the Street Laws brushed up against one of the Conquerors, displaying major attitude.

"You ever hear of the words *excuse me?*" the Conqueror questioned.

"Yeah," the Street Law replied. "I've heard it. I just ain't about to use it with the likes of you." With that she kept stepping.

Now, the Conquerors were well trained in discipline, so, not wanting to step outside of their reputation for discipline and holding it down, the girl who had been brushed decided to try to let it slide.

That was until another one of them came by and did it, too.

Brandi had taught them that the best fighters were the ones who knew how to fight but who worked to avoid the fight, not the ones who started it or felt insecure enough to show off their fight skills.

And they believed her.

Her teachings were deeply ingrained in those girls. However, no disrespect in blatant form could be tolerated because still and all, they were the Conquerors.

After the second brushing the Conqueror girl was starting to lose her temper. "What the hell is your problem?"

The girl from the Street Laws stepped right up to her. "You," she said. Then she shoved her. That was it. It was on.

Before anyone knew what was happening they were getting their scrap on. Gin and juice were flying.

The joint was closed down in record speed. Weapons were drawn. Fortunately nobody was shot because Brandi's girls were trained in the art of removing the opponent's weapons. They quickly disarmed the Street Laws.

Instead of shooting them the Conquerors settled for an old-school beat down along the lines of what the Street Laws had started. The Conquerors weren't even winded when they finished beating them up, due to their extensive battlelike training.

They consequently beat the Street Laws like they owned them, leaving a bloody, crippling trail that made for one very unhappy, ashamed Left Eye when she received the bad news. Apparently, she wasn't the law of the street that she thought she was.

She had kicked off a fight that she couldn't win, and now she would be the laughingstock of the streets unless she found a way to change that.

And change it she would.

Chapter 19

Upon hearing the bad news about her underlings and their public shame in the gin-and-juice joint, Left Eye slammed down the phone so hard in the cradle that the cradle cracked completely in half.

She'd have to buy a new cordless phone, thanks to her little display of anger. She couldn't believe her ears. These niggas were completely whacked.

She was sick to death of hearing about the snobbish, bling, blinging Brandi and her precious Conquerors. Brandi Hutchinson. Brandi Hutchinson. Brandi Hutchinson. Damn her straight to hell.

She wished Brandi would drop dead in her sleep.

Lately it felt like that was all Left Eye heard about day and damn night. Brandi this and Brandi that.

These niggas needed to get a life, they acted like Brandi was the only thing to talk about these days.

Now some of her girls had wound up injured. They were the talk of the underground circuit as well as the laughing-stock of the hood for getting their behinds straight up whipped in an after-hours joint.

A joint that she knew for a fact the very prissy Ms. Brandi's girls basically thought they were too good to even be in attendance at.

Left Eye's little score in locating their hangout spot for the night had backfired on her.

She needed a plan that was going to garner Brandi's undivided attention. She needed a plan that would make Brandi see her for the contender that she was. She needed a swing move that would bring major respect running to her door.

Brandi needed to be cut down to size. That needed to happen fast, like yesterday. Hell, this wasn't Wall Street, despite whatever grand illusions Brandi was suffering under.

This was Los Angeles, home to one of the biggest hoods in the country.

Where the hell did she think she was?

Left Eye kicked the broken cradle with her foot. This was the West Coast. With all of her Wall Street antics Brandi's slimy behind needed to be on the East Coast. Maybe them niggas back East would appreciate her, but this crap she was pulling made Left Eye wonder about her West Coast roots.

You had male gangs that hadn't tried half the crap Brandi was pulling. And she was a newbie. An off the hook schoolgirl who not too long ago had been running around flaunting her straight-A school status and hanging out at rap concerts.

What the hell was wrong with this picture?

Left Eye was pissed as hell. In her opinion Brandi had just rose up one morning and decided to make a place for herself, and them niggas in the Square had basically sat back and let her do it.

They were so stupid they didn't have a damn thing on lock. Now all of their possible profits were filtering back into Ms. Wall Street's bank.

Well, not Left Eye. She wasn't from the Square and it was a good thing she wasn't. Because she wasn't having it. Brandi had better ask somebody. She'd better ask anybody before she got smoked.

This was the hood. There were certain rules, regulations, and behavior codes that applied to the streets.

Despite Ms. Thang's popular belief and her spreading of

the new gang rhetoric, this wasn't a corporate boardroom they were dealing with here.

Brandi thought and acted like she was the creator of new life or something. Not. Besides that, she was also interfering with Left Eye's cash now, and that was a definite no-no.

Left Eye wasn't down in the Square messing with Brandi's money, and hell to the nah, she wasn't about to let Brandi's spiderweb antics keep dipping into her cash tills.

She conveniently ignored the fact that Brandi already had a major grip that she hadn't been able to prevent. Admitting this was much too much to ask at this point. Better to live a lie than the truth.

Even though Left Eye's operations were just outside of Brandi's turf, Brandi's moneymaking capabilities were extending far and wide, and they were cutting into Left Eye's profits on the real.

As well there wasn't a lot Left Eye could do about it because Brandi had paid for territorial rights, and her power was extending outside of the hood into areas that people like Left Eye never ventured into.

Despite it all Left Eye still had to hold it down, so that meant she had to come up with something. Something that could strike at the heart of the very capable Ms. Brandi.

She needed something that would make her sit up and really take notice.

As Left Eye sat across from the projects where Brandi grew up, she saw what might be the right opportunity materializing before her very eyes.

Left Eye was so low level compared to Brandi's status that it wasn't a big deal for her to be in a spot of observation, so she used this to her advantage.

Brandi's posse would rain down on her just as they would anyone else on the street who made a wrong move. That was just a fact of life, Brandi style.

The area was on lock, plain and simple. She knew she couldn't get in there looking like herself without them knowing she was there. So her plan had been to arrive in the midst of them, unidentifiable as either friend or foe.

Left Eye didn't make any out-of-the-ordinary moves or risk bringing any undue attention her way. In fact if you didn't know her personally you would not have identified her as a gangbanger. She was so disguised that she was not even wearing her easily identifiable eye patch. She had on a pair of regular seeing glasses. After she'd shed her gangster-style clothing, she looked rather matronly in her everyday getup.

She was a bit to the pudgy, plainer-looking side of things, anyway, and so the look she had chosen only enhanced this image.

She wasn't a fool—she wouldn't waltz onto Brandi's turf waving a red flag, saying, look at me, and risk getting killed. She was much too smooth for that. Since the gin-and-juice-joint incident she didn't for a minute underestimate Brandi's posse. She knew that would be a grave mistake.

All she wanted to do was blend in with any other pedestrians on the street and not cause any attention. She needed to get close enough so she could smell the real Brandi for herself.

So far it was all good.

As she watched she saw a bunch of kids playing in the streets. Some were running through an old sprinkler that had definitely seen better days.

The day was hot, so people were suffering under the sweltering temperatures, and that run-down sprinkler was better than nothing.

The small kids had young mothers who looked tired and wilted from the heat and humidity. But the kids were happy as they shrieked, ran, and pushed each other into the sprinkling water.

Despite the heat you still had some young knuckleheads out on the basketball court shooting hoops, talking junk to each other. Each of them was trying to be the man and bring attention to their plays.

Once some of the young girls showed up they would really start to strut their stuff.

Ari and her girls were jumping double Dutch again. Young police officers, straight out of the Police Academy, on bicycles with blue short-sleeved shirts and shorts, were pedaling alongside the streets, keeping an eye on the projects.

Left Eye wondered if any of the young rookies ever complained that that was where most of them wound up at upon leaving the Academy—out on the streets in shorts pedaling bicycles.

It was one helluva way to make a living as far as she was concerned. Usually when death went down on these streets, they were the first ones hit even when their air patrols were supposed to have the area on lock.

Hell, if she was one of them, but damn if she'd ever be, but if she was, she'd insist on being in the air, not on the ground in shooting range of some of the crazy death-struck niggas that occupied the Square. That was some ludicrous bull crap if she'd ever seen it.

She stopped watching the bicycling police officers as she saw Brandi stroll up to the double Dutch game along with Tangie and Tata and some other members of the very envied Conquerors.

She couldn't believe her eyes. Sure, she'd come there hoping for some tidbit of information that would help her, but at the same time she never expected to see the Queen of the hood herself, the very elegant Ms. Brandi, who even in her street gear gave off a certain presence, strolling around the Square as though she owned every damn square inch of it.

She'd hoped to get a sense or a smell of her, but she sure hadn't expected to see her in person.

This little turn of events meant the heifer was still slumming in her old neighborhood despite all the hype going on about her, Left Eye observed. Well, wasn't that extremely interesting.

Brandi watched Ari as she flipped, jumped backward, and

landed on her feet in the rope. Tangie shouted out loud, proud of Ari's accomplishment. "My girl be killing that rope!"

Brandi smiled proudly as though Ari were her daughter. However, she was her girl, and she was proud of her. "Yeah, that's my girl, Ari. She can go. There isn't anyone around here that's going to go head up with her in that rope, believe that. My girl can basically take it to the tournaments."

When Ari finished jumping rope another girl slid in the rope to take her place. Left Eye watched as Brandi beckoned Ari over to where she was.

When Ari arrived Brandi put her arm around her shoulder. She walked her away from the others so the two of them could be alone.

Left Eye watched the interplay between the two of them intently.

"So what's up, Ari Lynne?" Brandi asked.

"Ugh. Why you calling me that, Brandi? You know how I hate that name. Just call me Ari," she said with a bit of an attitude.

Brandi's attitude matched hers. "So what if you don't like it? I like that name."

Ari stopped walking to challenge Brandi. Looking her straight in the eye she asked, "Why?"

Brandi stared back at her, secretly liking her spunk but at the same time biting her lip to keep from telling her little young behind she'd better not get smart with her. Instead she said bluntly, "Because it's yours."

This answer threw Ari off course. A frown creased her forehead.

The sound of the Mister Softee truck coming down the street with its familiar music drew Ari's attention away from Brandi's answer.

Brandi followed Ari's gaze. "You want a ice cream?" She knew Ari, as well as many of the kids she played with, could be outside playing for days without a penny in their pockets to buy anything.

Ari smiled brightly. "Yeah." She hesitated, then proudly said, "I've got money. But my friends don't have none."

Brandi reached into her pocket. She pulled out a small wad of money. "Here. There's enough for you and your crew. You go hook them up. You can hook them up for a good while on that but don't spend it all in one place, okay?"

Left Eye sat back, contemplating while keeping a watchful eye. She couldn't leave the area because she knew Brandi had it on lock.

She'd have to wait to leave until they were gone, otherwise she would be spotted, and if that happened, well, if that happened she would be flirting with serious injury or death. Neither of whose doors she wanted to knock on right then.

Ari nodded, happy at being able to play bigshot with her friends on Brandi's dollar. She started to run off. Brandi called her back.

When she returned Brandi tousled her hair. "Ain't you forgetting something?"

Ari frowned. Then a big smile lit her face as she remembered. "Sorry."

She reached up and hugged Brandi tightly around the neck. Then she planted a kiss on her cheek. Brandi flashed her a smile as Ari ran toward the ice-cream truck beckoning to her friends.

They dropped the rope to run after her to the ice-cream truck. Brandi and her crew continued walking the projects.

After they all had gotten their ice cream, Ari and her friends went back to where they were jumping rope. One little girl named Tonya watched Ari as the two of them stood on the side of the rope waiting for their turn.

Finally Tonya asked Ari, "You going to have your own gang like Brandi when you get bigger?"

Ari screwed up her face while still licking the ice cream.

"Nah." She took another lick. "My mother says I'm going to college. Cuz I told her I'm going to be a doctor. I want to work with little babies and make them well when they get sick. So I ain't going to have no gang."

Tonya licked her ice cream before she could lose the dripping sweetness. "That's good. I think you'll make a good doctor, Ari."

"Thanks," Ari said, returning her attention to the double Dutch game.

Left Eye bit her lip in contemplation.

Chapter 20

Brandi, Tata, and Tangie strolled along through the projects. The heat was suffocating, but Brandi seemed oblivious as Tata and Tangie strolled on either side of her, remaining quiet as they always were while she assessed situations.

Her mind gathered as well as discarded information until she came upon just the right combination of things.

Both Tata and Tangie had the utmost respect for her peculiar brand of brilliance. Neither of them ever wanted to disturb it when they knew it was at play. After all, that mind of hers was what was getting them all paid, and paid very well these days.

They were both more than familiar with this contemplative side to Brandi, so they just lent her their silent support during these times. Their presence was felt yet it was unobtrusive.

Brandi observed Lisa doing her number again, begging for drugs while awaiting her checks. She had lost a lot of weight. If it was possible she looked worse than the last time Brandi had seen her.

This time Brandi looked away because if she had mentally followed the trail from Lisa's actions to hers it would have led directly to her own doorstep. Life had a funny way of turning around and coming back on you sometimes.

For some reason Brandi had been mentally wrapping herself in a cocoon of denial when it came to certain realities in her life.

Especially realities that were in direct conflict with the moral codes she had been raised with. She was in a constant battle, though she never mentioned it to anyone, to keep her father's voice of admonishments out of her life.

She also had to fight to keep her mother's constant little spiritual teachings from ringing in her ears.

Her dad had become like a ghost that she carried around with her. That was how much she heard his voice and saw his disapproval. It was like he was there but not really there.

He intruded on her thoughts at the oddest times, niggling away at her conscience. She stayed at war trying to keep the sound of his voice out of her head.

Brandi looked away from Lisa's actions, deciding to visualize the projects as something other than they were. Something she dreamed of them being. This was much safer ground for her to mentally tread on.

Her father didn't know what he was talking about, he just thought he did. The world no longer operated in his old-school, outdated way of seeing things. It was a new day.

And only the strong survived.

Hell, she couldn't eat her morals, nor could she trade them to pay the rent. This train of thought had become a constant form of justification for her. She brought her mind back to the present.

"Imagine what would happen if we had these projects bulldozed down to the very dirt they're sitting on?"

Tangie sighed. "Yeah. And, then where would these people live? All you'd have would be that bunch of dirt."

Inwardly Brandi sighed, wishing Tangie would get some real insight. She couldn't see past her nose most of the time.

"We'd create a new and better neighborhood right here. With new houses they could live in without graffiti on the walls and hallways that smell like piss. Hey, we could plant some grass and flowers," Brandi stated patiently.

Tata only smiled. In her opinion Brandi loved to live outside of the real deal at times. She was definitely a dreamer.

Sure, she had pulled off the gang unification and income factors, but what she was talking about here was far more and far bigger than marshalling together street gangs, and Tata knew it was a tall order.

Brandi hadn't experienced the other side of the fence the way Tata had. And Tata knew from firsthand experience it wasn't always a pretty picture.

Even when Tata had been in school she'd always been smarter than the other kids. That was why she'd always been in trouble. She could see what they couldn't.

She knew that crap they sold them in school was nothing more than that. It was a way to control them. To teach them only what they wanted them to know.

Then, when they went out in the world trying to make it on that fake tip, they could barely make ends meet. Tata had known they weren't teaching her how to own anything. They were only training her mind to work for those who did own, and she wasn't feeling that mess.

That was why she had been a terror in school. Her resentment had built like a storm inside of her. Schools were getting away with that nonsense in the name of education all around the country.

Sometimes it frustrated her that people couldn't see beyond the noses in front of their faces. That was what had attracted her to Brandi's plan in the first place. Brandi was talking about having and building your own dream. Not buying into someone else's dream.

If you wanted to rent one of these prison apartments in the projects that was fine. If you wanted to tear down the prison to build a real home, one that offered freedom instead of bondage and imprisonment, then that was a horse of a different color.

Tata's smile widened as she tossed Brandi's words around in her mind. That would be more than a tall order, it would be damn near impossible to pull off. Damn near but not totally.

Brandi stopped walking as she watched some little kids in another part of the projects dart through a fire hydrant that had been turned on to cool them off.

"I think Ari and her girls are good enough to sponsor for the double Dutch tournaments. What do you think?" Brandi asked, switching her train of thought.

"Hell yeah," Tangie said.

"That's what I'm talking about," Tata seconded the motion.

"All right. Tangie, I want you to hook them up. Get them to the trials and tryouts, and get them uniforms. File all the paperwork for them to enter the competition. Oh, and don't forget to get signed parental releases from their parents."

Brandi turned to Tata. "Tata, set up a nonprofit organization that can handle the sponsoring of the tournament. Let's do the same thing for some of the kids that play basketball as well."

Then Brandi looked around the projects taking in every sight, smell, and sound. "I think it's time we started to take care of our own. Don't you?" she asked, not really expecting an answer.

She already knew the answer. It was an emphatically ringing yes, and that yes was ringing loudly in her ears.

Her daddy would one day see that she could do something right.

She would teach him that instead of listening to somebody else's sermon, sometimes you had to create your own.

Chapter 21

That night a bunch of young boys were sandwiched between the Square's apartments shooting craps. Money and dice lay all over the ground while they strutted around hollering at one another.

The young boys were watching the roll of the dice intently as though their very lives depended on that roll. One of them, named Mace, picked up the money off the ground, and another one, called Cameo, stomped his foot in anger.

Mace threw his hands up in the air with the money held tightly in his fist. "Yo, man, ain't no sense in you copping no attitude. The money had my name on it. It's as simple as that. It's a C note with my name on it, and you know that."

"Shut up, nigga, and roll the dice," Cameo said, shaking his head, frustrated at Mace's win.

There was a chorus of laughter, and a clapping and slapping of hands in the air from the rest of the boys.

Hearing the sound of a helicopter overhead they all looked up. The helicopter was drifting very close to their action.

The lights were out on the helicopter, and the sound had been minimized as the machine drifted in the air toward them. They had been too caught up in what they were doing to notice it.

Before they could react the helicopter pinned them with a bright, powerful light that was blinding in its power.

A voice surged from the loudspeaker from the cop sitting in the passenger side of the helicopter. "All right, you little punks. Break it up. Now! This ain't Vegas."

The helicopter was hovering just above the rooftop.

All the boys scrambled to pick up the money and the dice. They knew they had better move fast because the next thing coming down would be gunshots, and most likely lots of them in the form of an automatic spraying the area.

They shoved the money in their pockets while shielding their eyes from the light.

Mace yelled at them. "Man, get that damn light out of our eyes. We can't see ya but we hear you, punk."

Cameo laughed, yelling, "Yeah, you punk Blue Boys. Kill that light."

The sound of gunfire rang out. The boys ran through the projects, ducking and dodging, using the buildings as shields as bullets ricocheted all around them.

That was just how it was in their hood. Death was always creeping and lurking around the corner. And you never knew when it had your name on it.

Chapter 22

Upon hearing the helicopter and the gunshots, Sloan Patterson padded out of bed with her hair wrapped tight in a silk scarf.

She looked up at the ceiling in her living room before covering her ears and dropping to the floor. She crawled cautiously to the window to look out.

You always had to lay low because you never knew when a bullet might come flying through your apartment. Sloan's apartment had several bullet holes in it, and she wasn't responsible for any of them.

The living room was extremely well kept as well as nicely furnished. You could tell extra work had been put into the apartment. The apartment reflected the fact that someone had pride and cared, despite its location in the very notorious Square.

The atmosphere reflected the pride of a woman who was struggling yet trying hard to hang on to her dignity. After peering out the window she crawled from the living room, crouching up against the wall, to go down the hallway to check on her children.

She had to be careful because more times than not, a stray bullet had wound up somewhere that it shouldn't have, regardless of who was doing the shooting.

Bullets didn't have names on them. And Sloan didn't have

any desire to add any more bullet holes to her decorating pattern.

She looked in the first bedroom and saw two of her children, ages five and six, asleep in their beds. She breathed a deep sigh of relief.

A couple of kids had been killed in the projects in their sleep from stray bullets.

Funny thing was nobody ever knew what had happened, or whose bullet it was or what gun it had come from. It was just a casualty of living in the Square.

Slowly Sloan crawled from her younger kids' bedroom, trying to ignore the gunfire, shouts, yells, and blazing lights surrounding the outside grounds as she made her way to the second bedroom to check.

She looked in to find the bed was empty. The room belonged to her fifteen-year-old son, J. She had known the room would be empty before she arrived. Call it a mother's instincts.

Besides, if J had been in the house he would have been trying to protect her. He was the one who had told her to always get on the floor when shots rang out so as not to get accidentally hit by a flying bullet.

He was so streetwise for his age. It hurt her to think about it, but she couldn't deny his built-in instinct for survival. And she was torn because she didn't want to kill his spirit for knowing how to survive.

J, the initial name by which friends, foes, and culprits knew him, had a penchant for the streets. He used every trick in the book including sneaking out of his room to be a part of them.

Sloan was so exhausted from trying to keep him safe from something that he didn't want to be safe from that sometimes she felt the weight of that burden hanging like a rock around her neck.

She often felt like she was fighting a losing battle. Still, she had to try.

She slid down the wall quietly, her face awash in tears when she realized J's bed was empty as she listened to the growing spate of gunshots outside of her window.

She pulled out her cell phone, beginning the ritual of calling all of J's friends, hoping against hope that he was safe, praying that he was, as she did every night, while she listened to the helicopter's blades move into the distance fading away.

"Please, Lord. Please," she whispered.

Chapter 23

As per the prearranged schedule, at the break of dawn all the Conquerors were out in full force. They were dressed in uniform standing at attention in front of Brandi.

Brandi walked around center stage in deep thought. They, too, had come to be used to her bursts of pacing, so not one of them dared to move or say a word during this time.

Secretly she was seething a bit over the gin-and-juice-joint incident but she had decided to keep this from spilling over into their routine.

She wasn't about petty, low-level street fighting and they knew it. She had received the report of what had happened. Everything would be dealt with in its time.

Finally Brandi stopped in front of the young women. "We are the Generation. It is our time. Nothing before or after matters. It's what we are now that counts. And you know that. We are the Generation. Say it."

The entire posse repeated in unison, "We are the Generation."

Brandi shouted at them, "Say it again! Louder. Say it like you mean it!"

"WE ARE THE GENERATION!" their collective voices chimed.

Brandi shouted with more intensity. "Say it louder!"

"WE ARE THE GENERATION! WE ARE THE GENER-
ATION! WE ARE THE GENERATION!"

The young girls' eyes never wavered from the center of the
room. There was not a sign of passion, with the exception of
their continuous chanting. "WE ARE THE GENERATION!
WE ARE THE GENERATION!"

After they had chanted this refrain so many times their
voices were almost hoarse, Brandi held up a hand calling for
them to halt.

They stopped the chanting on a dime. They could have
been conducted by a symphony director, their voices were
that in sync.

Brandi hit her hand to her chest, then back at them, indicating their unification with one another.

"You and I. We are the Generation. Each day we will
begin with this motto. We have to engrave this in our memories because we're taking over."

Brandi paced in front of the girls. Her black spit-shined
boots glistened from the rays of the early-morning sun in the
warehouse.

"We are taking over. Say it. Believe it. Know it. We're
doing this now. Because now is our time. You got it?"

She continued on, not really wanting or waiting for an answer to her question. All the girls knew that, so they remained silent waiting for her to continue.

She was passionate and convincing. She imparted as well
as instilled her convictions in those who were following her.

They bought in because it gave them—for most of them
the only time in their lives—something to really live for. It
gave them a place to belong. It provided them with someone
who understood and cared about their feelings.

The posse gave them something they were missing in their
personal lives. It gave them a common goal as well as a way
to get paid, and get paid well.

Brandi's vision was unique because up until her formation

of the Conquerors the female gangs had never really received much attention, notoriety, or mention, for that matter.

All of the focus had always been on the male gangs. That had changed.

Most female gangs, the few that existed, were considered to be only counterparts to the male factions.

Brandi had single-handedly changed all of that practically overnight. She possessed a warlike mentality, and she had garnered a very valuable asset—a talent for being persuasive.

When she spoke people listened.

She stopped pacing once again, her voice so low that even in the quietness of the warehouse they had to strain to hear her. She purposely orchestrated it to be that way. She was always onstage. She was always the consummate actress.

She looked each of them in the eye while speaking. Her presence was so overpowering that even the members who were way in the back of the formation felt as though she were looking directly at them, directing her words to each of them, privately.

She had a way of making each girl feel included as part of the group yet individual, as though each of them were special in their own right.

"The generation before us didn't do it," she whispered.

She had whispered those pain-filled words so very low that she knew they couldn't hear her. She also knew no one would dare to ask her to repeat them or speak louder.

But they needed to hear this. They needed to know the truth of it. And, most of all, they needed to feel it.

Tilting her chin while willing the threatened tears to be held at bay inside of her, she repeated the words loudly enough for the entire warehouse to hear them.

"The generation before us didn't do it."

She went back to direct eye contact.

"If they had we wouldn't be here. There wouldn't have been a need for us. There would have been a way made for us. No one fought for us, so that means"—and here she paused so long they wondered if she was ever going to finish the sentence—"so that means we're going to have to fight for ourselves. And this is where we start. We are the Generation."

Brandi looked at the sunlight streaming through the warehouse. She felt a profound sadness, as though there were an answer that was eluding her. An answer she couldn't seem to find.

But a true leader never showed indecision, even when they felt it. This fact was ingrained in her very spirit.

"We are the Generation!" Brandi shouted. "Got it?"

In unison they replied, "Got it!"

"I asked you if you got it!"

"Got it! The Generation. We are!" They replied in perfect rhythm.

Brandi surveyed the room for a last time.

"We will deal with the current situation at hand when it is time. Suit up. Make sure you're wearing your vests. Make sure you do a complete weapon check first. You're going to break off into your individual teams under your designated team leaders. Your team leaders will ensure procedure. The masks—I want them on your faces. No exceptions. Understood?"

"Understood," they all replied, eyes forward, their shoulders held straight back in an act of pride. Staunch conviction reflected in their voices.

With that the posse broke into formation, running around the warehouse, chanting over and over again, "WE ARE THE GENERATION!"

Chapter 24

Brandi had increased her frequency in visiting the salon to twice a week since Tata had approved all of the new security clearances. Her visits to the salon were fast becoming the major highlight of her week.

With all of the strenuous workouts she participated in, as well as the strict diet and the discipline of her routine, you would think this would have been enough to relieve a lot of her tensions.

However, the truth was she was increasingly feeling the pressure. Pressure that she had never calculated or anticipated before springing into diva action and deciding to tread ground that others dared not step foot on. Her drive had spurred her to strive for boundless limits.

She hadn't known just how stressful being a leader and in charge could be. The responsibility alone for shouldering other people's actions was huge for a girl her age. It would have been humungous for someone a great deal older than her.

Originally she had been driven by pure adrenalin, hatred, and anger as well as by a need for a sense of direction.

She had also been led by misguided pride, as were so many who found themselves in similar positions at one time or another.

Often those in such a position want and need to take action if for no other reason than for the sake of taking action.

The crossroads of a person's life are often fraught with
many emotions, missteps, and confusion.

Once she had chosen a direction Brandi was left with the
mechanics of developing her day-to-day plans.

She constantly had to anticipate the moves of the opposition before they happened. Which meant safeguards always
had to be in place just in case and in the event of. As good as
she was, no one could prepare for every eventuality.

It just wasn't possible.

Now she was dealing with the crabs-in-the-barrel syndrome. She remembered this syndrome being a favorite of
her father's, one of his discussing-the-issues platforms. Of
how people tried to keep other people down and from climbing out of similar circumstances simply because they couldn't
handle change or advancement.

Now, because she didn't deal with low-level gang beat
downs, she was feeling the appetite of the crabs-in-the-barrel
syndrome, especially since the gin-and-juice-joint incident.

Also, as much as she hated to admit it, she was beginning
to feel her father may have had a point when he was on this
particular soapbox.

The incident had become a shining example of the crabs
hanging around her ankles, trying to keep her from climbing
out of that barrel.

At the same time she was dealing with her own personal
appetite for growth that was astounding and could seriously
use some taming.

The more she actually accomplished, the less she felt like
she had accomplished inside, and the more driven she felt.

She was finding she constantly had to feed her need for
takeover in order to feel the original rush that had gotten her
where she was in the first place.

She was always feeling like she should accomplish more,

and so she lived in a constant state of animal-like hunger. It surged through her body from the moment she awakened in the wee hours of the morning until she shut her eyes at night.

It was very much like a personal haunting.

The takeovers were growing at an alarming rate as she extended her turf and fed her hunger.

She was exulting in the praise of others and in the impact she had on people merely by appearing. People like Frenchie, who orbited around her the instant she appeared.

The more they depended on her actions, the more she felt the need to protect them, so this also increased her expansion into areas where she felt people needed her services. Areas that she knew needed her own particular brand of protection. All for a price, of course.

That was the trade-off. It was part of the barter system. You always had to give something in exchange for what you got.

The constant adulation and worshiplike status was heady stuff for a young girl who was just about to grace the age of nineteen.

Chase Ajani considered it a stroke of good fortune that the very intense, gorgeous, and what he considered wicked, Ms. Brandi had increased her visits to the salon. It allowed him ample opportunity to increase his observation of her when she was at her most vulnerable.

He had a line into what she'd been up to, and truly he was impressed with that gold mine of a mind of hers as well as with the slick sheen of beauty she radiated.

The gold that hung from her neck and wrists paled in comparison to the golden light that lit any room she walked in to.

Chase was patiently putting together his plan for capture, and most of all his strategy for his complete dominance of her. He could, of course, settle for nothing less.

It was one thing to own a fine ruby. It was another thing to own the soul of it, to possess the very mine from which that precious gem had been unearthed.

The soul was the part that was more illusive, more difficult to capture. It was part of what made the chase so very exciting in itself; first the discovery and then the ownership.

Chase was sometimes called by his last name by some of his counterparts, the ones who preferred his last name to his first. For him it didn't really matter, either Chase or Ajani he would answer to.

He was a man who inspired awe in others.

He was also a man who demanded instant respect without ever speaking of it. His very presence spoke of accepting nothing less. So it was fitting that some would call him by the name in which he was victorious.

He allowed his name to roll off his own lips. "Ajani."

Ajani was the present character he was floating in and absorbed in, if anyone had been observing him, which they weren't. He floated in and out of different character personalities at whim.

The world was his stage, and he never missed a shot to perform, to illuminate the masses, or to draw the praises of those who were less than he.

Once again he stood as he always did behind the glass window in the salon with his hands pushed deep into his tailored light-linen trousers.

He was the perfect picture of a sensuous woman's dream. He was a portrait for women who salivated for men. Most of them never saw the blemish on the picture until it was too late.

Ajani was the epitome of respect. He was self-made. Few men could make this claim, because they followed in the footsteps of others, traveling along paths already created for them.

Ajani had a unique claim in this regard. He had treaded grounds that other men never even dreamed about. He was the creator of things often not seen but very definitely felt.

As such he was about to become Brandi Hutchinson's worst nightmare.

Chapter 25

Brandi tossed and turned fitfully in her sleep. She mumbled so loudly that if she hadn't been alone, surely the other person would have tried to awaken her.

Most likely they would have been a bit alarmed at the sounds that were emanating from her. Grunts of pain and distress rent the air.

As it was she was alone without anyone to hear her. She was wrapped tight, a bound, captured hostage, with no escape inside of her own nightmare.

Shadows, images, and voices invaded her unconscious mind, laying the foundation, the very format for a clandestine meeting. They opened a doorway between the conscious and the unconscious.

They were also planting vicious seeds of opposition in her enemies as only those who move in the spirit can. And, before too long, Brandi would be in a state of reaping. Reaping what she had sown.

The worst of it was she would have no recollection of this nightmare that had befallen her, and therefore no way to connect the dots of fate. It was a fate that was rushing her way at warp speed.

"My black Sleeping Beauty." A whisper floated across the winds of her unconscious without any frame of reference for her to attach it to.

While she had been remolding and remodeling herself on the outside, forces she'd never, ever dreamed of reckoning with were remolding her without her awareness—and most of all without giving her a choice.

The whispered words continued to blow through the recesses of her mind until they were like a gentle wind against her cheek.

Brandi kicked off the 1000 thread count sateen sheets she normally luxuriated in sleeping in. She wiped the sweat from her brow as her body temperature soared.

She kicked around in a fit of hysterics, thrashing on the bed as though she were fighting for her very life, yet she never woke up.

That is, she never woke until she found herself in the pine box with dirt being thrown over her while she was still alive, with the suffocating dirt filling her throat and lungs.

She clawed through the dirt, pushing with all her strength at the lid on top of the closed pine box, and with that she awoke.

She sat up screaming, only to find she was in the warmth and comfort of her own bedroom.

She caught a glimpse of the terror in her eyes reflected in the mirror sitting across from her bed. It was the same mirror that had captured and imprisoned her spirit without her ever being the wiser.

She was staring at a shell. Ajani smiled at her from the other side of the mirror.

The only problem was she couldn't see him.

Brandi's mother Rita sat straight up in bed in her bedroom at the same time that Brandi sat up in hers, when a picture of Brandi that had been on her dresser crashed to the floor, shattering into pieces.

Charles stared at the broken glass before pulling his shaking wife into his arms.

He had no doubt that the broken picture was an omen.

An omen of what was the question that bore asking.

Chapter 26

Brandi shaded her eyes so she could peek through the screen door of Q's apartment after knocking on the porch door. She knew Q's mother had the day off, so she wondered what was taking her so long to open the locked screen door.

Finally Renita appeared, worn and tired-looking. She unlatched the screen, waving Brandi inside.

"Hi, Brandi," she said without much enthusiasm. Defeat and weariness laced her every word. Her voice sounded as if she were doing her best to just put one foot in front of the other every day.

Brandi lowered her head in the face-to-face presence of Q's mother's very obvious pain.

Brandi would have done anything she could have to erase it, to take back that one night up to and including never attending the concert at all. How she wished she could turn back the hands of time.

She realized that there were many things in life that could be done, but changing things that had already happened wasn't one of them.

Time was elusive and waited for no one, nor did it turn itself back for any person. The only thing time could be counted on to do was to keep on going.

Brandi was at a loss to do anything other than what she

had been doing. The fruitlessness of the situation washed over her.

"Hi," she said softly, trying to keep all she was feeling from reflecting in her voice, burdening Q's mother even more.

Renita gave a small smile.

"I came to see Q. I wanted to take him for a walk."

Renita knew why Brandi was there. She was loyal and never missed a visit with Q. She knew Q looked forward to her visits. They were like brother and sister.

She nodded, again waving Brandi on.

Brandi was a nice girl who had done a lot to help out with Q. She was almost like the daughter Renita had never had. That was how close Brandi and her son had always been, and how often they had been in each other's houses before this all happened.

But seeing Brandi, unbeknownst to Brandi, was difficult for her. Because every time Renita saw one of Bobby's friends it reminded her of his condition, and Lord help her, but she couldn't help but to wonder why it had to be him.

Lately, every time she saw another healthy teenager taking their life for granted she asked herself this question.

She knew it wasn't right, yet she couldn't stop the thought from leaping into her mind. Try as she might she couldn't rid herself of the thought.

That was why, even with all Brandi was doing, she sometimes had a hard time seeing her or any of Q's friends.

Q's predicament had locked him and Renita into their own personal prison. Renita had no idea how to come out of it. She also had no belief that they ever would. She kept seeing Bobby in the before-and-after stages, as though he were some reality show makeover candidate.

Looking at Brandi she did her best to vanquish these thoughts.

"You know where to find him, sweetheart," she said softly, hoping her words would draw attention away from what she was really feeling. "He's in his room. You can go on in."

Brandi hesitated, thinking of saying something to ease her pain. Then she thought better of it. In reality what could she say that would take away Q's mother's pain?

Nothing. That's what. There was absolutely nothing at all she could say that would change that.

She walked down the hallway to Q's room. She could smell his sickness in the air. She could feel his frailness and the loss of his vitality. She wore the burden of it like a cloak around her shoulders without being totally aware of it.

It was too bad in a way that she could only follow the medicinal smell of his sickness. Because if she had been able to smell the foulness of it, the actual stench of the truth behind it, as well as the truth that lurked deep below the surface of these types of incidents, perhaps she might have chosen a different course to travel.

As it was she couldn't ascertain anything other than what was in front of her face. She was covering her ground in the only ways known to her. All that she knew and saw were the physical results.

In the same instant that Brandi walked down the hall to Q's room, Left Eye was trailing the scents of her life, and all she saw in Brandi's life were the sickness and the foul smell of Brandi's latest actions.

The more jealousy and hatred she harbored toward Brandi, the more her own motives for her imminent destruction were fed.

And the more the winds of Brandi's fate blew in the direction of Ajani's orchestration.

When Brandi reached Q's room she looked inside and saw that he was sitting by the window, looking out at the kids playing.

The room was sparsely furnished to make room for all of the medical equipment including a special bed and chair.

It was like a blessing and a curse. It was considered a blessing that Brandi had made these things possible, at least by some people.

Those who possessed more wisdom didn't consider it a blessing. However, wisdom was not running around in abundance.

All of those in the yeah corner, including Q's mother, forgot to consider the source of the income, which completely nullified what was considered a blessing in the first place.

If only they knew what a blessing really was, perhaps it could have been different, but they didn't.

It was a curse that a boy his age even needed these things. A boy who had once possessed great physical stamina and vibrancy.

And, righting one wrong with another hasn't ever been the proper way of doing things, as Frenchie's mother was in the minority trying to point out.

However, righting one wrong with another had become an acceptable way of life for some. There was no denying the truth of that.

It was beginning to look like the blessings were blocked. And that the curses were running around in abundance.

A poster of the lead rapper of the X-Masters still hung prominently on Q's wall, despite the bitter occurrence of his circumstances after the concert.

Regardless of the hype and regardless of the misguided images—not to mention the mind games they played with the youth who bought their music—rappers like the X-Masters would continue to hold the spotlight, never shouldering any of the responsibility for hyping up a young boy to the point of being out of control.

They would certainly never lose the spotlight or accept responsibility as long as places like the Square existed, where people like Q found their self-esteem and self-worth within the world of that music.

Directly opposite the rapper was a poster of Michael Johnson, the famous black track runner who held world records and in 1996 won two Olympic gold medals.

He was doing something Q would never do again, and that was run. Q had been on the track team and used to be a 100-yard sprinter. So he was a fan of running.

The contrast in the poster on the wall was stark and bold. Yet one would have had to have the sight to see it, and to see it beyond the surface for what it really was. A reminder of what had been lost, and yet in a sense never really gained.

Q sat drooling with his arm twisted at the usual odd angle while watching the kids playing outside the window.

Brandi waltzed in. She struggled to put a smile on her face, determined to cheer up Q regardless of the devastating circumstances.

She never wanted him to see her down, nor did she ever want him to have to look at his circumstances mirrored in her eyes.

She refused to pass on her sorrow to him, heaping it upon his own sorrow that was already there. In her opinion that was not something that good friends did to one another.

Sometimes she felt like there was nothing but burning fire where her heart used to be, a raging inferno, to be more exact.

However, she had no desire for Q to see or know this. It was what it was.

She walked over to him in her three-hundred-dollar jeans, matching designer shoes and handbag, with her hair shining and swinging from her visit to the salon.

She had a new body perm in her hair that was the bomb and envy of all those who couldn't pay its astronomical price tag. In any case you got what you paid for. And the salon, like her, was a rising star.

Ajani was innovative as well as sitting on the cutting edge of everything that was of any stature involving black hair care, just as Brandi was on the cutting edge of everything in her line of work.

She really didn't even want to think about the salon while she was with Q because then she started to think about the man who was the manager. A man who had practically made her heart stop beating.

Ever since she'd caught sight of him she couldn't get him out of her mind. She couldn't believe she'd never seen him before, but she had been told he was very low profile yet an important part of the salon's success. He was a poster boy as far as she was concerned.

A search of Tata's records had indeed revealed his presence as well as confirmed his position in the salon.

Seeing him was like seeing a mirage, but in that one heart-stopping moment she'd had to catch her breath.

She'd never seen a man that fine, even in the movies or in a magazine, and definitely not in any area of her life. He was so fine and smooth, he moved like liquid. Her belly quivered at the thought of him, and she'd never even spoken to the man.

She stopped herself short. She couldn't go there with her thoughts, but one thing was for sure: she definitely wanted another look at that man to be sure of what she had seen. She might have to step up her visits from two to three times a week to increase her chances of catching him there.

It was the first time in her life that she'd ever really noticed a man in that way. Instantly she detected the danger in that. That was exactly why she trained and disciplined her posse the way she did.

They couldn't afford to get involved with things that made their minds stray, even if wrapped in the finest package humanity had to offer.

Anyway, she needed to quell that for the time being. Q needed her full attention.

Besides, she had to be a shining example of the rules she had set. It was her staunch belief that you should never ask more of a person than what you were willing to give yourself.

However, she had to admit that until now she'd never thought her stand regarding men might be a hard one to keep. There was a magnetic pull that kept insinuating itself into her thoughts, and replaying that glimpse of him over and over again in her mind.

The pull was so strong it was like fighting against an upstream current.

Finally, through sheer willpower and discipline she managed to refocus her attentions on Q, although it was not without some effort.

"What's up, Q?"

Q moved his head slowly in answer. A sound that came close to sounding like *ugh* left his lips.

"Q, we're going for a walk. I've got to get you up out of this room. You need to feel the sun on your face. It ain't good for you to be in this house all the time."

Brandi was aware that she was the only person who took Q out of the house. His mother never did, and neither did any of the other people who visited him.

She didn't understand why they didn't see the importance of that. But it was all good because she enjoyed this private time with Q that belonged only to them when she took him out.

She grabbed the back of his chair, turned him toward the door, and then wheeled him outside.

Her posse was always in close proximity securing the area, but they never got close to her or even made their presence known.

Visiting Q, and her salon visits, which were close to sacred for her, were all made alone.

As soon as she conjured up a thought regarding the salon, there he was again, she could see him. Mr. Chase Ajani. She pulled her mind away from him, feeling like she was swimming against the tide. What a weird feeling.

In any case she knew she needed her personal moments alone like a fish needed water, and she fought for and guarded those times with all she had.

Her posse all knew for a fact that Q and his condition

were sensitive, sore spots for her, so they stood down, giving her space.

Brandi wheeled Q around the neighborhood, stopping here and there to immerse him in the atmosphere of the hood.

After they had strolled around for a little while she stopped in front of a grocery store.

She pulled a damp cloth from the side of Q's chair. She wiped the sweat from his face with it. She dipped the cloth in the cool water, and repeated the process to cool him off as well as provide him with the comfort of her touch.

She wiped his face and neck.

"You thirsty, Q?"

Q nodded. He released that ugh sound again. Brandi took this as the yes that it was.

Q looked at her, wishing she'd talk to him like she used to, but all he saw in front of him was a fine shell that looked like the Brandi he knew but that possessed none of the spirit of the Brandi he had known and loved.

Brandi was oblivious to his observations, choosing not to know. Q wouldn't understand the new her and she knew it. She saw the questions in his eyes whenever she visited, but she wasn't going down that road with him.

She wasn't going down that road with anybody. She didn't owe him or anyone else an explanation for her life. It was her life, after all. She decided she'd do what she wanted with it.

In fact she'd do more than that. She'd do what none of them had done with their lives. End of story.

Brandi exited the store with a 20-ounce bottle of Coke for Q and a bottle of Evian Natural Spring Water for her. She opened the Coke bottle, sticking a straw in it for Q to drink from.

It was a slow, painful process since he could swallow only a little bit at a time. She had to wipe his mouth after each sip. She didn't mind doing this. She considered it just a part of their friendship. It was what a sister automatically did for her brother.

Had the situation been reversed she knew Q would have done the same thing for her. They had been bonded to each other for as long as she could remember. She was patient through the process until she knew he'd had enough.

Once he was finished she turned up her bottle of water to her mouth. She drained it and then threw both bottles in the trash. Q watched her finish her water.

He released a sound that Brandi took as him wanting to move on. What he really wanted was more of her. Not the shell she was sharing but to be part of the heart she was now shielding.

They continued their walk, with Brandi none the wiser about what was going on inside Q.

She decided to wheel Q over to where she knew the double Dutch game was taking place. As well it was a talking place with a vengeance because they had all heard about the tournament and their participation. So they were hard at work, since they'd been given something to strive for.

They weren't just jumping rope for themselves anymore. They were repping for their neighborhood. This gave them a sense of pride and purpose.

Brandi was the first person who'd taken any serious interest in their skills. She was also the first to discover that double Dutch really meant something to them.

Sure, it gave them something to do, but it was more important than that. It gave them an arena where they could create as well as be themselves.

It was an arena that encouraged them to be the best they could be.

The game of double Dutch gave them back as much as it took in stamina. The jumpers in Los Angeles from the Square were among the first to demonstrate aerobic jumps within the ropes.

Their split-second timing was legendary as was their ability to pair off in the rope, matching steps and beats to the rhythm of the turning pieces of twine.

Though these days they were mostly jumping to sleek cordlike rope because it increased their agility and their ability to turn at a lightning pace, the sound of their clickety-clacking steps slapping the pavement.

Brandi took a seat on the bench in the midst of the heated warmups, positioning Q so he'd have a good view of the jumpers.

Ari ran over as soon as she spotted Brandi, throwing her arms around her neck and squeezing tight. She took note of the fact that Brandi smelled like Armani. On her the perfume gave off a clean, sensuous smell.

Ari loved the feel of Brandi. She also took note of the proud way Brandi carried herself with a tilt to her head and a certain fire burning in her eyes.

But Ari was smart.

She knew what Brandi was. As much as she worshipped the ground that Brandi walked on she never in a million years wanted to be like her.

That was why she had told Tonya she was going to care for little babies and become a doctor. And that was exactly what she was going to do. One day she would move both her and her mother out of the projects.

Brandi appeared to have it all but what she didn't have was real substance or a real future. Ari was positive of it. In fact she hugged Brandi even tighter as she realized this, wishing she could make it different for her.

She knew Brandi deserved better.

However, Brandi no longer believed that she deserved better. She had fallen into the pit of her own hatred and thus she had victimized herself much more than her enemies ever could have.

Finally releasing Brandi, Ari said, "I heard about the tournament. Thanks. You're the best."

"Nah. I ain't the best, Ari. It's all about you and yours. You and your girls are the best. There isn't anything I can do without your skills. Y'all jump like y'all invented that rope."

Ari just hugged her tighter, wishing she could make the pain go away that she felt deep inside Brandi. Brandi thought she was the consummate actress but she wasn't fooling Ari, not one bit.

Next Ari knelt in front of Q, giving him the black hand-shake for the hood. She held his hand up for the shake even though it was one-sided. He couldn't perform his part of the task.

Q smiled his lopsided smile at her. He knew she was a beautiful, giving spirit of a child. His eyes brightened, indi-cating she had cheered him up. Brandi loved her for that.

Upon kneeling in front of Q and patiently doing the hand-shake with him, Ari had touched Brandi in a spot deep inside her that was never penetrated, and certainly never recogniz-able, anymore.

Ari decided that since they had a warm, receptive audience she might as well show off big-time for Q.

"Q, check this out," she said, jumping into the rope, flip-ping backward twice, landing on her feet without missing a beat.

Ari was so agile, lithe, and skinny that it seemed as if she were at one with the rope when she was in it. It looked as if she exerted no effort. Her talent in the jump rope was limitless.

It was seamless, and just part of who she was. The girl had a body that had been made for gymnastics. If her talent had ever been spotted, and she'd been given the proper training, there was no doubt she could have been a serious contender in gymnastics.

Ari twirled and turned in the rope at the speed of light.

Q was so excited by Ari's skills that his ugh sound released more furiously along with the nodding of his head.

Brandi went to stand in front of him, putting jealous hands on her hips, just so she could see the shining gleam in his eyes. It was a treasured moment for her because it was some-thing she rarely ever saw in Q anymore.

She silently vowed to bring him to watch the double Dutch

game more often. She would also see that he was on the center floor of the tournaments when Ari's team was up.

Brandi reached over to hug Q close to her. Q could smell her warmth and perfume. She was so thankful to Ari and her girls for paying Q special attention.

They were all taking turns now jumping in doubles and triplicates strictly for Q's pleasure.

Q smiled again.

At that moment he had two wishes. One was that Ari would win the double Dutch tournament, walking away with every prize available.

Two, he wished that Brandi would never release him from her hug. It was the first sign of any real warmth he'd seen in her since that fateful night.

Brandi flashed Ari a warm smile.

Ari looked off in the distance as she heard her name. "My mother is calling me. I've got to go," she yelled, waving good-bye to Brandi. She ran off in the direction of her mother's voice.

When the day was over Brandi maneuvered Q in his chair back to the apartment turning it over to his mother, who wheeled him back inside.

Brandi stood on the porch smiling and waving at Q until she couldn't see him any longer.

Q, who was beginning to learn how important the small, often unnoticed things in life were, for his part decided to take his memories of the day with him, and tuck them away in his heart so he could pull them out for review whenever he needed them.

This was a time when he would need them often. He could still hear the sound of Ari's mother calling to her as his own mother wheeled him into his room.

For what seemed like the millionth time he wished he had listened to the sound of his own mother's voice more. Back when it was filled with hope for him, and not pain.

Chapter 27

Just as Brandi was about to step foot into her gleaming new car she heard her own mother calling to her. "Brandi! Brandi! Brandi, wait!"

Her car was shined to a high polish just like the black spit-shined boots she wore when she was in training. Things shining and gleaming on the outside, even if not on the inside, were beginning to become a personal trademark for Brandi.

She had hoped she could get off of the street without her mom's noticing she was at Q's house, but she should have known better. She'd probably been alerted the instant she'd stepped foot on the street. Her mother sometimes possessed the instincts of a panther.

Rita ran down the street to catch up to her, looking very pretty and petite in her light, summery warmup suit.

"Hi, Baby. How are you doing?" she asked, her eyes watering over. Rita's heart fluttered as she thought of the broken picture of Brandi that had thrown itself off her dresser.

She still didn't know what that was all about, but she knew Brandi's picture frame was lying in pieces in a pail she had swept them into. She didn't have the heart to throw it out.

For some reason she also hadn't removed the picture from the pieces of glass either. She wanted to but couldn't seem to bring herself to touch the picture as she looked at it through the broken glass.

The whole thing, pail and all, was now sitting beside her dresser.

"I'm fine," Brandi muttered without touching her or reaching to hug her.

Rita stepped closer, longing for Brandi to reach out to her but having trouble knowing exactly how to reach her.

"How come you didn't stop by?"

"Is Daddy home?"

"Yes."

Brandi shrugged her shoulders indifferently as though she could care less. "Then there's your answer. That's why."

Brandi reached into her purse, then put the same knotted cloth her mother had given her initially back in her hand, filled to the brim with what she had received from her mother plus a great deal more.

"That's what I owe you and then some."

Rita stared at her incredulously. What was happening to her child? She barely recognized Brandi. And by that she didn't just mean in those extremely expensive clothes she was wearing.

"What you . . . owe me?" she stuttered.

She stared at her daughter, wondering where the real Brandi was. An image of the fragmented glass with Brandi's picture lying inside it popped into her mind's eye.

"You don't owe me anything, Brandi. I gave you that money because I love you and wanted you to be all right."

Brandi looked away, unable to handle the love in her mother's voice or the hurt in her eyes. "Then mission accomplished because as you can see I'm just fine."

"That isn't quite what I see, Brandi," Rita said, taking a step back from Brandi, not even bothering to open the knotted cloth.

Sighing, Rita asked, "Were you visiting Q?"

This question automatically put Brandi on the defensive.

She couldn't stand for people to mention Q's name, especially her parents, after what her dad had said.

Whenever it came to Q she always got touchy. "Yeah. He's my friend. What of it?"

A pang ripped through Rita's chest at Brandi's disrespectful tone. She decided against feeding into it. The more you fed a monster, the more it grew, as she well knew.

"Nothing, honey. I didn't mean anything by it. I was just asking, that's all," Rita said as she retreated from what she could see was a losing situation with her daughter.

"I love you, Brandi," Rita said, her voice trembling with memories of the sweet little girl Brandi used to be.

"I've gotta go, Ma. I'll see you around."

Brandi got into her car. The conversation had been so brief and stilted Rita forgot to ask her about the new Lexus she was driving.

And she didn't even want to travel down the road of how Brandi could afford that car plus give her back the money she'd given her.

She just hoped and prayed the things she'd been hearing weren't true.

Brandi turned the ignition. She took off down the street without a backward glance. Rita stood at the curb watching her until she disappeared from her sight.

When Rita entered the apartment Charles turned from his paper, giving his wife a sad smile. The kind of smile that summoned up all they had lost together without him speaking one word.

In their bedroom Rita dropped to her knees. "Our Father, who art in heaven. Hallowed be thy name. Thy kingdom come. Thy will be done. On earth as it is in heaven."

Rita sometimes wished with all her heart that things would one day be done on Earth as they were in Heaven.

She wasn't at all sure just how much more pain and heartbreak she could stand. And as she well knew, most people wouldn't understand this on a spiritual basis, so there was nowhere to turn.

Her only recourse was being where she was, and that was on her knees. Perhaps in the end it would be all that she needed.

After all, she knew the Lord Jesus Christ was all power. Sometimes it just had to be in his time and in his way.

"Amen," Rita said when she finished her prayer.

She took the cross she had been clutching to her bosom during the prayer and dropped it into the pail on top of the broken picture of Brandi.

And that was where it would stay, she vowed to herself, until her child was returned whole.

"She's in your hands now, Lord. She's in your hands. I've done all that I can do."

Rita sat on the side of the bed, her face awash in tears. Her husband silently watched her from the doorway, his face awash in tears as well.

The only thing he could hear was the sound of the cross hitting the glass inside the pail where Rita had dropped it.

The metal cross hit the fragmented glass. All he could think of was the blood.

" 'By the blood of the Lamb,' " he whispered by way of his own prayer.

Charles would give his own life if he could just so Brandi could have hers back.

I'm willing to trade in my life, Lord, just so Brandi can have a chance at repentance, he thought.

Chapter 28

That night in the warehouse it was far from business as usual. Their operations were vastly increasing, so now considerably more product had to be continuously cranked out within the same span of time.

Reaching the end of her process, one of the girls stamped the money envelopes with a special sticker. Ironically enough the stickers had horns on them, not that anyone cared or noticed the significance of that.

It was all about the money and what that represented.

It was about eating, paying their bills, and surviving. Most of all, it was about being on top, and not being at the mercy of anybody's whim like you were when you didn't have bank.

Someone handed the stamped envelope to Tangie, who dropped it through a slot in the floor.

Meanwhile, a group of the Conquerors including their infamous leader were creeping up all over an industrial building whose façade was a storage facility.

Inside there were numerous dollars as well as a cache of valuable drugs. The Conquerors were moving in. They were taking over. They were doing what they did. What they did was conquer.

They operated under the same premise as advocated in the *Street War* games, which Brandi still played on the computer.

They had automatic weapons. Everything was in place.

Inside the building a group of the Pagers were milling around. This was their operation. The money, the drugs, all of it belonged to them. They owned it all, as well as the turf, or so they thought.

In reality Brandi owned it now. They just hadn't received their eviction notice yet. But they would.

Up until that point there had never been a breach of their security. And you could tell that they weren't expecting one.

They had made the ultimate mistake often made by people who had gotten away with too much for too long. They had gotten comfortable. Comfort was an unaffordable luxury if for no other reason than you let your guard down.

The sound of Brandi's voice broke through the orchestrated stillness in the air, slicing like the sharp edge of a razor. It carried urgency, seriousness, and it was laced with great strength. "Take it down. Now!" she said, giving the order.

The Conquerors hit the door once, twice, and it flew off the hinges. They entered the industrial facility as though they were from the Drug Enforcement Agency and like they just had it like that.

It was certainly a coup that the DEA would have been proud of, had they been privy to this display of power but, of course, they weren't.

However, many of the agency's tactics, maneuvers, and strategies were employed by the ever-resourceful Brandi.

The Pagers were caught completely off guard. Before they could blink, their grounds had been seized and surrounded, inside as well as outside.

The takedown of their fortress was full and in effect. Tata didn't make any bones about it. Her commands were loud, clear, and definitely not to be disobeyed.

"If you don't wanna die, don't move. Get down on the floor. Put your hands out in front of you. Move it!"

Her weapon clicked, ready to fire.

The Pagers took one look at the show unfolding in front of

them. The Conquerors were dressed from head to toe in black including the masks they wore. They moved like lithe ballerinas—orchestrated and in control.

The Pagers knew they were outgunned, outmanned, and outsmarted. They hit the floor as they were told to do.

Their only recourse was to try to limit the casualties.

They had been hearing about all the takeovers.

They had precautions in place. For some illogical reason they hadn't figured in a million years they'd be hit. Such was their power and comfort level. Now they were learning the price of such a comfort, but it had come to late. It was way too late.

They also had made the mistake of thinking they were too far outside the turfs that were being taken over for this to happen.

Apparently they were wrong, and someone was getting very greedy as well as power hungry. They all knew that could be only one person.

Before the Pagers could fully calculate what had hit them they had been relieved of their drugs, their money, and their weapons.

In one poof Brandi had shut them down. She put them completely out of business. They could forget about buying or starting anew because that just couldn't happen. There was nowhere to buy that Brandi's group didn't have on lock.

Before hitting the heart of their operations, all of their operatives, both on the street and off had been taken down as well.

It was beginning to be clear that those gangs who had opposed or had not been invited to join in with the Conquerors were slowly being eliminated, one by one.

Later that night Brandi walked around her warehouse, surveying the people who were a part of all the takedowns including the one that had taken place that night. She checked to make sure that not one person was missing, injured, or otherwise touched.

"Good work, Conquerors. Good work."

So far she had pulled all this off without the loss of any life. For that she congratulated herself.

After all, she wasn't a murderer. She was a Conqueror. She was in fact the Conqueror of Conquerors.

She smiled at the very thought.

Earlier she had been sad after running into her mother. But now she was back to herself.

That was what she had been training her girls on. You had to empty your minds of personal problems because one split second of your mind wandering could cost you more than you were willing to pay.

Brandi vowed to never let one of those split seconds happen. That was just before Chase Ajani crept into her mind once again to occupy her thoughts.

Chapter 29

The following morning in the warehouse Brandi led the new chant. "We are?"

"The Generation."

"I can't hear you!"

"WE ARE THE GENERATION!"

Brandi smiled.

That was so much better. She wanted to feel the conviction in their voices. They had to know who they were. They had to feel it in their bones.

It wasn't enough for her to tell them. They had to know it, and more than that they had to feel it. They had to feel the importance of it.

Once they had completed all their morning rituals Brandi said, "You all are doing a bang-up job. You have perfect control. There are no body drops. Taking over things without taking people out is no easy feat but you guys are doing it. Because of this there are envelopes here with cash bonuses for all of you. And, that's because we are . . ."

"WE ARE THE GENERATION!" the Conquerors yelled with great conviction, psyched about their cash bonuses.

Brandi nodded her head. "We are in control. Check that out."

She signaled to Tata and Tangie. They passed out the fat cash bonuses to each member. Brandi believed in sharing the wealth.

She knew that she could create pride and honor. She didn't believe in the ones at the top being the only ones benefiting while those considered lower on the pole worked but reaped no rewards.

In her eyes they were all created equal. That was why she went on a lot of the takedowns. She wanted them to know she was one of them. She wasn't talking at them, she was talking with them.

They had to be one for all and all for one. That was her motto. And her girls had the utmost respect for her because they could feel her. She was true. And she cared about them. They knew it by the way she treated them.

If someone in her group had a personal problem, then Brandi considered it her problem. They all worked out a solution to take care of it. They took care of their own at any and all costs.

Rents had been paid. Nasty landlords had been put in their place. Bail bonds had been funded. College funds had been provided. Babies had been fed, and Pampers had been bought.

Whenever Brandi's family of Conquerers needed anything they would all put their heads together to make sure they got it. And Brandi was well known for going in her own pocket to ease the personal situations of her girls, their family members, as well as their extended family and whoever else in the neighborhood had problems.

When there was a heat blackout, and elderly people were getting sick, Brandi bought air conditioners for everyone who needed one. She personally saw to it that they were installed.

The Conquerors were growing in numbers as more and more young women decided to sign on to their dream.

More and more of the young women wanted to be a part of the plan.

And Brandi felt they had only just begun. In reality they were at the beginning of the end.

Chapter 30

Brandi ran alongside the Santa Monica Pier under a brilliantly shining sun. The water was sparkling. It threw reflections her way. It rippled freely as only water can do.

Her iPod was firmly planted in her ears as she jogged on her own with the type of freedom she gained only during her moments of rare solitude.

She jogged along the pier as if her very life depended on it. In so many ways it did. She disciplined herself to become one with her own mind as she jogged in her heavy black military boots that were shined to the hilt.

The pier was one of Brandi's private spots.

She didn't share the pier with anyone. She always went to the pier alone.

No security, no entourages, no war generals or the like, just her. Tata didn't like it, but she had learned to live with it after Brandi had discovered the secret detail she'd sent once and given her the tongue lashing of her life.

That discovery had backed Tata off. Brandi was a bit more resourceful than she had given her credit for. She figured that if Brandi could spot one of her details, then she could certainly handle any trouble that came her way.

As well Tata knew she had to give Brandi what she wanted, and that was respect for another's privacy. After all, if Brandi had done that same thing to her—loading her with a private detail at the wrong time—it could have cost her her mother's life.

She wasn't willing to risk her mom's life. She was always careful with this one and only treasure in her life.

So she gave in to what Brandi wanted—privacy and some time for herself. It was a fair exchange as far as Tata was concerned because the price for her to keep her particular brand of privacy was so much higher than Brandi's.

The personal time at the pier gave Brandi time to reflect on things, time to contemplate. Most of all it gave her an opportunity to run freely. Not in the same manner as the training and regimen of her posse.

At the pier she was a singular entity. She could become one with the wind. And when she received what she called her second wind while jogging it was almost as if she could fly. She felt like she had grown wings.

There were no restraints, no rules, and nothing to live up to. There was her music, and there was the wind. It was all she needed.

She was smart enough to know that this time alone was a security risk. However, there were some risks that had to be taken. You couldn't live as she did without having some private time, without having some stolen moments that belonged only to you.

She couldn't be on 24/7.

There had to be dry spots. The Santa Monica Pier was one of them.

There, without all the attention she constantly received and without all the demands of her position, she had time to spend with her own mind.

That was both good and bad. As long as those thoughts were kept to the business at hand it was fine. It was only when they strayed that she found herself troubled.

Like when she thought about the day she'd sold that old

heap of a car her daddy had bought her. Along with it, she'd wanted to get rid of the Bible her mom had given her, which was still in the car.

For some reason the Bible disturbed her even though she hadn't looked at it since the day she'd left home and thrown it in her trunk.

But at times she was acutely aware that it was in there. So, she decided to leave it in the trunk of the car to be taken away with the vehicle.

What use could she possibly have for it with all that she was doing?

It distressed her to just lay eyes on it, which was why she had thrown it in the trunk in the first place.

But like a bad penny that just kept popping up, after she'd sold the car, just as she was about to pull out of the lot in her new Lexus, the salesman had run up to her out of breath, with the Bible in his hand.

"Miss," he'd said, "you forgot your Bible. It was in your trunk."

Brandi had stared at the Bible as though she'd seen a ghost before taking it with a smile.

She'd taken it only because she didn't want the salesman to think she was a raving idiot if she reacted in a way that would reveal its real affect on her.

As soon as she was out of sight of the car dealership the trunk of her new Lexus had become its new resting place, just as the trunk of her old car had been.

It was things of this sort that haunted her when she was at the pier.

She couldn't get rid of that Bible, try as she might. She had even contemplated leaving it on the church steps like an abandoned baby, but she couldn't bring herself to do it. So she was still riding around with it in her trunk.

She mostly fought against the tide that tried to sweep her away into a land of thoughts she didn't need to have, but it was an uphill battle all the way.

It was particularly a battle when she was alone. She ran harder, turned her iPod up louder, and fought to turn off her daddy's voice in her head.

She always heard his admonishments when she didn't want to. This time she could have sworn she'd heard him whispering, " '*The blood of the Lamb.*' "

Why were things always bothering her when she was striving so hard to empty her mind?

As well she fought not to see that Bible lying in the dark of her Lexus trunk. But see it she did, and once again she heard her daddy whisper, " '*The blood of the Lamb.*' "

She turned up the volume on her iPod even louder in an attempt to drown out his voice.

She looked out at the water, blinking because it couldn't be. It looked just like her Bible from the trunk of her car was floating on the water before her eyes.

Chapter 31

"It's time to pay the piper," Left Eye whispered as she spotted Brandi walking toward the double Dutch game. She saw Ari wave excitedly at Brandi.

Brandi waved back, smiling while her posse pulled up the rear behind her.

Brandi was back in mode after her private visit to the pier. She struggled valiantly against the ghost of her own mind.

The Mister Softee truck chimed its way down the street. Ari yelled, "Hey, you guys, Mister Softee's here." She was still hoarding the money for their ice-cream treats that Brandi had given her.

They had doubled their consumption of ice cream since training for the tournaments and since Brandi's money kept them well supplied.

Brandi sat down in her usual spot on the bench. Her posse fanned out around her, milling and blending into the projects.

Ari ran over to the ice-cream truck. She had a good head start on the other girls. She was the first one to arrive excitedly at the truck.

Tonya wasn't too far behind her.

Just as Tonya gained on Ari she saw her fall onto the sidewalk directly in front of the ice-cream truck's serving window.

Tonya yelled out at her. "Ari, quit playing around. We're coming." She laughed because she knew Ari was somewhat of a prankster and liked pulling little jokes on them at times.

Before Tonya could reach the ice-cream truck it pulled off. That was strange.

"That's what I'm talking about," Left Eye said to no one in particular as she melted into the crowd on the street, disappearing like a genie in a bottle.

By this time Brandi had looked in the direction of the ice-cream truck just as she heard Tonya yelling at Ari. Something was wrong, she felt it with every instinct in her body.

Some might say like mother, like daughter, because Brandi's mother was known for her instincts as well, but say what they might, Brandi knew what she felt.

And she felt like something was wrong even though she couldn't spot a thing that looked out of place, with the exception of the ice-cream truck pulling away.

Why would the ice-cream truck pull away before the other kids could reach it?

Tata spoke into a high-powered walkie-talkie. The whole of Brandi's posse went into what they called their Stage 2 Alert.

Tata had made the call simply upon making eye contact with Brandi. She read her instincts and immediately went into action.

Brandi could feel that their territory had somehow been invaded even though she couldn't see the results of it yet. That's how subtle it had been.

Tonya's screams confirmed that something was definitely wrong as she reached Ari to discover this wasn't a joke. Ari was lying on the ground with her throat slit, dead.

Tonya's continuous screams that hadn't broken octave since she saw Ari lying in her own pool of blood brought people in the area on the run including the bicycle cops.

As far away as she was Brandi ran so fast on her way to

Ari that she arrived even before people that were closer to the scene than her.

She looked down at the beautiful child with the lifeless eyes. Her face was slashed in what looked like a hundred lines neatly crisscrossing each other with a singular line of blood seeping from the slit in her neck.

Everything in Brandi froze. She couldn't move. She couldn't make her mind reconcile the child lying on the ground with the full-of-life Ari that she had seen waving to her and running to the ice-cream truck only moments ago.

She felt Ari's arms around her neck. "Bye, Brandi."

She heard her voice soft as a whisper as she sat on the ground like a statue staring at Ari.

For all of her discipline and training she found herself at a crossroads with it.

She heard her own voice reflecting back at her, *"It only takes a split second of the wrong timing and you could lose your life."*

There was mass confusion as the police started backing people away, securing and roping off the area.

Brandi gave the signal to her posse to back off. She finally got up from the ground. There was nothing they could do for Ari.

Ari was dead.

Brandi's cell phone rang. The number was blocked. She never, ever received calls from blocked numbers. Her line was private. She knew everyone who had her number.

She stared in shock at the block that popped up on her cell phone screen. She pushed the TALK button, smearing it with some of Ari's blood that had gotten on her hands when she had put a gentle hand to the slash marks on the child's face.

She had touched her as though she could bring her back from the dead, but she couldn't.

"Bye, Brandi." She could still hear Ari's voice.

She bit back the sob as well as the scream of hatred that was forming in her throat.

Before she could say anything into the phone a voice calmly questioned her. "How does it feel to have signed Ari's death warrant, Brandi? You're the bomb."

The phone went dead in her ear.

Seeing the look on her face Tata questioned her. "Who was that, Brandi?"

Brandi didn't answer.

Tangie jumped in, very distraught over Ari's killing as well as at the ashen look on Brandi's face. "Brandi!" Tangie stopped walking and got in her face.

"Brandi, who was that on the phone?"

Brandi deadpanned her. "That was the enemy. The enemy who killed Ari."

All they were left with was the sound of Tangie's surprised gasp.

That and one little girl with her throat slit and her face cut to smithereens, behind them lying on the ground.

The police were already looking for the dead girl's mother.

Chapter 32

Left Eye had pulled off an incredible coup, and she knew it. She was going to blow up. There was no doubt about it. The ice-cream truck idea had been brilliant on her part.

When the truck had arrived as it innocently did every day on the street, not one person had suspected it. Left Eye's hand-selected young gangster killers had been positioned in the truck.

As soon as Ari approached, before she'd even had an opportunity to ask for an ice-cream cone, they had cut her throat with a straight razor clean through her jugular vein, killing her instantly.

Then they had destroyed her face, slashing it to ribbons.

It was one of the neatest murders they'd ever pulled off. Left Eye was proud of herself and her hand-selected gang members. They ought to put her in the *Guinness Book of World Records* for what she'd just pulled off.

Hell, she'd be willing to bet there were serial murderers in prison that weren't that smooth.

Her young gangsters had performed like the professionals they were. She might be able to take the gang to the next level, kicking it up a notch, now that Brandi had raised the stakes on what constituted a gang and given it such an elegant makeover.

Elevating the gang wasn't something Left Eye would have thought of before but it was worth thinking of now. Basically she was a street gangbanger but, hell, everybody could use a little promotion sometimes.

Surely the almighty Conquerors hadn't thought their asses were going to get away with the beat down in the gin-and-juice joint. They couldn't possibly believe their own hype that they were untouchable.

Them heifers must have lost their minds completely. They better ask somebody. Because Left Eye kicked behind and would always shine.

She didn't need the damn *Wall Street Journal* to teach her how to whip somebody's behind. That was Brandi's thing, not hers.

All she needed was what she had—her street instincts. They were the same instincts that had kept her alive this long.

The Mister Softee crew was already ghost. And you better know that.

Damn if she wasn't good, because they had pulled off the murder of the century, and then gotten out of the area even with the bicycle cops patrolling the streets.

Left Eye knew they were some bad muthas.

It just went to show you that nothing was impossible. Left Eye was really feeling herself. It was too bad she couldn't get her bragging rights on right then. However, it was too risky.

She knew she'd have her spotlight when the time came. Besides, she'd be all that with the young gangsters she had selected for the job. They'd be showing her nothing but mad love and respect.

She knew the police were going to be looking for a suspect, so it would be too hot to try to gather props. And the cops were good and pissed off that the murder had taken place right in front of their eyes with them being none the wiser.

She also knew that Brandi would be a threat, undoubtedly thirsty for revenge. Despite Left Eye's personal hatred for her, she knew Brandi could not be underestimated.

The good thing was that her second plan of action might at least knock the very in-control Brandi off balance, at the very least for a short period of time.

It was worth a shot. And she'd be damned if she wasn't going to take it.

"Round two, Brandi Hutchinson. It's almost round two."

Left Eye smiled at her own projection. Brandi wouldn't be able to look down on her as some low-life gangbanger once the plan was wreck and in effect.

Far outside of Los Angeles the Mister Softee truck chimed its last chime as it went up in flames.

As it did Left Eye sat at her kitchen table writing her own little rhyme. She was a clandestine ghetto poet, and she had a whole notebook filled with little rhymes that reflected different events in her life.

She wrote:

> Mister Softee was up in flames
> Tell me who's to blame
> For this dark and very vicious
> game.
>
> The Conquerors don't even
> demonstrate shame.
> And Ms. Brandi Hutchinson too
> late she came.
>
> Much too late to chain the
> hate that was spewing around
> as though it had a date,

no chains or locks to keep it
in place.

No love to save Ari's face.

Left Eye finished writing, closing the notebook until the next chapter.

Chapter 33

Q's mother heard terrifying sounds emanating from her son's room. The sound of ugh that he usually released had gone up an octave as well as increased in volume. It sounded like an animal had been wounded and was releasing a war cry for help.

Immediately following this particular noise was a release of air as though he'd been punched and lost oxygen.

Wondering what was wrong she quickly tightened her bathrobe around her waist while running into his room. Every step of the way her heart pounded a little harder, and though his room wasn't that far away it felt like it was a mile away until she reached it.

When she did Bobby was sitting at the window. Tears were streaming down his face. She ran over, instinctively wiping his tears, checking for what might be hurting him before noticing that his attention was riveted to the scene outside the window.

Following his line of vision she saw that the cops were all over the place. The Square was covered with them, milling around in various stages of police procedures.

There was mass hysteria outside from both the onlookers and the authorities. And just as she digested this piece of information she became aware of the helicopters zooming overhead.

"Oh my God," she stage-whispered.

She took a cloth to wipe the tears from Bobby's face. "What happened?" she asked as though Q could answer her.

The next thing she heard was a loud, insistent banging on her front door.

Distraught at the timing of this she put down the cloth. She gave Bobby a quick hug, indicating that she'd be returning. She ran to the front door to discover her neighbor from across the street standing there.

"Renita," the neighbor huffed as soon as Q's mother opened the door. She was completely out of breath from having run all the way. "They done killed that little girl."

"What little girl?"

"Ari."

"No!" Q's mother put a hand to her mouth. Tears immediately sprung to her eyes. She heard a drumming in her ears, she was so startled by what she'd heard. It couldn't be true.

Then she remembered the sounds emanating from her son's room. It had been the sound of pain of a different nature than physical pain.

A small voice chimed inside of her, though she said nothing. *Dear Lord, please don't let it be that Bobby has seen that child get killed.*

"Yeah. It's true, all right. They done cut that child up like she was yesterday's meat, I'm told. You can't be too safe these days. You might want to keep Bobby in the house until this dies down. I just wanted you to know cuz it's gonna be a nasty mess around here for a bit."

"Thanks, Lady Bird," Q's mother said before closing the door to go back to her son. Everybody called her neighbor Lady Bird because she was a slight woman who spoke quickly and was always fluttering her hands around like the wings of a bird.

She was also known for her ability to gather information and pass it around quickly.

Upon entering Bobby's room the true nature of his tears really started to sink in for her.

He was sitting at the window. He always sat at that window. That meant he must have seen what happened.

It was a bit of a distance but at the very least he must have recognized that Ari had gotten hurt. Well, not hurt, actually, but killed.

Dear Mary Mother of Jesus.

"That was Lady Bird. She was here about what happened to Ari."

"Ugh," Q said.

Renita wrapped her arms tightly around him. For the first time since everything had happened she was glad that he was alive.

At first as cruel as it may have sounded she didn't want him to be because she didn't want her child to live the life of a suffering vegetable. However, after seeing what had happened to Ari, suddenly she was glad for another opportunity to hold her boy close.

She couldn't bear to think of the pain of discovery awaiting Ari's mother. They were close, and everybody knew it. Ari was an only child. She'd had her whole life ahead of her.

She was one of the Square's brightest spots. Everyone knew Ari. She was a beautiful shooting star cut down before she could shine.

"Who would want to kill an innocent child?"

Renita couldn't believe the squalid conditions they were living in, and this time she was thinking more of the squalor of their spirits than of the actual physical living conditions they all lived in.

It was just so insane, the killing of innocent people. It had absolutely no rhyme or reasoning to it.

She had never been a rich woman. She had grown up herself in the midst of very rough economic times, but even amongst those conditions of the daily struggle to pay bills and keep food on the table she'd never witnessed the thirst for blood that seemed to motivate these kids.

She'd never seen this horrific brand of moral decay. It was at its very worst. It was growing more deeply by the day if that was possible.

She shook her head at the sheer insanity of it.

She knew Bobby had acted foolishly in his circumstances. But she also knew that she and her son were victims of circumstances that neither of them could control. Those circumstances were created by forces that were malignant and had been built over a long time.

Q continued to moan, emitting sounds of sorrow over Ari's passing.

Unbeknownst to Renita, Bobby's distress level was also heightened as his thoughts got around to his best friend, Brandi, and her reaction to the death of a little girl that Q knew she loved so very much.

He'd seen her cradling what must have been the already-dead Ari in her arms just before total chaos broke out.

Chapter 34

The patch of land known as the Square had seen many sad days. It had seen too many. The day that Ari Simms was murdered was truly among the worst.

It was one of the most devastating days the projects had ever seen. It was another dark mark upon its already-scarred history.

If the skeletons inside of its bricks could talk, even they would have howled at the pain. They would have screamed at the sheer injustice of it all.

You could hear the echo of lost souls shouting out from their vanquished places from their forgotten, unknown graves.

Upon hearing the news from the police of her daughter's brutal slashing out on a public street, Ari's mother, Tanya, promptly fainted.

The police had conducted door-to-door interviews, questioning, searching for answers, but still hadn't come up with anything concrete.

They had questioned everybody that they could prove was on the street at that time but still there was nothing. They came up time and time again with a big, fat zero.

The black neighborhoods, they knew, had a thing about clamming up when something happened. People didn't like to talk whether they'd seen something or not, for fear of reprisals.

Also, many of them had been raised in a culture that taught them not to talk to the police under any circumstances because they could not be trusted.

That attitude coupled with the difficulties of an investigation that happened on a crowded street produced little to no results.

The amazing thing was that although Q's apartment had a direct view of the murder scene, even though from a distance, the police never showed up at his apartment with any questions. They never made the connection.

Eventually the case would become cold. It would end up being another unsolved murder with a file an inch thick that had produced no results.

It would remain open in order not to add insult to injury in an already sensitive situation, but that was all it was—open.

No one was going to go the extra mile for Ari.

The only thing that seemed certain was that the attack originated from the ice-cream truck, but nothing could be learned about the occupants of the truck or the truck itself. It was as if both had vanished into thin air.

A pall had come over the neighborhood like a black cloud drifting overhead before the start of a severe rainstorm.

All of Ari's friends were in various stages of fright and depression without any means for learning about coping mechanisms or finding clinical support to deal with the loss of their friend.

As the eleven-year-old Ari lay in cold storage at the morgue— her once-beautiful features frozen in slash lines of red from the horrific butchering job that had been performed on her— her closest relatives were planning for a closed-casket funeral.

Her mother was in a near-comatose state since fainting at the disclosure of Ari's death. She couldn't even perform the basic functions of preparing for Ari's departure.

She sat rocking in her favorite rocking chair, holding a picture of Ari to her chest with one of Ari's blankets draped over her shoulder, moaning.

Her eyes stared straight ahead as though they were blank. In many ways they were. She couldn't see anything except whatever was in her direct line of vision.

Fortunately she and her sister were very close. Her sister was attending to every detail of the funeral arrangements, decisions, and house, up to and including brushing Tanya's hair and teeth in the morning.

She force-fed orange juice down Ari's mother's throat just so she would have some form of nutrition in her body.

Brandi had gone into total isolation.

Tata was running the warehouse in her absence. Brandi refused to talk to anyone. Basically she hadn't been seen or heard from since the day of Ari's murder.

Brandi was in fact in a similar state to Ari's mother. She kept hearing Ari's soft whisper in her head, "Bye, Brandi."

She kept feeling Ari's arms around her neck. And she kept seeing her jumping in that rope and running to the ice-cream truck.

She saw the inside brightness of Ari's star. She couldn't cope with the fact that it had been put out. She remained in a state of mourning and solitude.

She didn't attend Ari's services. Brandi deciding not to be in attendance was a huge surprise to everyone. She didn't care. She preferred to remember Ari the way she was.

She wasn't going to sit there in front of a box imagining what Ari had been like. She couldn't do it. She wasn't going to stare at the picture of her they had on display, either. Of course, what remained of her couldn't be shown.

Hell nah. She wasn't going to do that. But she was going to do something.

Only time would tell what that something was.

Chapter 35

Several weeks after the murder of Ari Simms, Brandi emerged from her self-imposed exile to rejoin the world physically, though not completely in spirit.

She hadn't done a thing to her hair or appearance during her mourning period. This in itself was not like her. She was already thin but now, with an additional loss of fifteen pounds since Ari's death, she appeared skeleton-like.

She had eaten very little. She had slept less than that. She had also spent a great deal of time doing something that she publicly denounced to her posse all the time: wallowing in self-pity.

It had been something that she couldn't stop herself from doing. Hence her intense need for privacy away from a world that could see her carefully built façade crumbling.

She emerged in a wig to hide her wrapped hair that was desperately in need of a perm and some color.

She wore large black Gucci sunglasses to keep the sun out of her eyes. More than that she wore the sunglasses to keep the world from seeing her eyes. She was hiding the sense of desolation and the deep hurt that was lying behind them.

Her first stop on day one was, of course, the salon. She had continued to work out like a fiend at home because she had needed an avenue to let out her pent-up energy.

However, that was all she had done, so upon her emergence into public, she looked as though she owned a patent on the very idea of mourning.

Upon stepping into the salon she was immediately informed that there had been a change in her normal routine and prep area, and that a private area of the salon had been set up exclusively for her visits going forward.

Cristal had been designated to lead her to her new quarters. And she did so in an extreme state of excitement, for this kind of treatment had rarely ever happened.

The very magnetic Chase Ajani, the man himself, had had this room especially prepared for Brandi. He had declared quite frankly that no one else was to use it at all for any reason with the exception of preparing it for Brandi.

The room was to be used exclusively for her services. Nothing else would be tolerated. Cristal was brimming with excitement upon relaying this news to Brandi.

When she opened the door she awaited Brandi's reaction with bated breath because the room was filled with beautiful plants of orchids in a wide variety of glorious splashes of color.

Specially selected African-American art hung from its walls. As well there was plush, thick wallpaper, rich in quality and texture, in just the right colors to harmonize with Brandi's skin tones.

The pile carpeting was every bit as rich, and thick as the wallpaper. The porcelain sinks, and pedicure stations were a beautiful black and bronze to complement the wallpaper and the carpet, and every tool in the place was either shining gold or sterling silver.

The entire space was designed to pamper. it was designed to make a woman feel nothing but good about herself, as though she were the only worthwhile female on the planet. The room was definitely fit for a queen.

It was only natural for Cristal to think that once Brandi learned of this lavish treatment from this man—a man who left women drooling simply by passing them on the street—would excite her.

Upon Brandi's entrance, Cristal could instantly see she was wrong. For all of the excitement Brandi showed, one would have thought that she had stepped into nothing more than a public restroom.

"Don't you like it, Brandi?" Cristal whispered in awe. "Chase Ajani has gone to a lot of trouble to make this room exclusively yours and very special for you."

Brandi stared at Cristal seeing her but not really seeing her. Cristal was such a child. "And why would your Mr. Ajani go to such lengths, Cristal?"

Before Cristal could provide an answer Chase Ajani strolled into the room, bringing with him his own electric charge as he made his way over to stand in front of Brandi.

"Cristal, thank you. That will be all. I believe that I am the only one who can truly answer Ms. Hutchinson's question," he said, smoothly dismissive.

Cristal knew her exit when she heard it. She was gone without a whisper. But not without disappointment. She really didn't want to miss the sound of just listening to Ajani's voice. He had a voice that could make you drift off into a daydream just listening to it.

Chase Ajani lifted the Gucci sunglasses from Brandi's face. He took note of the faint shadows under her eyes. He tucked a hand under her chin, raising it a bit. Then he raised one of her hands and lightly grazed his lips over the back of it.

A tingle that Brandi had never felt before hit the pit of her stomach. She audibly sucked in a breath. Chase smiled as he looked into her wounded eyes.

"You are one of our salon's best customers, Ms. Hutchinson. I am aware of your loss as well as of your accomplishments. I thought that a lady such as yourself deserved a better accommodation than merely being served in a public area, regardless of how thorough your security is." He paused. "It seemed fitting that you would deserve some privacy."

He grazed her other hand with his lips, treating Brandi to another one of those tingles way down deep.

"And, by the way," he continued flawlessly, "my name is Chase Ajani. Why don't you call me Ajani, as only the most special of people are allowed to do?"

He took her hand and led her over to a luxurious couch, where she sank immediately into a plush pile of cushions.

Brandi was reminded of the glimpse she'd had of this man the last time she had visited the salon. And yet as fleeting as it was, it had made an impression on her even then.

His gesture was very touching. However, precaution was a way of life for her. Smiling at him she punched in Tata's number on her cell phone.

Before she could say one word Tata assured her that she was aware of the private accommodation provided by Mr. Ajani, that all had been checked out, and that she hadn't been told because it was a surprise for her. Security clearances had been made. All was well with the new arrangement. She was to do nothing except enjoy it.

Brandi clicked off the call.

She smiled, swept into the deep current of electricity she felt from looking into Ajani's eyes. That tingle swelled from her stomach into her chest.

"Well, Mr. Ajani, it seems that you have thought of most everything," she said as she looked around the very classy, elegant setup.

"No 'Mister.' Just plain old Ajani for you, Brandi." His voice caressed her name.

Ajani gently rubbed a thumb under one of her eyes, where he could see very light swelling, possibly from tears that had been shed. Ms. Brandi Hutchinson had a human side.

"I haven't yet thought of quite everything for you, Brandi, but I assure you if you give me a chance I most certainly will. For now, please enjoy the masseuse, the spa, and facial treatment, along with the makeover as well as the other treats we have made available and at your service."

Briefly he lightly grazed a thumb over the inside of her palm before rising to leave. Brandi's insides fluttered at his very touch.

Ajani was a dangerous man to her in her current vulnerable state. And every instinct she had was telling her to run from this man, and run fast.

But, as every woman knows and as Luther Vandross has crooned many times—a heart does what it wants to do.

Chapter 36

That night the party was cranked and in high gear in a single-family home not too far from the Square. There were crowds of young men and women hanging out, dancing, sweating, and gyrating to the beats from the DJ.

There were a few low-riding vehicles pumping up and down the street showing off their hydraulics. Regardless of what happened this trend constantly continued.

In fact when something happened like what had been done to Q, it just seemed to kick this stuff up another notch or two.

Word had leaked on the street about the party, and cars were double-parked, lining up to be a part of the in-crowd.

In the driveway there were several young men sitting on the hood of a convertible, clowning around, ranking on each other, and hurling insults—their basic entertainment for the night.

There were quite a few people on the front porch of the house, laughing and talking. All in all it was a nice night for a party in L.A.

The weather was warm but with the kick of a balmy breeze. Everyone was feeling good for the night. A couple of the Conquerors walked down the street laughing and talking with each other.

They were wearing regular street clothes. Shamika was

wearing a long white designer silk shirt with jeans tucked tight into rhinestone-studded cowboy boots.

She was wearing her fashionable lumberjack look as though she had just stepped out of the pages of *Vogue*. Her long hair was swept back in a single ponytail that was black and shining like an ad for a perm commercial.

Her girl Dierdre was looking like an abs commercial in her black leotard with her cap flipped backward. She had huge, thick gold hoop earrings dangling from her ears, and four-hundred-dollar Gucci sneakers on her feet.

As they walked, one of the hydraulic low-riding vehicles pulled up next to them. The young man on the passenger side focused on Shamika. Everybody called him by the name of Shock-T.

He looked Shamika up and down, from head to toe, leering in her direction. "Hey, sweet lady, my name ends in a T. Cuz I be called Shock-T. Why don't ya spend some time with me?"

For some reason his boys found this corny line of crap hilariously funny. The driver hit the hydraulics, driving the car up and down. Shamika rolled her eyes. She didn't even slow her pace as she pranced along the sidewalk as though the sidewalk itself should be graced because she was on it.

"I don't think so, B-boy. Not tonight."

"Ah, Baby. Why you dissing me like that?"

The car suddenly took off, causing Shock-T to fall backward as his boys continued laughing at his antics with Shamika.

One of them said while laughing, "Man shut up. That fine girl doesn't want you. Look at her, man, really look at her, she's as fly as one of them video models on BET, and you know doggone well you ain't with that."

Shock-T ignored him. He leaned out of the car looking at Shamika with a smile. "Ah, Baby. Please."

One of the other young men in the backseat pulled Shock-T by the back of his shirt back into his seat.

Shamika smiled. She kept walking.

Against Dierdre's warning glance she stopped to look at Shock-T, addressing him directly. "You've got to learn to lighten up on a lady, my brother."

Dierdre pulled her arm to hurry her along in the midst of the cat calling and whistling that had started to go on. "Come on, girl. Don't pay any attention to them. Keep your eye on the prize."

The passenger in the backseat shouted, "Yo, Shock. The lady said light, man. You heard her. You done struck out again, partner. Check it out."

Then they all laughed.

"Shut up!" Shock-T yelled at them. "Just shut up."

He turned to the driver and thumped him on the shoulder. "Come on, man. Drive. Will you?"

The driver laughed at Shock-T's predicament, too.

"Man, shut up. You're always trying to get your rap on, man. You've got to learn to let things come naturally sometime."

Shamika and Dierdre exchanged glances, laughing, too.

Eric, who was Shamika's boyfriend, was standing at the window of the party house. He had been watching the Li'l nigga getting his flirt on with his woman.

Although the Conquerers had all agreed to abstain from certain activities, this didn't include hanging out publicly with their boyfriends.

The girls just tried to keep the boys at bay by impressing upon them the importance of their vows and forming solidarity within their posse.

The beauty Shamika radiated captivated Eric. He could hardly believe she was his girl. Hatred raged in his heart at the thought of any other man touching her.

Hell, he wasn't even touching her these days, so he definitely wasn't feeling this flirting nigga trying to get his groove on with his woman, of all the women. Dierdre was right there, too, yet this Li'l nigga had passed on her to go after his Shamika.

As Shamika and Dierdre approached the party—one they shouldn't have been at, anyway, but they thought it wouldn't be a big deal if they stopped in for a minute—Eric watched them intently.

The party was straight up jamming by this time. Shamika and Dierdre finally reached the house. They walked up the front steps.

As soon as they reached the porch Eric stepped out, grabbing Shamika's arm. His anger was boiling. He could barely contain it. "I gotta talk to you."

Shamika gave him a surprised look. She looked at Dierdre, who shook her head in the negative, giving her a warning look not to go with Eric. She didn't like his vibe.

Shamika shined her on so as to cut down on the embarrassment of Eric's behavior. "Dierdre, go have a good time, girl. I'll catch up to you when Eric and I finish talking."

She couldn't imagine what was wrong with him, but she was going to tell him he'd better check himself. However, she didn't think doing that so publicly would be wise.

Dierdre smirked in Eric's direction, not feeling him at all. She definitely disliked his little abusive public display of ownership, but he was Shamika's man so she'd let her fly with that nigga.

"Yeah, okay. I'll check you later," Dierdre said as she moved through the throng in the party to try to find a bottle of water.

She sure hoped they had some water because everybody was so busy blinging, gyrating, and sipping from various glasses she knew none of what she was seeing was even close to the category of water, or at least no closer than the starting liquid.

Brandi's rules were definitely putting a strain on their partying and love lives. Yet, at the same time it felt good to have a goal. It felt good to feel like you were stronger than a lot of the mess you saw going on around you.

Eric tightened his grip on Shamika's arm. He led her through the crowd of tightly packed bodies and dancers and down a long hallway away from everyone.

He opened a door, looking inside. He closed the door, apparently not at all satisfied with what he had glimpsed in the room, as a look of disgust plastered itself over his already-angry features.

Still gripping Shamika's arm he tried another door a little farther down the hall. Upon looking inside he could see the room was empty. Satisfied that he'd finally found a private spot he pulled Shamika inside with him.

The bedroom was modestly furnished. Posters hung all over the walls. Eric yanked on Shamika's arm. He pushed her in the direction of the bed, where she landed in pure surprise.

"Eric, what is wrong with you?" Shamika asked, starting to become just a tad bit touchy regarding his abusive greeting of her. He'd asked her to come, and he knew that she didn't usually hang out at parties, so she'd thought he would be glad to see her.

She didn't know what was wrong with him. She'd never seen him like this. "Why are you acting like this? What is wrong with you?" she repeated herself.

Eric stood before her, staring down at her in a rage. He had never been so filled with anger before in his life. He had hurt a lot of people in his time without ever experiencing the level of outrage that was surging through his body.

The range of anger Shamika had moved him to was near indescribable. He didn't tolerate women disrespecting him, and she knew that.

"Who was that nigga, Shamika?" he finally managed to spit at her.

Shamika took a step back from the palpable rage that was rolling off Eric in waves. Astonished, her mind a complete blank, she asked, "Who?"

Eric slapped her so hard and viciously across her face that her ears rang.

Before Shamika could recover or say a word or do anything in her own defense, he followed that slap up with a vicious backhand.

He didn't give a damn about all the noise he was hearing about the Conquerors. Nor did he care about all that they thought they were. Shamika was his girl. She'd better ask some damn body cuz he wasn't feeling her disrespect.

Behind them the muffled sounds of the jamming party were going on outside the door. Shamika was not only hurting. She was mad as hell.

Slowly she rose from the bed where she had landed once again after the vicious slap she'd received.

Eric stared at her. Spit welled up in the corner of his mouth. "Answer my question, ho. I said, who is that nigga?"

Shamika was angry and humiliated. She couldn't believe that Eric had put his hands on her, slapping her like she was some punk-ass nigga he had rolled up on on the street.

She let her anger get the best of her. Eric had not only stung her with his attitude and actions, he had hurt her feelings so bad that she couldn't think straight.

Ice formed in her voice. Belligerently cold she said, "I don't have to answer to you for nothing I do, nigga." The *nigga* she dragged out to sound as nasty and low-life as she could possibly make it. "You-don't-own-me."

A look of malignant madness, even of insanity flashed through Eric's eyes. His anger surged like a spurt of water just before it tumbles over a waterfall.

He yanked Shamika's ponytail with extraordinary strength with one hand. He slapped her face with the force of ten men with his other hand.

The continuous slaps to her face resounded like echoes, they were so hard.

Because he had a grip on her ponytail, the force of the

slaps twisted her head back and forth as she bore the full brunt of the harshness of each and every slap.

He slapped her like she was a whore in an alleyway, without concern or thought for any shred of dignity she might have had.

Shamika looked into his eyes as he continued to slap her, unable to free herself. There was nothing there she could appeal to. He was caught up in his humiliation of her, caught up in punishing her.

His eyes were empty shells.

She was hurt beyond words. His continuous slaps had rendered her immobile. Her face was stinging. It was blistering from the force of each slap.

Both the palm of his hand and the knuckles from the back of his hand were imprinted on both sides of Shamika's face from the sheer force of the slaps.

Still enraged Eric stopped slapping her. He let go of her ponytail so suddenly she fell to the floor.

He dragged her by her ponytail across the floor as though she were nothing more than a bag of garbage that needed to be hauled out to the trash.

He slammed her up against the door as he released his hold on her.

Shamika rose to her feet. She took a step away from the door, allowing room to maneuver. She gave Eric a deadly look. Eric had underestimated the shape she was in due to her grueling training with the Conquerors.

When she was steady on her feet she reached behind her back. Eric drew his automatic down on her, firing at her chest. He shouted at the same time, "Don't even think about it, ho. Nobody disrespects me."

He continued to spray her with automatic bullets until she was forced back against the door. She landed with her back against the door at the exact same time that Eric's gun clicked on empty.

Shamika's body gave a last death jerk.

Eric walked over to Shamika. He lifted her head to look at her. Outside the door the party was still in swing. Shamika's white silk shirt was covered in red, flowing blood.

Eric moaned.

He looked shell-shocked, like he had awakened from a nightmare. One that he didn't know he was in.

"Shamika, I'm sorry. I love you. You know I didn't mean it. I don't know why you made me so mad. I'm crazy about you. You know that."

Shamika, of course, didn't respond.

When she didn't Eric started to cry.

"Shamika, get up. Please. I'm sorry. Get up!" he screamed at her.

Suddenly the door to the room opened and a young girl from the party stood there.

She took one horrified look at the mess in the room. That was it. She screamed at the top of her lungs.

Eric looked at her as fear shot through him. He released his hold on Shamika's body.

He ran out of the room.

The girl continued to scream, her yelling now formulating into words as she assessed the situation.

"Oh my God! Oh my God! She's dead! Oh my God!"

Chapter 37

Out in the living room the crowd was finally becoming aware that there was some type of problem. Eric ran through the throngs of people, pushing and shoving people out of his way in his pursuit of the front door.

People panicked.

They started to run and to duck behind furniture. Shouts of "What happened?" and "What's going on?" could be heard.

Out on the front porch Eric pushed through the screen door. He hopped down the steps. He ran right past a startled Dierdre, who had been chilling out front waiting for Shamika.

"She's been shot! She's been shot!" were the only words that Dierdre heard as she saw Eric running.

Upon hearing those words and not seeing Shamika, Dierdre ran down the steps behind Eric. She ran out into the street.

Just as Eric ran up into the driveway of the house across the street and was looking to scale the fence, he heard Dierdre's voice calling out to him, "Eric!"

He hesitated for a fraction of a second. When he did Dierdre went down on one knee. She aimed her gun directly at his back. She emptied her clip on him.

She calmly watched him fall. She heard his screams of pure agony.

"Justice," she whispered as she smiled.

There was total panic as cars revved up to get out of the area. People were running in every direction.

Dierdre ran back into the house to see about Shamika. The music was still booming as though the party were still going on. The living room of the house was in a shambles.

Dierdre shoved her way past the few people who were still inside. When she reached the hallway she ran searching through different rooms.

A feeling of foreboding shot through her when she reached the bedroom door where Shamika's body was. She hesitated a moment before going in.

She had to push against the door because something was up against it. It was Shamika's body.

Squeezing through the door she had to turn away at the sight of Shamika's blood there was so much of it.

It was all over the place as though somebody had emptied her body of its entire blood supply. It was splattered all around the room.

Dierdre got down on her knees, tears flooded her vision. She closed Shamika's eyes.

Just as she ran out of the room she heard the sirens in the distance.

Chapter 38

Outside on the street Dierdre moved swiftly. Just as she was running a group of the Street Laws spotted her. One of them started yelling hysterically.

She was holding Eric in her arms. "Why you shoot my brother? Why did you have to shoot him?" she sobbed.

In that instant the other Street Laws opened fire on her. Dierdre ducked behind some vehicles while continuous gunshots rang out behind her.

Some of the Street Laws yelled at Eric's sister, Shellie, who was sitting on the ground holding a very dead Eric in her lap. She cradled him, moaning over and over as she rocked him back and forth. "Why you shoot my brother? Oh God! Why did you shoot my brother?"

The sirens were gaining ground and getting closer.

Soon the helicopters would be flying overhead, and the police cruisers would be there.

"Shellie, get up! Come on! We gotta go!" one of the Street Laws shouted.

Another one of the members yelled at her. "Yo. Let's do this. We've got to get out of here."

Shellie screamed at their ignorance. Couldn't they see? How could they be so stupid? "No! I can't leave my brother. I can't. Oh God! He's dying. Help me."

He was already dead. It was just that Shellie was in shock.

Another one of the gang members screamed at her, trying to break through her fog, attempting to get her to understand. "You can't do anything for him. There's nothing you can do! Shellie! Come on!"

She ran over to Shellie, pulling her up off the ground by the arm. Eric's head slipped out of her lap. A slow, steady stream of blood dripped from the corner of his mouth.

His eyes stared into the twilight of the sky, unmoving.

"Come on, Shellie. The Boys in Blue are on their way. You wanna be here to try to explain this setup to them?" She shook Shellie. "Well! Do you?"

Shellie looked at her, tears streaming down her face. "But, he's my brother," she moaned.

The girl softened a bit. "I know but you can't help him now, baby girl. You just can't help him. We've got to go. Okay?"

"My mama wouldn't want me to leave him. And he wouldn't leave me. I can't. I just can't leave him. He's my brother."

She took Shellie by the shoulders. She looked deep into her eyes, trying to connect with her.

"I promise you we will take care of this. Word. We got this. And we gonna take care of it. But we need you to come with us for now. Okay?"

Shellie gave a slight nod of her head before looking for a last time into Eric's sightless eyes.

The girl didn't wait, she yanked on Shellie's arm, making her feet fly into place.

It was just another night in the hood.

Chapter 39

While Shamika and Dierdre had compromised the position of the almighty Conquerors, Brandi was sitting on the edge of some very tempting compromising herself while she licked the wounds of death from her pores.

She had promised herself that it would be dinner, and dinner only with Ajani. Thus far that was what it had been.

A very wonderful seafood dinner in an exclusive part of Malibu. And it had proved to be a delightful evening with Ajani as he reveled her with light anecdotes and stories to keep her amused as well as to keep her mind off her current sorrows.

After dinner they sat out on the rocks under the moonlight chattering away. Brandi found herself wondering what she was doing there with him.

She was shivering at the mere nearness of Ajani, and he hadn't even touched her. He was an intoxicating man for her. She'd had to remind herself numerous times during the evening that she had better not play with fire because those who played with fire eventually got burnt.

At the same time she was undergoing a warring conflict with her own convictions because she felt like she had been stripped bare with the murder of Ari, and she was fighting for ways to uphold her posse without resorting to or falling into the age-old art of murder.

She didn't want to live with a murder on her hands if it was at all possible to avoid. However, people were making it increasingly difficult for her to avoid these positions with their actions.

She was absolutely numb inside from all of the considerations, the planning, and then the strategies that she had had to reassess as well as discard as not good enough.

Then she found herself in a position with a man she barely knew whose mere presence had the ability to make her forget her own name.

She knew there was no way in the world that she needed to be with him, nor did she need the conflict of feelings that he aroused in her.

Yet, it was as if someone had dangled an illusive, addicting drug in front of her, and though her mind screamed don't touch it, her body craved just one touch of it.

With great difficulty Brandi struggled to focus on Ajani's voice.

"So you think I like sitting under the moonlight alone even though there's a beautiful woman at my side?"

Brandi smiled. "You're not alone, Ajani."

"Aren't I?" he volleyed back at her. "You're sitting beside me but you're not here."

Brandi didn't respond.

"Why don't you take me where you were? At least this way we could spend the time there together." He smiled his easy smile at her.

Brandi felt a tug in her chest.

But then she thought about all those who had trusted in her leadership and loyalty, and she knew, regardless of what she wanted, that the vows she had made, the ones she had taken with her girls, were what had to come first.

There was no room in her life for a man like Ajani. "I'm sorry, Ajani," Brandi said as she stood up.

With great difficulty she glanced into the dark, liquid pools of his eyes, the same eyes that had mesmerized her from the first glance.

How could one man have that much power in a look?

"I can't take you there. Where I'm traveling I must go alone."

With that she left Ajani standing on a rock under the moonlight alone as she made her way back to her own car for the drive back.

Ajani watched her departing footsteps. He watched the very shape of her, her form and how she moved. He loved her fluid motion, loved just watching her move.

"There's no such thing as alone for me, Brandi."

He knew his time would come to face her again.

It always did.

Chapter 40

Just as Brandi climbed into her car she got a distress signal from Tata that put her on a direct route to the warehouse.

Something was very wrong. They had agreed to use that signal only if there was a major emergency.

Once Brandi arrived she sat behind a glass shield with a small television monitor in front of her, flicking from screen to screen, watching different areas of the operations.

She flicked to an outside screen that showed the Conquerors patrolling the outside of the warehouse. The patrols had been greatly increased. Everybody was strapped down.

One of the private phones next to Brandi beeped.

She picked it up and clicked on, listening intently. Her eyes flashed in icy anger as she listened to the conversation on the other end.

"Dierdre, go to the hideout. I want you to go there right now. And I want you to stay there. Do not move from that spot under any circumstance. Lay low. I'll be in touch shortly."

Brandi clicked off the phone. She hit a button. She stood up, getting her pace on. "Tata, come on in. Bring Tangie with you."

While Brandi was waiting every phone in the room rang at the same time. She answered call after call from various trusted sources.

Finally she took the last call.

Upon hanging up she heard a discreet buzz. She pushed a button, opening the metal sliding doors to admit Tata and Tangie into the room.

Once they stepped through Brandi pushed the button to close the metal doors shut behind them.

"Totally confirmed, as reported," Brandi told them. "There's going to be a war on the streets. First there was the gin-and-juice-joint incident. Ari's dead. Now Eric has shot and killed Shamika. The war can no longer be avoided."

They all sat down.

"Tata, you're already aware that Dierdre killed Eric in retaliation for Shamika's murder and that Eric is the brother of one of the Street Laws, Shellie."

Tata jumped in to finish the story. "Yeah. They spotted Dierdre. They shot at her. She had to break camp to get out of there alive. They're out for blood. I don't see how a war can be avoided at this point."

Secretly Tata's blood was racing. She loved a good fight. There was nothing that got her more psyched and pumped up than an opportunity to let her skills shine.

Of course, now she was disciplined with these actions since she had joined the Conquerors. But blood as well as slinging and banging would always be part of her makeup.

Tata's mother had gone down like a prizefighting champ when her time had come and so would she when her time came.

Tangie's throat was hurting with unshed tears because she knew this was not a good course of action. There would be a lot of devastating losses. The type of losses that could never be recovered from, and she knew it. Deep in her heart, though, she had always known that the possibility existed. She had just hoped that it would never happen.

Tata on the other hand stood rigid like the soldier she was, with blood in her eyes. The Street Laws had spilled some of her blood by spilling the blood of her family. The Conquerors were her family so she would spill some of theirs.

It was as simple as that.

Brandi looked across the table at both of them.

Silently she arrived at a decision she had been trying to avoid making since Ari's death. Her hand had been forced. There was no other choice.

She, like Tangie, had hoped deep inside it would never come to a street war. But she hadn't been unrealistic enough not to consider the possibility.

That was why she had been so drawn to her *Street Wars* game. It had taught her a lot about the mentality of those who inhabited the streets for a living.

It had also shown her how to gain the best advantage for taking down an enemy. It was funny in a way. A mere game had taken her into the minds of cold-blooded killers as well as making her aware of the lengths to which people would go to win. It had shown her exactly what having an appetite for blood could do.

"We're going to the mattresses for an all-out, bloodbath war. You need to be prepared."

"That's what I'm talking about," Tata said.

Chapter 41

Brandi had purposely avoided this particular visit she had to make, primarily because she thought she already knew the answer to her main question.

However, believing that you knew something and actually having that something confirmed definitely put things in a different light.

Yeah, she had been playing the game. Her hatred had reached grave proportions. She was aware of that.

She was moving in a direction that was contrary to everything she'd been brought up to believe. For reasons unknown to her, that direction had put her in dire conflict when it came to certain decisions.

She had agonized over this specific visit during the many weeks she had spent in isolation after Ari was murdered.

She had sent money but had avoided her regular visits with Q to evade what she knew would be the inevitable, a confirmation of the truth.

She had evaluated the layout from every angle regarding Ari's death. She knew enough to follow the unfolding events that led up to her killing.

But as it is with life, the inevitable eventually becomes unavoidable, and when something must be done, it must be done.

Especially, she felt, if you had held yourself up to be accountable to many others for your actions.

Once inevitable's time arrived there wasn't much more to be said or done. Brandi knew this deep down inside, though she had never in her wildest imagination thought that she'd ever turn out to be such a philosopher.

She could clearly hear her mother's voice urging her to be true to herself, but she knew she'd given up that right long ago.

Her photograph sitting in a pail of broken glass with a cross on top of it next to her mother's dresser was a confirmation of a different kind, though she had no way of knowing this.

From the time that picture frame had fallen from its place, shattering into so many pieces, the omen for Brandi's direction and the place where she was now had been established.

That was the funny thing about the spiritual world; it operated under a different set of laws than the world of the flesh. Brandi was on a collision-course path.

Brandi knew for a fact that the police had never questioned Q during their interrogations, and had botched up their search for questions and answers regarding Ari's murder.

Once she was done with Tata and Tangie for the evening and once all of their plans were solid and in effect, she'd made the trip to visit Q.

Under the circumstances she could no longer put off that visit.

On her way over there she thought about how glad she was that she had set Ajani straight. She didn't need the complication of him in her life right now.

And she didn't need another potential target that she cared about and would be obligated to protect. It would have been different if they had just targeted her, but instead they wanted to take down everything around her so she could experience the agony of watching it crumble. And they were not to be underestimated.

It was personal, not business, and as such she had a duty to protect and serve those that she loved.

Once she arrived at Q's apartment she sat next to him at the window, looking over at the area that had turned out to be Ari's personal graveyard.

She had known without stepping foot into his room that Q would have been able to see the murder scene if he had been in the window that day. And instinctively she had known that he was in the window, even though she had no confirmation of this.

They had always been like that with each other since they were little kids. They could feel each other without speaking or talking.

She had known that Q had seen her while she sat on the ground holding Ari.

She could feel his eyes on her as she held the dead little girl.

And a part of her hadn't wanted to act on the information, as much as she had loved Ari. She had been in abject agony regarding the honoring of her death by the rules of engagement applied on the streets.

The reason for that agony was because she hadn't wanted to cross a bridge of absolutely no return. She was at war with her own flesh.

But under the escalating circumstances, on the brink of no return was where she stood.

So far she'd pulled off everything without any loss of life whatsoever. That fact in itself was quite amazing, considering the reputation she'd established and the coup she had pulled off.

However, to her credit she had been very careful with her handling of things to ensure no loss of life. There were no guarantees with what she had been doing, but somehow fortune had smiled on her.

But any true soldier knew that if you entered a war there were bound to be casualties.

The only thing she could think about that was reassuring at this point in time was that neither she, her family, her extended family, nor any more of her girls would become one of those casualties.

They'd have to strike in a way to minimize impact as well as injuries and death to their own side.

It was time to get down. She positioned herself directly in front of Q so she could read his eyes.

She'd always been able to read him in a way that no one else could. His injuries hadn't changed that. If possible it had made their bond stronger because of his limited communication skills.

She'd learned to read his eyes, the windows of the soul, in order to know how to help him. Now she had to read them for a message she didn't want to receive.

For his part Q wasn't surprised about her absence during the time that he hadn't seen her. He had expected as much under the circumstances.

He knew what the real Brandi was made of, and that was more than most people could say of her, even her own parents.

He'd heard she was holed up in solitaire after Ari's murder. Truly speaking, he hadn't expected any other reaction on her part.

As well he wasn't surprised to see her on this day, either. He had known she'd show up sooner or later. He'd also known that when she did she'd be seeking confirmation, and that her visit wouldn't be in the light of her regular visits.

He'd already known since the day Ari died that one day Brandi would show up to ask the questions that not one other person had dared to ask.

That was just who Brandi was. He also knew she was smart enough to have already figured out the answers.

There was no way she would just rely on Tata Davis or any member of her posse to handle everything, and he knew that as well.

He had a sneaking suspicion that his mother had suspected exactly the same answers that Brandi was searching for the day she had come into his room to find him in tears. He had seen her glance out of the window to look at the murder scene.

But by silent agreement she never dared to ask, and he never tried to communicate the truth of the little girl's death to her.

He knew they were better off left alone as they were. He didn't want to bring more tragedy into her life regarding his knowledge of the murder.

Most likely the police would have written him off even if it had crossed their minds, simply because of his limited, nearly nonexistent communication skills as well as their role in causing them.

However, if that was the case they had gravely underestimated him.

The truth be told Q wouldn't have told them, anyway. He would have used his disability as a means of not telling them because he wasn't going to cause his mother any more grief under any circumstances.

That information could have gotten a hit put on him, and then she'd have to deal with that in addition to his already-intolerable circumstances.

Brandi looked across at him. Water welled up in her eyes but didn't spill onto her cheeks.

Q was the only person on earth that she'd ever dare to let see that side of her. She knew she could trust him not to exploit what others would consider a weakness.

Not even Tangie and Tata, as close as they'd become to her, would ever witness this side of her, and Tangie was her best friend.

But Q was different. Q was her brother.

Finally, swallowing hard, her throat constricted with un-shed tears, Brandi got around to asking the ultimate damning question.

"Q, were you in this window the day Ari was killed?"

She searched his eyes, seeing the pain of his yes answer re-flected there.

She nodded her head, wishing the answer could have been different.

Then she looked out of the window, seeing the scene ex-actly as it had transpired on that day.

She saw the Mister Softee truck pull up to the curb. She could see Ari running delightedly toward it.

Though she didn't see the next part, she asked the question that her gut instinct had led her to during her retreat from the world following Ari's death, prior to it being confirmed by the perimeter security team she'd hired.

Q's confirmation of this detail would erase any and all doubts.

"She was in disguise. But by any chance did you see Left Eye out on the street from the gang called the Street Laws on that day?"

The answer yes was immediately reflected in Q's eyes.

She nodded again.

Both her gut instinct as well as her resources had been cor-rect regarding Left Eye's carefully planned execution of Ari as well as the level of Left Eye's vicious jealousy of her.

Brandi had taken the extra precaution, without even Tata's knowledge, of hiring perimeter security that reported directly and only to her.

The team she had hired and had laid out major, major paper to have, were known only as the Shadows. They had a reputation for blending into an area or scene without anyone being the wiser.

As good as her people were, even her posse hadn't ever spotted them. Nor had they spotted the disguised Left Eye, but the Shadows had, and so had Q.

She had figured in advance that the Street Laws might present a problem in the future, being the ghetto hood rats they were, and so she found insiders from their gang who she had paid off to get information regarding their activities.

That was a part of the information she had used to take over their income.

Of all the other gang factions in the city whose turfs had been taken over or who hadn't been asked to join the Conquerors, the Street Laws were the ghetto equivalent of the bottom of the barrel, even from the hood standpoint.

They were true hood rats, and that meant they had a dangerous mentality that could not be ignored.

Brandi had anticipated their "hell to the nah we ain't rolling over" attitude. She had also anticipated Left Eye's anger at not receiving an invitation to join the Conquerors.

Brandi had rejected them for the same reason she was about to go after them with a vengeance now. They were too low-life for her standards.

She stayed up nights long after her posse was asleep, anticipating the moves of others. That was why she had hired the Shadows.

They protected her and her posse from a distance. But their main objective was collecting valuable information without anyone even knowing they were there.

She had received reports of Left Eye's personal feelings regarding her and her accomplishments. As well she knew she was a great source of irritation and embarrassment for Left Eye.

Brandi flicked her tongue to the inside of her cheek before hitting Q with her next question. "Was it the people in the ice-cream truck who murdered Ari?"

This was a source of great pain for her because she felt like she should have seen it coming. But it was such an innocent occurence. That ice-cream truck was on the street every day serving the kids, but that was precisely why it should have been checked out.

That had been a grave oversight on her part.

Every day they should have checked it because somewhere along the way Left Eye's gang had murdered and gotten rid of the body of the real driver.

They then took his place. They pulled up to the curb. Ari was the first to arrive at the truck. They most likely had been watching her pattern of always being the first one to arrive at the truck.

They used this information to gain an advantage to kill her, and then vanished into thin air once they destroyed the truck. The truck still hadn't been found.

Nor had the body of the driver. But Brandi knew as sure as she was sitting there that he was dead, too.

Q's eyes spilled over with tears, giving Brandi her final answer of the murder occurring from the ice-cream truck.

Brandi nodded.

She felt like a statue whose heart had turned to stone. She could have been the TinMan that Nipsey Russell had played in his role with Michael Jackson and Diana Ross in *The Wiz*.

If she only had a heart.

The answer was she'd had a heart at one time but it no longer existed. In fact she'd still had one. It had just been hidden until she had taken a seat across from Q. Until the confirmation of Ari's death had dropped into a steel bucket like icicles dropping from a tree.

The last shred of her heart had died while she sat in that chair across from Q.

"Q, after tonight I most likely won't be able to see you for a while. But I'll make sure everything is okay for you and Renita," she had carefully told him. "I'm also going to have someone move the two of you away from here once I speak to her. Because after tonight, Q, life is never going to be the same."

Q released the most painful, awful sound of ugh that Brandi had ever heard. She was slowly losing life as she'd known it, and she knew it.

She'd already arranged for her parents' departure. They were safely in the southern part of the United States, though her father, from what she'd understood from her mother, was furious with her.

So be it.

At least her mom had had the good sense to listen when Brandi told her that she had made arrangements for them to get out of Los Angeles because their very lives depended on their getting out right then and there.

She'd had to do it. She couldn't bear it if anything happened to them because of her actions.

And now she couldn't risk anything happening to Q or his mother, either. To protect them she would have to give them up as a part of her life, at least for the time being.

Brandi put her arms around Q. He felt the warmth of her tears. He could hardly bear the thought of never seeing her again.

But he knew her mind was made up.

His tears mingled with hers.

Chapter 42

Later that night Brandi, Tata, and Tangie were again in another meeting, this time outside of the Los Angeles boundaries that they normally traveled in.

Brandi looked at Tangie, searching for another answer that she needed to a very important question. "Where's Fishbone? I heard he's not in the city."

Tangie nodded in the affirmative. "Yeah. He's not in L.A. That's true. But you know Maestro will know where he is and how to reach him."

"Okay, then talk to Maestro. Right away. He needs to make the connection so I can talk to Fish. Tell him this can't wait. Fishbone will not appreciate hearing about this from anyone but us, and the news is escalating and traveling fast, so I need to talk to him like yesterday."

Tata glanced briefly at Tangie.

Then she put the whole of her focus on Brandi. She was disturbed as hell about the Shamika and Eric incident. It kept bothering her even when she tried not to think about it.

For one thing Shamika and Dierdre had no damn business hanging out that openly, and at a party at that. They both knew that. Parties were off limits unless they had a specific reason for being there in terms of visibility, like they had had at the gin-and-juice joint.

But more than that, the manner of the killing was bothering the hell out of her.

"What I wanna know is how the hell did Eric kill Shamika? She was back-strapped Brandi. Her knife was still in her sheaf when Dierdre found her dead. She slept with that thing. You know that. I don't understand how the hell she got killed without ever taking it out of the sheaf."

Tata imitated Brandi's habit of pacing the floor. "I mean seriously, Brandi. She could have stuck that knife in that nigga's heart before he had a chance to blink. The girl was well trained."

Shamika's death was turning into a personal affront for Tata.

Brandi flicked her eyes over Tata's face. Her features were frozen in icelike hatred. A cold determination reflected from her eyes.

Brandi took a deep breath before answering. She was learning that being right didn't always make you feel good. There were times when she was beginning to wish she'd been wrong about some things.

"Apparently, because it was Eric she took that extra second that I've been talking about."

Tangie jumped in. "Eric went off on some jealous rage because of some Li'l nigga's hollering at Shamika on the street in front of the party. At least that's the word that's coming down. It sounded like parts of their argument were heard outside in the hall. But I guess nobody thought it would get that out of hand. You know how people don't like to mess with a man and his woman's personal business."

"Well, it's too late. It doesn't matter now. That split second of hesitation cost Shamika, her life. And I can tell you both right now I'm not willing to lose any more lives over it."

Brandi addressed Tata directly. "Tata, I need you to oversee the shutdown of the entire warehouse operation. Do it according to plan, girlfriend. I want it ghost. There's not to be a trace of it left."

"Brandi, we're talking major paper here."

Brandi turned to Tata coldly. She was not going to debate this with her. "Shut it down."

Tata nodded, respecting her position as well as her wisdom.

"Tangie, go make the connect with Fishbone. Tell Maestro that this needs to happen yesterday, like I said earlier. We've got to get all the accounts in order, and make sure none of them get splashed with this nonsense so that in the future we can reopen shop."

Tata smiled, now understanding Brandi's plan.

Brandi nodded in her direction. Then she picked up a pager and sent a signal that simply said, "Code Red."

Chapter 43

Outside the warehouse the patrols were out in full force. The yard was constantly filling up with more and more patrols by the minute.

They moved as if they were in a silent, synchronized, choreographed dance, one in which they could not miss a step. And due to their intense, elaborate training they *were* in a dance, and missing a step could be crucial.

In fact missing a step was something that just could not happen.

Fishbone was walking through Los Angeles International Airport past the lounge area when a television newscast broadcasting its breaking news caught his attention, stopping him midstride.

He slowed his brisk walk to view the scene just as other patrons in the lounge area turned to look at the television, wondering what was going on.

The newscaster stood there looking grave as well as pensive as he relayed the sad events of the evening. "There has been an outbreak of violence in Los Angeles today. South Central L.A. has exploded in what appears to be gang-related warfare."

They flashed an aerial shot of the area where the party had

taken place. They flashed the house as well as the street outside the house.

"Surprisingly enough, from what breaking news we have filtering in at this time, there appears to be a breakout among the female gangs in Los Angeles including acts and threats of retaliation for two gruesome murders that took place tonight here on this street and in the house shown behind me.

"Two people are confirmed dead. That was just the beginning. We are told the body count is tallying up. Blood is running in the gutters in this unusual turn of events. We don't believe there has ever been female gang warfare or bloodshed in the history of the city of Los Angeles.

"Historically, as we all know, there has been unrest from time to time among the male gangs, but never before now have we even recognized female gang membership at this level of participation. Our sources have now confirmed that the female gangs are a fact, and that this is only one of the areas of gang life that has now changed."

A closeup shot of Shamika's body lying covered in the house flashed across the screen. Then a shot of Eric's body that was covered as well, lying on a stretch of grass just shy of a fence, flashed across the screen.

From there they went to a shot of all of the EMS vehicles on the scene as well as the news trucks and LAPD milling around in full force surrounding the area.

The newscaster finished up his segment. The grave manner in which he had been speaking suddenly turned to excitement at his dawning awareness of being among the first reporters to deliver the news of the start of a gang war.

"We are advising residents in these areas to stay inside their homes for their own safety and well-being. These streets are very dangerous tonight. We will have further news later."

The entire lounge erupted in conversation at once.

A look of pure astonishment crossed Fishbone's face, just as his cell phone and private pager went off.

What the hell was going on?

He took off at a dead run through the airport. It was crucial that he get into the city, and get there fast. This he knew before he clicked on his phone and pager to receive the details firsthand.

He started issuing orders straight away as well as instituting layers that would minimize any impact.

Frenchie couldn't believe her ears as she sat on the couch listening to the evening news.

Pearl cleared her throat and looked over at Frenchie. "Would you like to take any bets on who might be at the center of this first historical female gang-related activity in Los Angeles?"

Frenchie rolled her eyes at her mother. Then she said a private prayer for Brandi Hutchinson. She was going to need it.

"And when they fell great was the fall of them," Pearl muttered under her breath.

Brandi was going down, and Pearl knew it. Only she knew it wouldn't be the gangs who took her down.

She would be taken down by a different entity. It was written all over her. One just had to know what to look for.

And then Pearl did a strange thing. She too decided to pray for Brandi Hutchinson.

"Lord forgive her for she know not what she do," she uttered, beginning her prayer. For the first time in her life she now understood why Jesus had uttered about those same words on the cross.

Jesus Christ had truly been a man of great mercy.

Chapter 44

Tangie stepped out onto the front porch of her house just as her older sister, Jackie, turned the corner of their street coming home from work.

It had been a long day but Jackie was looking forward to spending some time with Tangie. As far as she was concerned they didn't spend enough time together these days.

They were always running in different directions for different reasons, upsetting the balance of time they could spend together.

Jackie was a hard-working lady. She worked in the bank, and didn't tolerate a lot of the attitudes that went on in their neighborhood regarding work ethics and having a job.

She didn't approve of the welfare system because she believed it made people less productive and lazy. People didn't seem to want to get out of bed if they thought they could have the basic necessities of money, food, shelter, and medical care practically delivered to their front doorstep.

Welfare reform was something she heartily approved of, but even with that there were still issues of this type affecting people.

She didn't believe in street hustling either, because to her that was climbing a ladder of fake success inevitably inflicting pain on other people.

How could one consider themselves a success if they had

to snatch the crumbs from someone else's mouth to do it, or sell them their own death broken up in little portions just to own a piece of the pie?

She was a firm believer in what goes around comes around. She wasn't going to go out like that.

They had lived in their neighborhood all their lives, only a few blocks from the Square, and someone had always worked in their family.

First, their mother had worked.

She had had two jobs. The stress of that was one of the things that had killed her. She dropped dead of a heart attack. She died on the job, of all places.

She also raised three kids single-handedly. In the end it had proved to be too much. She had always been a woman of somewhat frail health.

After her death Jackie had stepped up to the earning plate to take her place, since she was the oldest and their mother was gone. Fishbone and Tangie were still young then.

Her job didn't pay enough for her to move them from the area. When Fishbone started getting money she flat-out refused to take any of his tainted money.

She ended up struggling, with little in the way of comforts but a peace of mind that she was doing the right thing.

Her only wish was that she could have prevented both her brother and her sister from being so infatuated with street life and all its so-called benefits, but it was like fighting an uphill battle all the way.

All they saw were things like the independence and the income. They never stopped to consider the other side of the coin.

Fish had been down in the street life and gang life for a very long time.

Even when he was very young, before their mother had died, he was always doing things that she couldn't do anything about.

She was powerless to stop him. He was headstrong and believed in going his own way. Period.

He also believed in paying for his own circumstances, and there was nothing Jackie could say to make him think any differently.

Now she was dealing with the fact that Tangie had gone the same route, walking down that same street paved with false dreams, due to her affiliation with the infamous Brandi and that damn gang called the Conquerors.

And Jackie had to admit there was no getting around it: Tangie had been blindsided by Brandi. For as long as they had been friends, Tangie had never witnessed anything in Brandi's personality to indicate that she would one day become one of the most formidable and fiercest gang leaders in Los Angeles.

Yet the fact remained that she had become exactly that.

Tangie had told Jackie that they weren't a gang, they were a posse. Whatever the hell that was. She said they were more like a family.

They were a family that bonded together regardless of the circumstances. That was exactly the type of gang rhetoric, Jackie knew, that sucked a lot of young kids into the life. The desire to feel needed and wanted as well as a part of something.

However, she didn't care one iota what Tangie said about the Conquerers or what she called it, for that matter. She knew a gang when she saw one. They were a damn gang with a touch of glam and polish on them. They were that and nothing more. A gang was a gang.

Jackie had been losing sleep at night trying to come up with a way to disentangle Tangie. She had witnessed firsthand her attachment and growing involvement with them on a day-by-day basis.

As well she couldn't believe Fish had let Tangie's involvement with the Conquerors go down like that, thinking it was building her self-esteem.

She was frustrated with the fact that people could talk

themselves into believing anything as long as they wanted to believe it.

Fish's reasoning was pure garbage in its truest form, if she'd ever heard it. It was trash in all its ugliness.

Being a member of a gang was absolutely dangerous from the moment you entered to the point of never being able to get out. Fish ought to know that, since he'd never gotten out.

It was a personal choice of his not to leave gang life, and eventually he had graduated through the levels to the top leadership position.

But even though, he had "achieved" this at his age, there was no ignoring the fact that few of them got the privileges that he had received, and he knew it.

She had a feeling there was a hidden, self-serving purpose for Fish in allowing this involvement of Tangie's that he wasn't revealing.

But that was just her feeling. It was nothing she could prove or put her finger on. It was just something she felt.

Jackie looked over at Tangie standing on the porch just as she pulled onto the street.

Jackie loved her baby sister. She planned to spend the evening having dinner with her, trying to talk some sense into her about that gang nonsense.

She knew it would continue to be difficult because Tangie's accumulation of designer clothes as well as the cost of the designers she could now afford, coupled with her casual attitude toward money, were all a testament to the fact that she, like Fishbone, had discovered the financial benefits of gang life.

Jackie still had her heart set on trying. And she would continue to try as long as she had breath in her body. She wasn't just going to sit idly by watching Tangie travel down the same road as Fishbone. It was a miracle Fishbone was even alive.

Just as Jackie smiled at Tangie and Tangie waved at her, a Cadillac Convertible drove up, pulling in front of her and cutting her off.

Jackie cursed under her breath.

She was just about to back up to pull around it when she realized there were two vehicles in back of her, and she was sandwiched in between them.

The Cadillac slowed directly in front of Tangie.

There were four members of the Street Laws riding in it. One of the members, named Latifah, who was sitting in the front passenger seat, climbed out of the car to sit on the window ledge and yelled, throwing her hands up in the air. "Hey, Tangie! So, what's up, Bad Girl?"

Tangie spotted the dark shadow of the automatic weapon pointed at her from the backseat a split second before it exploded in her direction.

She took a step backward as the explosion ripped through her body like a cannon being fired.

Round after round after round was fired on her as her body did a strange death dance, and the bullets prevented it in a ludicrous sort of way from falling and hitting the front porch.

She was being held on her feet by the impact of the bullets that were lodging in her body.

There was a look of total surprise on Tangie's face. As though she couldn't believe what was happening to her, and she was trying to think of how to get out of harm's way but she couldn't come up with an answer fast enough.

This was another of those split-second timing situations that Brandi was always talking about. The very danger of hesitation itself. And shock—the kind that rooted you in place.

Jackie's car was trapped between the Cadillac in front of her and the two cars in the back of her while the Street Law hoods were gunning down her sister.

She couldn't move her car, try as she might. She was a hostage in her vehicle.

Jackie was so stunned at the quick turn of events that for an instant she couldn't move at all. She was paralyzed with fear as she watched the bullets hit her sister, jiggling her around like some grotesque puppet.

Jackie finally started screaming Tangie's name. "Tangie! Tangie! Oh, no! Please! Tangie! Noooooooooooo!"

The car with the shooter finally sped off, satisfied that Tangie was dead. Her body hit the porch with a dull thud without the spray of bullets to keep her on her feet any longer.

The cars that had trapped Jackie's car sped off, too, leaving her car free to move.

Jackie watched as though she were seeing everything in slow motion. She hit the door handle and climbed out of the car.

On wooden legs she walked slowly toward the body of her dead sister lying on the porch. Finally she ran so she could get there faster.

She reached the top of the stairs to look down at the bullet-riddled corpse of her sister.

It was the type of murder no family member should have to witness. The bullets had torn through Tangie's flesh, ripping it damn near to pieces.

She was unrecognizable because she had also been struck in the face, losing a portion of it completely to the explosion.

It was a senseless, vicious act, and Jackie unfortunately had been given front-row tickets to the stage play of the death of her own sister.

Jackie turned away from the sickening sight and the mess they had made of her sister. She started retching and crying at the same time.

She sank down on the stairs, covering her face with her hands, not wanting to see any more.

Neighbors ran up on the porch to try to comfort her and to stare at what had once been a human being.

At that moment Tata pulled up. She had been coming to pick up Tangie.

She took one look at what was going on, and ran up on Tangie's porch with her heart pumping pure vengeance.

Tata had never been a praying type of girl. She was cold to

the bone through and through. Her lifestyle had left her without much ability to feel.

However, at that moment for the first time in her life her mind screamed for the mercy of the Lord. "Oh, God, please no. Please, God, don't let it be. Don't let her be dead." The words never actually left her mouth but they were written in her heart.

Tata ran up on the porch. She looked down at the dead Tangie, or what was left of her. She kneeled down beside her.

She looked at the scar on Tangie's wrist where she had cut herself as they had all vowed to be one for all and all for one.

Then she took off her jacket with *The Conquerors* emblazoned on the back of it. She closed Tangie's eye, the one that was left. Then she gently laid her jacket over her so people would stop gawking at her.

With that she jumped into her Jeep with only moments to spare before the cops and the emergency service workers arrived.

Chapter 45

Jackie sat in the recliner in her house staring at absolutely nothing after they took her sister's body away, and once all the police activity and the medical furor had died down.

She sat with every light in the house on, shivering even though it was a warm night in Los Angeles. She was cold in a way that she had never experienced cold before. She was cold internally.

It felt as though an ice glacier had parked itself inside her skin, refusing to be moved.

The living room was full of pictures of their mother along with them as little children. Then there were various pictures of Jackie, Fishbone, and Tangie in various stages of their lives while they were growing up.

There were a few pictures with Jackie and Tangie both together smiling brightly. They had come from a family that believed in preserving memories.

It was a good thing because memories were beginning to be all they had left.

Jackie shook her head, unable to quite believe that now there were only two of them left: her and Fish.

There was a knock on the door. Jackie didn't answer it. The knocking persisted. Still she didn't answer. She wished whoever it was would just go away.

She wasn't in the mood for company. She most likely would never be in the mood to see people again.

She was getting to the point where she couldn't do people anymore. It seemed the more involved with people you were, the more hurt and pain there were to splash around.

She hadn't yet recovered from the news of Ari's death. Everybody had known that beautiful child, if not personally, then by reputation. Now her own sister's name had been added to the death list.

Jackie's tentative faith in humanity for the time being was shattered beyond all belief. How could her very own people gun each other down so mercilessly? With no thought for each other or the consequences?

Did they truly hate each other that much?

Didn't they realize what they were doing? Didn't they realize the destructiveness and harm that they were causing? Couldn't they see this behavior was a problem?

It really didn't matter how many times these same questions crowded her mind, she always came up without an answer.

And she knew that for as long as she lived she would always see the cars pulling up, blocking her in. She would always see her sister's body in the throes of death, the life quickly leaving her.

She would never be able to get the sounds of the automatic rounds of shots out of her head.

The knock at the door sounded again.

Jackie finally realized that whoever was knocking would refuse to go away unanswered. With great effort she finally willed herself to rise from the chair to answer the knock at the door.

She looked through the window to find Brandi standing on the porch. Pure hatred flashed across Jackie's face at the sight of her. Brandi's face was the last thing on earth that she wanted to see.

Slowly she opened the door. She stared her hatred at Brandi for a serious hot minute before even trusting herself to address her. Speaking to her, she was finding, was quite difficult.

"What do you want?" she finally managed coldly.

Brandi stared back at Jackie, quite unperturbed by her hatred. She had expected nothing less.

Out on the street it was completely full with patrols from the Conquerors.

Tata hovered at street level in total command of the heavily guarded street presence.

Also in attendance in full force was Fishbone's gang, the L.A. Troops, although there was no visible sign of Fishbone.

The street as well as all of the surrounding blocks were on lock. Nothing was coming in or going out. Not even the LAPD patrol cops in the area, because they had been very generously compensated to be exceptionally busy at that particular moment.

Jackie stared at the street patrols with bitterness and disgust. Bile rose in her throat. She hoped she wasn't supposed to be impressed by this street military tactic because she was anything but impressed.

Enraged at Brandi's sheer audacity would have been a more accurate description of what she was feeling.

The only thing she truly felt now that she could easily identify was revulsion. She spat at Brandi's feet she was so mad.

Brandi didn't budge or flinch.

She allowed Jackie her anger. Tangie was her sister, and as such Brandi knew Jackie was entitled to her anger. So if she had to endure some disrespect on that ground, then so be it.

Jackie shot daggers at Brandi with one look. If looks could kill, then Brandi would certainly have dropped dead on the spot.

When Brandi didn't respond to her question she asked her again, "I-said-what-do-you-want?"

"I want to come in."

Jackie took a step back as she surveyed the very dangerous Tata at street level as well as all of the rest of the Conquerers Brandi had brought with her.

Black currents of unrest and danger rolled off Tata surging through the air. It was so palpable you could feel it.

Jackie could tell that Tata loved her job and was itching to kill somebody in retaliation.

She finally pulled open the door, growing almost bored with assessing the truth of things, and a very dark truth it was proving to be.

"Suit yourself."

Jackie walked away from the door, leaving it open for Brandi. She went back to sit in the recliner. It seemed to be the only spot in the house where she could park herself, as though all of the other areas of the house were invisibly closed to her.

Brandi walked over to stand in front of the mantel in front of Jackie. The television was on and suddenly a newscast broke into the middle of their silent conflict.

They both turned simultaneously to look at it.

This time a different newscaster, unable to maintain the grave look of the first one to report and unable to hide the growing awe in his voice, said, "The gang violence in Los Angeles is reaching an all-time high. There have been repeated reports of shootings, beatings, and stabbings."

Then they showed the shots taken earlier of Shamika, and Eric's demise. They followed those with shots they had obtained right after Tangie's murder on her street.

"Again, we are warning all of the residents in these areas to please stay indoors. The sister of Los Angeles's revered and top gang leader, Fishbone, was murdered this evening, and law enforcement agencies are gearing up for fearsome retaliation. I repeat, please stay indoors . . ."

Brandi walked over to the television. She grabbed the remote control. She clicked it off just as a picture of Tangie's face flashed across the screen with surely only a second left before they described her gruesome murder in detail.

Brandi quietly observed that Jackie must have given the authorities that picture they were showing of Tangie.

Jackie jumped out of her seat in the same instant that her sister's face flashed across the screen. She screamed at Brandi. "Just who the hell do you think you are?" She refused to allow Brandi to answer. "I'll tell you who you are! You're some fake want-to-be leader. One who doesn't care about anybody but herself."

Brandi stared at Jackie without a drop of emotion. After a gap of time that one could have ridden an elephant through, she said, "You're very wrong, Jackie. Tangie was my best friend. I cared."

Jackie was beside herself with rage. She hit full-stage anger alert. "With friends like you who in the hell needs enemies?"

Jackie finally struck a chord. Brandi's eyes flashed briefly with pain. However, her stance did not change, showing both pride and conviction.

She stood with her booted feet planted slightly apart. Her head was tilted upward. She was in total control.

A beat passed before Brandi spoke while looking directly into Jackie's eyes. There was only the two of them. She had known that to show major respect, that was the way it had to be.

Brandi knew Fish would have also expected nothing less of her. He knew how Jackie was, and he would expect Brandi to deal with her accordingly under the circumstances.

Brandi looked at Jackie as though she pitied her, as the most astounding words found their way out of her mouth. "I suppose you've been patting yourself on the back for being a good big sister." She made sure she dragged out the last word good so her message to Jackie could not be mistaken or misconstrued.

"I'm going to tell you, Jackie, before you go patting yourself on the back too hard, Ms. I Have Overcome Because I Wear a Suit. You'd better give some major thought to the fact that if Tangie had thought you'd found the perfect way, she wouldn't have been in the Conquerors, and for that matter Fishbone wouldn't be heading up the L.A. Troops, either."

Brandi didn't miss a beat as she watched Jackie's mouth open and then shut in total surprise.

Brandi played her full leverage. "Tangie was a member of the Conquerors because we were her family. You're going to have to accept that. And she was there because she wanted to make a change."

Jackie looked at Brandi with nothing but pure venom springing from her eyes as a picture of the practically decapitated Tangie lying on her front porch flashed before her eyes.

"And now she's entitled to a closed-casket funeral because two wrongs don't make a right. Isn't that right, Brandi?"

Jackie stepped to the Ms. High and Mighty Wall Street-Thinking Brandi. "I'm not saying that I've found the way, Brandi. I'm sure that there are a few that find it. I'm just saying that you haven't."

Jackie had hit her mark.

For the very first time since Brandi entered the house she showed a slight trace of anger.

She took a step directly into Jackie's face. "Now you wait a minute!"

"Hell nah, Brandi. You wait a minute! Have you done the body count yet? Or have you been too busy running around giving orders and being important?"

Brandi stopped in her tracks. She stared at Jackie without speaking.

"Do you dare to think that because you're not pulling the trigger that you're not committing the murder?"

Jackie was on a roll.

Sarcastically, and reverting to the language of the street that she knew so well but had refused to use most of her life, Jackie said, "Well, they be adding up, Brandi. And don't look now but you're the scorekeeper. Now get the hell out of my house!"

Jackie had taken Brandi down in a single stroke with the one weapon you couldn't buy or pay for, and that was the truth.

Brandi headed to the door without saying another word.

Before she could step through it Jackie decided—out of the love they used to share in the past, ever since Brandi was a little girl coming to her house—to share some wisdom with her before she left.

Jackie was aware that she had taken Brandi down a few notches with her remark. She'd known her long enough, since back in the day when she was just a crumb snatcher, to realize this.

And she knew Brandi was right about the love she and Tangie shared. But that didn't change the circumstances of Tangie's horrific death, partly caused by all their thoughtlessness.

Brandi put her hand on the doorknob. She hesitated as Jackie's voice rang out. "If you want to make a change, Brandi, try preserving life. Because where there is life there is also hope."

Brandi turned to give Jackie a long, searching look. Then she stepped out the door, closing it softly behind her.

Jackie turned away. Tears cascaded down her cheeks.

Brandi was as lost as Tangie. Jackie realized with a pang they had both been lost on that night.

The tragedy of that loss pierced Jackie's heart.

Brandi stepped to the street with Tata orchestrating. She slid into the specially ordered bulletproof car. The Mexican guys at the chop shop had done a good job. Nothing short of a bomb would take a person out of that car.

Brandi closed the door to the car softly. Jackie's words rang in her ears.

But regardless of the penalties or circumstances she knew without a doubt that she was the new head nigga in charge.

Chapter 46

Under the rising tragic and very lethal circumstances, Tata had to do some mighty tall and fancy footwork to make sure that proper information was sent to where her mother was being kept.

She had to reach the right people with the right information or it could be fatal to both her and her mother. She knew they wouldn't hesitate to use the situation to their advantage.

She wouldn't go down in a hail of gang gunfire, though they would certainly allow it to look as if she had. Instead she would go down under untraceable circumstances, and the Street Laws would receive all the credit as well as the blame for it.

People like the Street Laws were out of their league with these people. They weren't even on the same playing field, and Tata well knew it.

She could not under any circumstances risk a visit to her mother. It might cause a security breech, given the murderous circumstances that were dancing around her in her life.

And those people who called the real shots most certainly would not appreciate it.

In light of this she had had to come clean with some very dangerous people in order to secure her mom's safety, and to assure them that no matter how this went down, and what the outcome was, there wasn't a shred of anything anywhere that would lead to them or her mother.

She lucked out.

They checked, rechecked, and evaluated the situation as well as brought it to the proper parties, and decided, considering her past history as well as her mother's history, that they could afford to sit out the situation and wait to see what happened—as long as Tata understood that her physical visits had been terminated for now and were on hold pending the outcome of the situation.

After all, these were just street hoodlums killing each other. There was no way they traveled in the elite circles they were in.

Because she put up half of every dollar she had ever earned in the Conquerors, and that was plenty, this earned her the privilege of communication via notes with her mother that would be passed through a series of decoys, which was to be expected, given the extraordinary circumstances.

Tata knew her mother's handwriting down to the last stroke. So she knew when she received a correspondence from her mother telling her to be stand-up, and to do what she had to do, though she missed her terribly, that it was actually her mother's handwriting and that she was well.

Besides that, Tata knew that not one person on earth could have duplicated the tone of her mother's voice in that letter.

Her mother's voice, as well as her personality, had always been unique. They remained her strongest assets.

Tata burned the letter after her many readings of it.

Out of the half that was left of her earnings she put up half of that for the personal upkeep of her mother.

It was enough money to take care of her comfortably for the rest of her life in the event that something happened to Tata.

Tata's secret prayer had always been that one day they would release her mother, even to live in another country under an assumed identity. And because Tata knew there was every possibility she could be killed just as Tangie had been, Tata had suggested this possibility to them.

She had also provided enough money in case by some stroke of luck they someday considered it. They hadn't terminated Tata or her mother, so who knew what the possibilities were?

There was a time that they would have executed both of them for a lot less than what was going on with the gangs.

Tata's mom had been gunned down on the street in an incident similar to the one in which Tangie had died. Tangie's murder dredged up painful old memories in Tata's life.

Only her mother hadn't been playing with street gangs, or anything in that realm. She was in a league very far removed from street gangs.

She had been part of an underground operation. It was an operation that could not under any circumstances be spoken about.

Her "murder" had been a public display to convince some very scary people that she had died, and that their positions wouldn't be compromised.

Tata's mother's decision to be stand-up had changed both her own and her daughter's life forever.

Tata knew she was traveling down a similar road. Perhaps it was just in the blood.

Whatever it was, a person had to do what they had to do. That was just the way it was if you were born both black and poor in the hood.

Chapter 47

After pulling the necessary strings Fishbone finally stood alone in a sterile room with fluorescent lights bearing down on him before the remains of his sister Tangie.

Maestro stood directly outside the door, respecting his privacy but near enough to lend his silent support.

As he stood in front of the body Fish took off his cap as a means of respect for his sister.

He had been in gang life for as long as he could remember. During that time he had seen many things. Those things that were spoken of as well as a great many things that were not spoken of.

He'd dealt with each of them in his own private manner. However, with the shooting death of his baby sister, death had taken on a different meaning for him from the moment he'd been informed of her demise and the horrific exit she had received leaving this world.

Though he had been continually advised not to view her body in its current condition, he had insisted as her next of kin that he be allowed to do so.

There was nothing phony about him. There never had been. He'd always dealt with any blow that came his way. He would deal with his sister's body as it was, not after it was dressed up to suit the family and the public's perception of how it should look.

He bowed his head with his cap in hand. Finally he raised his head after a few seconds. He reached over and put a hand to the cover that was shielding the sight of Tangie from him. He yanked back the cover without further hesitation.

He couldn't believe what they had done to his baby girl. She had been nothing less than destroyed. The vibrant beauty she had possessed in life was nowhere apparent.

And unfortunately, his last living sister as well as his last living family member had been a witness to the hate-filled situation.

Fish wasn't sure just how he would face Jackie, but he knew without a doubt that she deserved to be next on his list once his last visit with Tangie was done.

After all, he and Jackie were the only family each other had left.

The word *destruction* roamed around Fishbone's mind in a way that it never had before. It was funny how the full consequences of gang life had never bothered him before that night.

He reached down to pick up his sister's cold, waxy hand while glancing away from the area where the whole of her face should have been, where it had been partially blown away.

As he held her hand his mind screamed in total rejection of her fatality. He kissed her hand, wanting to bring some warmth back to her body as well as her life.

He used his free hand to lift the cover completely for a full view of her body. Truthfully speaking he would have been better off if he had just chosen to forego a glimpse of her bullet-riddled body.

However, that was not who he was.

She was so torn from the impact of the bullets that it was difficult to tell what you were really seeing because pieces of her flesh were completely missing.

The forensics people had mercifully bagged some of those

pieces, the ones they could find, anyway, to be buried with the girl.

Later, long after the ceremonies were over, they would find pieces of her flesh embedded in the porch, in the dirt, and in the surrounding area where she had been shot.

Some pieces of her had been lodged and hidden in parts of the dirt and concrete, unrecognizable as body parts.

Fishbone found himself trembling without even being aware that he was. He covered her back up. He didn't move from her side.

A part of his mind screamed for revenge.

A thirst for it rose up like bile from the pit of his stomach. Tangie was his family. She was his blood. In the past he had protected people that were less than that to him as well as taken up their battles.

But for some reason Tangie's death was affecting him differently. It was affecting him in a way he would have never thought was possible. Her death was like an omen. It was like a personal sign for him.

If he didn't make a move that was extraordinary the killing would never end. It would just go on, and on, and on from generation to generation.

The realization of that thought slammed into his chest like the force of an impact from a speeding train.

He owed it to his sister. He owed her a change.

He had been her role model. He had gotten her in. It was up to him to get her out even if now it could be only in spirit.

Fish bowed his head and did something he hadn't done since he was ten years old.

He cried.

Chapter 48

Fishbone entered the house to find Jackie in the same recliner she had sat down in after Brandi had left the house.

The instant she saw him she rose, tears glittering in her
eyes. He approached her and took her into his arms. She col-
lapsed in his arms, sobbing in deep, heart-wrenching tears.

She'd done her best to hold up the best she could. But once
she saw her brother it broke the last of her willpower and resolve for a strong front.

Fishbone, she knew, was a lot of things that he shouldn't
be. But the one thing he was and had always been was a
tower of strength for other people.

That fact still remained about him even under the most
hideous of circumstances.

Outside their house, as well as for blocks and blocks away
in the surrounding area, the streets were covered with even
more layers of security than what had been present when
Brandi had arrived.

The Conquerors were the inside as well as the first layer of
security, due to respect for Tangie's position in the posse.

As he held a weeping Jackie in his arms, Fishbone stared
over her head at a picture of his smiling baby sister that was
sitting on the mantelpiece.

There were no words. What could he say?

He led Jackie to the couch to sit down. He held her, just letting her cry it out. He knew she needed that.

Maestro, of course, was directly outside the door, along with Tata.

Jackie was well aware of her brother's status in the gang as well as in the community, and not to be left out was his apparent affiliation with certain civic-type matters.

So she knew without a doubt that he had been apprised of every last detail concerning their sister's death, and that she didn't need to relay the events that had led up to her being killed.

She suspected Fish knew even better than she did, even though she was there, how she had been blocked in while the Street Laws slaughtered her sister in front of her very eyes.

They hadn't touched her because there was an unwritten law in street code: You didn't touch people's families who had nothing to do with the life. They were off limits.

They never would have touched Brandi's family, either, as wild and reckless as they were, because they knew better than to incur the wrath of all the gangs for violating a sacred street code that everyone abided by.

Ari hadn't been related to Brandi, so they had skirted the edges of the law with her.

Tangie had not been exempt because she was a member of the Conquerors. If you were in the life, then you were fair game.

Even someone of Fish's stature had to accept this, although Tangie was his sister. He had been a part of the writing of that law.

The stupidest of thoughts entered Jackie's mind. She thought about the steak that was sitting out in the kitchen for her and Tangie's dinner.

She had been going to grill a steak and toss a salad for them while she once again tried to talk Tangie out of her affiliation with the Conquerors and her fascination with fast money.

Ironically Jackie had planned to tell her that those things could be the death of her. Now she wouldn't have to since they already had been.

She had no way of knowing that Tangie wouldn't have been there anyway because Tata had been on her way to pick her up.

She laid her head against her brother's shoulder, soaking up the warm comfort of him, something she knew she would never again be able to do with her sister.

Her tears soaked his shirt and she said not a word because they both knew there was really nothing to say.

Chapter 49

Brandi stepped out of the shadows of the alleyway at the same instant that Fishbone did. He touched her gently on the shoulder under the star-filled night.

There was a single star that was shining so brightly in the sky that it illuminated the area of darkness in which they were standing.

At one time in her life, Brandi would have stopped to acknowledge and reflect for a moment on the star's unusual brightness. But that part of her life didn't exist anymore.

When she was a child she used to look up at the stars all the time with her daddy while sitting on their front porch. Sometimes they would sit there for hours on end after dinner, talking and dreaming with each other.

He used to make up stories, creating magical worlds for her and including the stars as some wonderful characters. He was pretty good at it. He had actually been a great oral storyteller. She had believed some of those stories.

And it was during those times that she had dared to hope as well as dared to dream, sitting under the stars with her daddy, locked in a magical, star-filled universe of one, together.

That was until reality had set in once she'd gotten older. Old enough to realize that all her daddy had been telling her was just that: made-up stories, pure fantasies that he spun for her private enjoyment.

A shining star and its magic had no place in the real life of someone like her. There were no shining stars or magic in the hood.

She shook her head to clear it of the memory. This was neither the time nor the place for the recollection of fantasies. One of her best friends had just been gunned down by gang fire. The other one had been completely paralyzed by the LAPD, able only to sip from a straw.

Life was what it was.

Her rage built with a bitterness that she could actually taste in her mouth. She'd been a little girl when her daddy had been weaving those stories but she wasn't a little girl now.

She had believed in the magic of life then but she no longer believed in it now.

And as her understanding of life and some of its circumstances grew, she was beginning to realize the fact that her daddy had wanted her to feel like dreams could come true. That was why he had made up those stories for her. But in reality dreams didn't come true.

The only thing that came true in the lives of the people she knew were death, tragedy, and broken dreams for those who dared to step foot on the magical carpet of hope.

She definitely wouldn't be that damn stupid or gullible anymore. Your dreams were what you made them. She had money because she had taken the initiative to take it by whatever means was necessary, plain and simple.

Deep inside she recognized the fact that she was feeling sorry for herself. She was also feeling sorry to a degree for all the others she knew.

That still didn't change the truth of the matter that she was right even if she was feeling sorry for herself.

If they didn't feel sorry for themselves who the hell would?

Their parents' generation? Not.

They couldn't help themselves. If they could have, then her generation wouldn't be struggling to make ends meet.

Perhaps it would be the generation after them. Brandi shook her head in disgust, thinking of Ari. At the rate things were going they wouldn't be around to bring in another generation.

Fishbone tilted her chin toward him in the brightness of the star, bringing her back to the present, reminding her she was still standing in the alleyway.

For the first time in her life she realized how very handsome he was and what a special draw he seemed to possess.

He'd always been like a brother to her, so she'd never noticed this aspect of him before.

She was a little bit amazed with herself for noticing at this particular time. One of life's little idiosyncrasies, she guessed. She kept noticing things after the fact, it seemed.

Fishbone put both of his hands on her face in a gentle gesture. He positioned himself so he could stare directly into her eyes, giving her the impression that they were the only two people in the universe.

The alleyway had become eerily quiet.

As contrary to the truth as the impression was—that they were the only two people in the universe—he managed to pull it off quite nicely, just like her daddy used to do when he created those other worlds for her.

In reality they were completely surrounded by layers and layers of armed, well-trained security.

Security that was blending into the shadows just as they had been taught to do. You couldn't even hear the sound of your own breath at that moment.

Fishbone brushed a speck of imaginary dust from Brandi's cheek as he looked into her eyes, and saw reflected back at him the eyes of his dead sister Tangie instead of Brandi's eyes.

Tangie's eyes were urgent as well as supportive. They shimmered with tears. They also nudged him with a power that only those eyes possessed, toward a goal he had struggled to reach.

He had no choice.

He knew it was the thing to do. He couldn't turn back now even if he had wanted to. He had already put it out there. He had started the wheels turning. There was no going back. He hesitated for a moment as he was overcome with a feeling of indecisiveness.

However, in the instant that he hesitated he found that now Brandi was no longer standing there at all, and in her stead was his sister Tangie in her full body form, just as she had been before she had died, black and beautiful.

"Fish, it's not worth it. Trust me." The words floated through his consciousness as though on a current of water.

Fishbone stared at the mirage of his dead sister.

He blinked and closed his eyes. Reopening his eyes he expected to see Brandi. But he didn't. Tangie was still standing there.

She reached up to put her arms around his neck, hugging him.

"It's time to do what's right," she whispered in his ear. There was that current of water again containing her words, filling his conscious mind.

With those last words Tangie faded away.

However, there was no mistaking the fact for Fishbone that it was her voice come back from the grave to warn him.

My God he had seen his dead sister.

Not as she was in death but rather as she had been in life. Fishbone had never seen a ghost before in his life, but he knew on that night he had witnessed a young girl come back from the grave to issue him a warning to try to save himself as well as others.

He thought about her friend Tamika. Tamika was in awful shape over Tangie's death. They had been very close. She was blaming herself for not trying harder to warn Tangie, to make her see what she had seen.

It had been a pitiful sight seeing Tamika and her babies huddled together among the unopened shopping bags that his sister had brought them, crying because she was never coming back. They were huddled among the bags because that was all they had left of Tangie.

Looking deep into Brandi's eyes Fishbone saw something that took him completely for a second loop of surprise. It was him. He saw himself. He saw the little boy he had once been. The scared little boy who had joined a gang just so he could survive the streets.

Fishbone hadn't seen himself in this form in so long; he had just about forgotten that that boy existed inside of him. It had been years since he had stared at that boy in the mirror.

As he squinted into Brandi's eyes in disbelief at all that he had seen, he saw Tangie before her final departure standing next to him as he was then, as a little boy.

She kissed the child on the top of his head, and then hugged him as though she never wanted to lose him.

Fishbone was bugging.

In reality he was older than Tangie. So how could that be? But it was and he knew it.

The realization dawned on him that he was receiving a golden opportunity to reach out to that boy now in a way he'd never been able to do before.

Only through great mercy and grace could that have been at all possible.

"Do it for him, Fish," Tangie said, releasing the little boy, and then she was finally gone.

The scared little boy who had been left all alone looked out at Fishbone. Then the boy reached out a small hand toward him.

Brandi couldn't believe her eyes as she saw a teardrop slip down Fishbone's face. Fishbone was hands down the most feared gang leader in the city, and was most likely among the top ten feared ones in the country. And he was standing in the alleyway crying.

If Brandi hadn't witnessed it with her own eyes she would never have believed it.

Softly he said, "Brandi, I've decided to give up gang life. I think you should, too."

They were such simple words but they hit the air with the impact of a double-barreled shotgun.

Brandi stared at him in astonishment, not believing her own ears.

She took a step back from Fishbone in a state of disbelief. "We're in the middle of a war, Fishbone, in case you haven't noticed. There isn't any getting out. And there ain't no turning back. Nobody knows that better than you."

Fishbone looked down the alleyway to see the little boy still looking at him, having stepped out of the depths of Brandi's eyes now, standing on his own.

His plea was loud and clear as he stretched out his arms once again toward Fishbone.

Fishbone looked up at the one, lone shining star sitting in the sky above, shining so innocently and brilliantly in a dark ghetto alleyway.

He heard his sister's voice blowing through the air racing toward his ear, *"Keep it right there. Yeah. Yeah. Yeah. Yeah."*

Fishbone gently touched Brandi's shining hair. "There's a time for all things, Brandi. The time for this is now."

The little boy in the alleyway smiled at Fishbone as he rose toward the star. Then he was gone.

Brandi eyed Fishbone coldly, seeing none of what he saw. She felt none of what he felt.

All she felt were a keen sense of rage and betrayal on a level she had never expected to see.

"You came here to tell me that?" she questioned.

"Yes."

"Then you shouldn't have," she said without a reflection of any feeling in her voice.

"Brandi, I make my own choices about what I should and shouldn't do."

Brandi rolled her eyes in the air.

"Some choice. Tangie was my best friend and your sister.

I've got to take them down, yo. And you know that. That's all there is to it. And they killed Ari, too. This is the only way, Fish."

Fishbone shook his head, no longer accepting the negative as he had so easily done all of his life. He was no longer buying it.

Under a shining star, the same star that Brandi felt offered no hope, he had found a spark of something special and a reason, even after all that had happened, to still hope.

They had both been standing on the same exact ground, and yet they were worlds apart as though they were not even a part of the same universe, never mind sharing some of the same space.

"Peace, Brandi. You've gotta bring it. Peace. There's too much blood being spilled."

Brandi faced off with him, her mind made up. It was too bad Fish had taken this position, but it didn't have a thing to do with what she had to do.

"All the blood that's going to be spilled is not on the ground yet, Fishbone. But it will be."

She turned away from him, her heart hardened, walking off alone down the alley.

And she was truly alone.

She had lost one of her best friends as well as her closest ally in the streets in one fell swoop.

When she reached Tata all she said was, "Tata, I want all of the Conquerors off the streets. Now. There is to be no further delay. Our attendance to personal matters is over. The streets are too hot."

Her decision had been made.

"We have to go to our hideout. I need to plan the executions of the Street Laws. Beginning with Left Eye."

Chapter 50

Brandi and Tata walked through the abandoned building. It was a hideout in the San Gabriel Valley that had been selected long ago in the event of just such a circumstance.

They, of course, arrived under the cover of deep nightfall. Neither of them had spoken a word after Brandi's initial order that they needed to get off the streets.

The few dim lights they had chosen to use cast eerie-looking shadows on the walls in the pitch-black darkness.

Everything they needed by way of survival gear—food, sleeping bags, dim flashlights, water, various means of communications—had all been provided to protect them from the dank elements of living inside an abandoned building, regardless of how brief a time it might be.

All the members of the Conquerors who were not critically injured were in attendance. There were layers of perimeter security as well as layers of interior security.

Some of the posse had been assigned to do nothing except guard the slots in the boards that had been nailed up against the windows and doors.

Brandi had sent some of her members ahead of the others to reenforce the security on the windows as well as the doors.

This had taken quite some doing because the building was huge. Their occupation of the building had also required quite a bit of cash, up to and leading to their finally arriving at the building, in order to keep the prying eyes of law enforcement officials away from the building and from a general patrolling of the area.

Everything it seemed was in place so all they had to do for the time being was to lay low. It had been reported all over the news that Brandi Hutchinson was the mastermind behind the female gang the Conquerors, and reporters were scrambling for any scrap of information they could get their hands on about her.

Tidbits of fascinating information about her had been filtering out to the press from her various enemies, and they had become intrigued with a nineteen-year-old phantom young girl who was known among the underground for ruling with an iron fist.

Her family as well as her best friend Q (who had been paralyzed in an earlier incident with the LAPD), along with his mother, had apparently vanished into thin air without a trace.

Try as they might neither the whereabouts of Brandi's family nor of Q's family could be unearthed.

Brandi's father was in a complete state of disbelief about where he was and about what his daughter had become, though he was fast admitting to himself there had been warning signs as she received blow after blow of tragic news.

Contrary to Brandi's belief he wasn't so much furious with her anymore as he was at himself. He was the parent, he should have seen it coming. He should not have assumed that she could take as much abuse as she had without there being some kind of fallout from it.

For her mother's part she just stayed on her knees in constant prayer that her daughter's life would be spared, that she would not be murdered.

It was the best she could hope for in the unfolding circumstances. As well she had plenty of time because she and Charles were lying low, keeping to the plan that had been laid out for them surrounded by the people Brandi had sent to protect them.

And there was no denying the fact, given the escalating news reports, that the protection might be necessary. It was a complete nightmare.

Since the Conquerers had nothing except time on their hands Tata sat down on the floor, pulling her knees up to her chin, reflecting on the note from her mother.

She was glad that she had set things up the way she had because there was no telling with the way things were going if they would get out alive or not.

The pendulum could swing either way, and Tata knew that.

Chapter 51

Brandi looked over at Tata, grateful for her loyalty and friendship. She was also happy that Tata was still alive, considering the circumstances.

Then Brandi did something that was quite out of the ordinary for her. She went over and gave Tata a warm hug. Tata looked at her strangely.

"I'm going to take a walk through the building. I need to be alone for a while."

Tata nodded her understanding. "It's been secured. Go ahead."

Brandi turned to look at the room full of her posse and encouraged them before she left. She hit a hand to her chest. "We are?"

"WE ARE THE GENERATION!" they replied in unison just as they always had.

"Yeah," was all Brandi said before she walked away.

The building they had chosen was huge and cavernous.

Brandi walked deeper and deeper into the building, not realizing, with her limited ability to see, that she had ventured somewhat off the path and stepped into a different realm of the building—until she heard a soft voice behind her, the sound of which not only startled her but also put her in a state of shock.

"Brandi," came the whisper of Ajani's voice. She thought she was hallucinating. Ajani was haunting her. There was no way she could be hearing his voice.

Brandi turned in confusion at the sound of his voice to find that she was not hallucinating in any way, shape, form, or fashion.

Chase Ajani was indeed standing directly in back of her.

He was so close that she could feel his breath right next to her ear. Brandi's heart pounded at his closeness.

But more than that it pounded at the possible implications of what his presence meant.

Had she been betrayed? Was he working with the other side? How the hell had he gotten in here? And more than that, how did he know she was here?

All those questions rushed at her at once. They crowded her mind in the fraction of the second that it took for her mind to process the information that he was really there.

She took a step back from Ajani. Her confusion and disbelief were apparent in the dimly lit room as they flashed across her features.

Ajani smiled at her as he might an errant child. "Don't be afraid, Brandi," he said, his voice melodic and laced with a mesmerizing, almost hypnotic quality.

Brandi drew her shoulders up to her full height of five feet eight inches. "I'm not," she stated indignantly. How dare he assume she was afraid of him? Who the hell did he think he was?

She was no fool. She was strapped. And she'd kill him dead on the spot if she had to. True, she would hate to see all that fineness end up as waste but it would be what it had to be.

Ajani shook his head at her childish whims. There were many greater than her, a mere child, who had feared him. He took a step in her direction.

Brandi's mind screamed for her to reach for her weapon

but she was rooted to the spot. That split second that she talked about that she had spent so many days and hours drilling into her girls popped into her own mind.

Yet through no power of her own she was helpless to unleash that weapon, although her mind was screaming for her to do exactly that.

The entire area had become darker, danker, and was filled with a presence that was very much alive and yet unseen other than that of Chase Ajani.

Ajani reached out a hand to touch the silk of Brandi's cheek. "I am not here to harm you, little one. I am here so that you can win."

For some reason his touch on her skin made her recoil instinctively. Everything inside her was screaming out a warning.

That fly smoothness of his that had originally had her mind in a state of ecstatic confusion was fast turning into revulsion, and she wasn't sure why.

She reached up to remove his hand from her cheek.

"How did you get in here?"

She had touched a spark in him.

"Brandi, you don't have time to waste on trivial things. How I got here is not important. The only thing that is important is that I am here for you."

"No," she said as she stared into the shimmering depths of his eyes.

Without warning she saw her mother hand her the Bible.

Then Brandi heard her mother's voice, almost in a whisper, repeating what she'd told her when she'd given it to her. *"The most important thing I have to give you is this,"* she had said.

"This will take you places that neither your father or I can. It will protect you when neither of us can, either. The words in red are living life. They are the words of Jesus, the living Christ. You'll just have to trust me on that for now, since you don't know for yourself."

An extremely queer feeling hit the pit of Brandi's stomach while at the same time a scream lodged itself in her throat, though it didn't release from her mouth.

Ajani wasn't happy.

He felt a shift around him that he found quite disturbing. He needed Brandi to come completely over to his side of her own free will.

He had wrapped her in the art of seduction, and now it was time for him to get paid. What the hell was this rejection he was feeling when he knew she was almost there?

Ajani's entire being turned black right in front of Brandi's eyes. This time a scream did release from her throat, but since she had stepped into a realm that was on the other side, no one, not even her posse, could hear the scream.

She heard a voice. *"Cross back over, Brandi."* It sounded like Tangie's voice.

Brandi shook herself but knew she didn't have time to debate it. The mesmerizing look of desire and want in Ajani's eyes had turned to a malevolent hatred, the likes of which Brandi, even in the imposing position of being a gang leader, had not ever seen before.

That was why he had been re-created so many times, to disguise who he really was.

The blackness of who he was reached out a bony finger, trying to capture her soul. With that Brandi ran for her life.

Suddenly she knew without a doubt that pulling her weapon would not kill this man. He was of a different element, of a different world, and she couldn't kill him by being strapped.

Words from her childhood rose up involuntarily out of her mouth. "My Lord Jesus Christ."

Ajani blanched in his spirit at her words. Intense hatred welled up in him. He hated the sound of that name. He hated the power that it evoked.

Brandi ran as though it was the last run of her life.

Ajani didn't chase her.

She had unknowingly evoked the very words that raised a wall between them. It was a wall that he had no way of scaling.

He let her go because he had to.

At that exact moment Brandi's foot touched the ground of the building she had been in originally, placing her back in a realm that was removed from Ajani.

Chapter 52

Brandi shivered from her experience of coming face-to-face with one of the many faces worn by the Spirit of Darkness. The evil had walked right into her life as though she'd had an open door.

Evil needed an invitation to hang out in people's lives. That invitation was issued in a variety of ways, and a person could easily be caught unawares.

That was a trick of the Devil; to blindside people, playing them until they were caught up in a spiritual web of deceit. He preyed on people's weaknesses. It was a lifeline to him. That was how he had been able to walk through the door of Brandi's life.

Brandi walked with her flashlight, shining the dim light. She tried to draw comfort from the little light that she saw. She didn't want to run back to her posse like some scared rabbit. She definitely needed to collect herself before facing them.

She listened to the strange sounds generating from the building. She was keenly aware of every little nuance. She had no desire to come back into contact with the likes of Ajani.

He truly made her think about how people projected images and how they could be so far removed from what they appeared to be. She realized in this assessment that projected images were dangerous.

She was only a hop, skip, and a jump from having to evaluate her own image as well as all that she had projected.

Up ahead of her she saw flickers of light as though the flickers were rising from a flame of fire.

Puzzled she walked a little faster, looking for a safe spot where she could see up ahead. After her frightening experience she didn't want to veer off the path again.

She finally spotted a corner where she could stand to watch what was going on.

She saw an extremely old black man. He was dressed in ragged clothing. There was a small fire burning in an old, antique-looking fireplace in front of him. He was warming his hands.

Brandi was getting mad. Security was supposed to have checked this building thoroughly. But then again the building was so huge, she supposed there could be squatters who had ways of entering.

Still, this was sloppy work. The only people who were supposed to have been residing in the building were them. She couldn't really count Ajani because try as she might she could not explain his appearance as anything close to rational, considering the way he had appeared.

The flames leaped from the fireplace, casting their shadows upon the walls in various shapes and sizes. The fireplace was the only form of light in what was otherwise a pitch-black room.

The abandoned building had actually once been an extremely active mansion in its day. Brandi wondered if this room might have been considered some type of ballroom because you could see a huge hole in the ceiling from where perhaps a chandelier had once hung.

She studied the old man. He had skin that looked like soft leather. He had a mustache, sideburns, and a goatee.

He continued to rub his hands before the fire, warming them. He acted like he was on the East Coast, where they had real winters.

They were on the West Coast. They didn't have that kind of weather on the West Coast. Still he persisted in warming his hands.

His back was turned to Brandi. Yet his presence was so powerful that it not only filled the room he was sitting in but it filled the entire space including that in which Brandi was standing.

His eyes, though Brandi couldn't yet see them, were of a startling, deep-hued brown. They were also of a penetrating nature. His voice was deep, almost resonant, and lyrical in pitch.

Brandi peered at him strangely from her hiding place.

Without turning around the man said to her, "Come out and sit with me, child. There is no reason for you to hide there."

Brandi's mouth dropped open in surprise.

She stepped out of her hiding place. She didn't know why but she did. Then through no will of her own she took tentative, cautious steps to where the man was sitting.

When she finally reached him she wondered what she was doing standing there after the harrowing experience with Ajani she had just had. Yet she stood there gazing into the fire in a daze.

The old man slowly looked up at her. He moved as though he were a century old, yet as though he had all the time in the world.

"Sit with me, child," he repeated.

Slowly Brandi lowered her tall frame to the floor in front of him. That was when she became aware that he had the most piercing, startling-looking eyes she had ever seen.

Yet again something, elusive as it was, drew her to his very presence.

She didn't feel the same fear as she had with Ajani. She had an odd feeling, like a person had when they were exactly where they needed to be when they needed to be there.

Brandi struggled to find her voice. "What are you doing here?"

"I'm warming my hands before the fire."

"That's not what I meant."

The old man smiled. He looked deeply into her eyes as though he could see her soul and all that she was.

The feeling he evoked as well as the deep look of wisdom that beamed from his eyes startled Brandi.

"Perhaps I should be asking you that question."

Brandi bowed her head. A feeling of deep-rooted shame overcame her. The feeling was so powerful she couldn't speak for a minute. Finally she glanced over at the blazing fire.

Her voice when she did speak sounded shaky and barely recognizable even to her own ears as it choked up with unshed tears.

"I'm here because I can't face what is out there."

"And what is that?" the old man asked kindly.

"My life."

"Hmmm. A lot of people run away when they are faced with doing what is right."

Brandi placed her chin in her hands. The tears finally came rolling down her cheeks.

"How do you know what is right and what is wrong?"

The old man gave her a deep look. Then he pointed to his heart. "That is simple. You know it because you feel it in here. Often we just don't listen to it."

Brandi was silent for a long time. Finally she asked the million-dollar question. "And if I do listen?"

"Then your foot will have landed on that narrow path that few ever find," the old man said, his voice laced with the conviction and truth of his words.

Brandi spoke slowly. "I've got to go. You've helped me more than you know."

The old man smiled in her direction.

Brandi stood and walked back the way she had come. On her way she continuously saw pictures in her mind's eye of the old man. She couldn't get him or his words out of her mind.

The old man still sat warming his hands before the dying embers of the fire.

In its ashes he knew there was both life as well as death.

Chapter 53

By the time Brandi got back to the area where she had left her posse, daylight was just breaking and beginning to shine in the room.

Except for the security patrols the Conquerors were getting some much-needed rest and sleep. Brandi knew better than to even admonish the security about either Ajani or the old man being in the building because she knew inside of her they wouldn't have seen them nor have had a clue as to what she was talking about.

Her security hadn't been breeched. Her life had.

Brandi went over to shake Tata awake. Tata sat up, rubbing the sleep from her eyes. "Where've you been?"

"It's not important. I need you to get in touch with Fishbone. Tell him to set up a Peace Conference. He'll know what I'm talking about. Tell him it has to be set up outside of L.A. on neutral territory. Then tell him the information about a coming cease-fire needs to be filtered into the law enforcement agencies and the media."

Tata was fully awake now. The sleepiness she was experiencing had flown right out of her body upon hearing Brandi's words.

"Why?" she asked, startled by Brandi's change of heart regarding the situation of a street war.

"Because I want to call peace. Tell Fishbone I said there

are to be no weapons of any type, and to put someone he can trust without a doubt on the job to do the searches and secure the location. We can't risk any kind of a security compromise here."

Tata got to her feet. "Peace?" She shook her head and then lowered her voice to keep those who were awake from hearing her challenging Brandi. They needed to always put on a show of solidarity, otherwise they could lose control.

Tata pulled Brandi out of the area into another room where there was only the two of them.

Stage-whispering she asked, "Are you crazy?"

She couldn't believe what she was hearing. She had heard the words leaving Brandi's mouth but surely she must be hallucinating.

This was not the Brandi Hutchinson who had come to her with a plan. Hell, this wasn't even the Brandi Hutchinson she was with last night as they arrived at the hideout.

Brandi saw the storm rise in Tata's eyes as she spoke. "There will be no peace until they're dead, Brandi. Do you hear? Dead. They killed Tangie and Ari."

Tata was so pissed off she was hyperventilating.

Brandi snatched Tata by the arm. "Let me see your wrist, Tata."

"Why?" she asked, resisting a bit in her anger.

More firmly Brandi said, "Let me see it, Tata."

Tata thrust her wrist out in front of Brandi in pure anger. You could see the cut mark across her wrist. Brandi stared at it before touching a finger to it.

"This scar says that you and I are one and the same. I don't want to see your blood spilled. In addition to that your mother needs you. You're all she has. And this is the only time you're ever going to hear those words from me," Brandi said in a whisper, thus assuring Tata of her silence.

Her manner of speaking revealed to Tata that Brandi had been aware of the high security risk of the matter that she had just spoken about.

Tata entered a state of extreme shock. How could Brandi have known?

One look into Brandi's eyes told her that neither her nor her mother's position would ever be compromised by Brandi.

Her mother had been an underground, ghostlike serial killer infiltrating people's lives at the highest level in a covert, underground operation, one that operated outside the perimeters of any laws that were on the books as people knew them. She had been a distributor of vigilante justice.

Somewhere along the line there had been a double cross. Now her very life depended on Tata's silence as well as on people continuing to believe that she was dead.

Tata searched Brandi's eyes.

Again she saw without a doubt that Brandi would never repeat those words or the knowledge regarding her mother again.

If Brandi had to she would die protecting that secret. Without a doubt Tata knew Brandi was get down.

She also knew in a flash that Brandi was doing what she felt she had to do to protect them all. Tata put her arms around Brandi.

Then she took a step back, hitting her chest. "I'm with you."

Chapter 54

Not long after the conversation that took place between Brandi and Tata, a meeting was set up to take place in the dead of night in an office building outside Los Angeles.

The door to the conference room was open. Inside was a long table surrounded by chairs. Fishbone and Maestro were at the door. Up and down the long corridor members of the L.A. Troops lined the hall.

Fishbone reiterated to Maestro, "Make sure you check them thoroughly, man. You're the last check. We don't want no bodies left up in here. I need to keep this clean. I had to call in some serious favors to get this spot and make this happen without any police surging in."

Maestro laughed. "I feel you, Fish. I'll let them in wearing only their underwear if that's what you want."

Maestro already knew that Fishbone had been making arrangements to leave the life, and that this was his last act as the leader of the L.A. Troops.

The news of his stepping down had hit the underground with shock waves. But Fish had not wavered. His mind was made up. It was what it was, as shocking as it had come to be for some people.

Fishbone laughed at Maestro's words. "Nah, man. You ain't got to strip them down to their undies. Just check them thoroughly like I said. I don't want any of these women going whack on us. Some of them are death struck as hell. And we can't afford any mistakes."

Fishbone looked down the hall to see all the players arriving.

"They're in the house, man. I selected the drivers to pick them up and to ensure there would be no leaks on the where-abouts of the location. All right, Maestro, let's do this."

After passing through the various stages of rigorous security checks that Fishbone had initiated himself, to leave no doubt in regard to the safety of everyone, they all took seats in the conference room.

There were six people in all who had the power to agree to a cease-fire as well as the power to really make it happen. Each and every single one of them was seated at the conference room table including Left Eye.

That hadn't been easy but she hadn't been given much of a choice, either. She either complied or the other gangs would initiate an order to terminate her. She'd opted to comply, thereby also taking a walk on the other charges of what she'd done.

The noticeable absence in the room was that of Brandi Hutchinson. She and Fish had met for a private conference prior to this event. He was both proud of her as well as happy with her position of being stand-up and of stemming the possibility for more loss of life.

The conference room was so quiet you could have dropped a pin and heard it fall. The tension was so thick in the room you could cut it with a knife.

The dishonor that had occurred between the Conquerors and the Street Laws had rolled into all the gang factions that were left, affecting them all as well as potentially involving them in an all-out war.

It had gotten quite nasty.

In light of everything the opposition in the room was not accustomed to being housed under one roof unless they were stealing income, injuring, or killing each other.

In what felt like an eternity but really was a matter of only a few minutes, intended to allow all the players time to adjust to the atmosphere, a door opened. Brandi walked in with her second in command, Tata Davis, right behind her.

Tata alone and on her own struck fear in the hearts of those around the table because they knew she was a killing machine. She was just like her mother had been. Like mother, like daughter. The fruit didn't fall far from the tree, and they knew it.

Tata Davis's mother was still a living legend on the street. She had taken down people whose names were barely whispered when she was alive. The only reason some of those people were still alive now was because Tata's mother was supposedly dead.

Brandi struck terror simply because she had the power to say yes or no to a person living or dying.

It had at first crossed their minds that they had been set up. But then they remembered Fish's word was golden, trusted, and bond on the streets, so if he said this was a Peace Conference, then a peace conference it was.

Brandi was draped in black from head to toe. But she wasn't outfitted in her gang gear. Instead she had on black fashion boots, a black silk shirt, black jeans, with a wide gold belt fitted round her waist, topped off with a black brim, and black and gold sunglasses. She was walking with a cane with a brass-handled hook on it.

Her demeanor took them all by surprise. A hushed silence deeper than the one that was already in the room fell over all of its occupants at Brandi's sudden appearance.

Fishbone was stunned by her bearing. He was unable to take his eyes off her. It was very obvious that she was in total command.

Fishbone, who by then was seated at the table, rose. Following Fishbone's lead, one by one all of the leaders in the room rose in order of rank.

When they were all standing Brandi walked to the head of the table. She took a deep breath. Tata stayed a respectable distance behind her.

Brandi nodded her head in thanks for the respect. She then indicated they should take their seats. They all sat down in unison.

Then Brandi took her seat. Before she spoke she looked out at each and every one of them individually.

Tata remained standing.

Brandi took off her sunglasses. "I asked you all here at great risk. The reason I did is because only the people in this room can truly put a stop to the violence that's going on in our neighborhood."

Toy, a serious-looking black female, spoke out. She evaluated Brandi coldly. "It's too bad you didn't think of this little meeting before Eric got shot down, and before some of my girls were beat and shot down. Nor did you think of it before SWAT and the LAPD Blue Boys came to set up camp on our streets. And you're the one who kicked this off, Brandi, trying to control all of the operations."

There was a collective nodding of heads from the other females in the room in a chorus of agreement with Toy's position.

Brandi acknowledged the truth of Toy's words respectfully. There was no denying the truth of what she'd said.

She raised her hand for the floor.

"You're right, Toy. It is too bad that I didn't think of this earlier. It's also too bad so much blood had to be spilled in order for us to sit in a room and talk like we've got some sense."

Brandi took a deep breath before continuing.

"If you think we need more injuries and bodies on the streets of our neighborhoods before a truce can ever happen, or if you think there needs to be more babies and children stabbed and shot down in our streets while we're pulling the knives and the triggers, then you can leave this room now, and you're free to forget about our agreement. All bets can be off."

Brandi stared at them all individually once again. They all

looked around at each other, evaluating the weight of her words, but no one made a move to leave.

Another of the girls piped up. "I guess that's why we're the leaders because we know what moves to make, and when to make them."

Left Eye smiled, satisfied that she would now be recognized for what she was. She had decided that remaining silent would be her best course of action under the circumstances.

Brandi allowed herself a small smile in the girl's direction. She didn't miss Left Eye's smile, but she knew the healing would have to begin somewhere. For her it would begin with Left Eye.

"Yeah. That's exactly right," Brandi finally said, agreeing with the girl.

There was a general murmuring in the room amongst the ladies. When they were again silent Brandi spoke. "The blood we spilled is our own. One day it will be our kids blood if we live that long. If not we could be the end of the generation."

Maestro looked at Brandi. "What is your fascination with the generation? It's all over the streets this generation stuff and you. What's up with that?"

Brandi took off her brim. Then she laid her cane up against the table. She tilted her head slightly before she grinned at them.

"Before I answer that question I'd like to have a vote to stop the violence."

Brandi looked at them, shrewdly aware of the position she had placed them in. They all looked back.

"A show of hands. Please," she requested respectfully, sticking hers up in the air first. Fishbone and Maestro followed suit.

Tata's hand shot up behind her.

Some of them were slower than others but eventually there was a unanimous show of hands in the room.

Fish flashed Brandi a deep look of love and pride. Brandi

returned the look. She knew Fish's position hadn't been an easy one, from the night he had made her the first one to know he was giving up gang life.

Brandi said softly, "Thanks for a unanimous vote."

She stood up and reached for her sunglasses, putting them back on. Next she placed her brim on her head and reached for her cane.

"Our generation is the one who isn't going to lay down or roll over. We're the fighters. And today we have just found the most powerful weapon of all to fight with. The one I guess I've been searching for all along."

"And what's that?" Maestro asked, the softness of his tone matching hers.

Brandi pointed to her heart. "The ability to listen to what's in here. When we win that war we can all truly be the new Conquerors."

Brandi took a step back from the table as the entire room rose, giving her a standing ovation.

Even Left Eye realized that she had underestimated Brandi's true leadership. She grudgingly admitted to herself that she could see why Brandi had become a leader.

This time there was no hesitation in the room regarding her standing ovation.

Brandi had struck a chord deep inside each one of them. They all wanted to be leaders and wanted to make changes. In many cases that was why they had become affiliated in gang life, but they had been misdirected, and they hadn't known how to make effective change in a positive manner.

Brandi looked at each of them, hitting her chest. "Peace be unto you all."

She searched Fishbone's eyes, which hadn't left hers, and then just as suddenly as she had arrived, she was gone, with Tata right behind her.

The door shut behind her, leaving a silent room full of reflective faces.

Chapter 55

Later that night deep inside of the abandoned mansion Brandi sat in front of the fire talking with the old man once again.

She had purposely gone back to the building alone to seek him out. Instinctively she had known he would be there just as he was, waiting for her.

Before speaking Brandi wrung her hands together in front of the fire as he had been doing. Now she understood why he had been doing that, though it wasn't that cold.

It was a motion that enabled reflection. It indicated a deep thinking pattern.

"There are a lot of things I did that I wish I hadn't. I wish I could give that Brandi back," the new Brandi said without looking at him.

Shame raced through her body.

Brandi let out a long sigh. She looked over at the old man. "What can I do with that Brandi?" Her bottom lip trembled with the weight of those words.

The old man looked at her through the reflection of the leaping flames of fire.

In that instant she saw flames of fire leap deep from the depths of his eyes, not from the fireplace.

Brandi shivered internally.

That shiver made its way slowly from her insides to the

outside of her flesh until her flesh was covered in goose bumps.

"Perhaps you can be reborn," the old man said.

Brandi looked at him in astonishment. "I'm already born. How could I be born again?"

He watched her steadily.

"Child, there are many different types of births. Something inside of you dies, and from the ashes of that death something more powerful is born."

Brandi was silent.

She swayed back and forth.

"Perhaps you were lost but now you are found," he continued. "Come, child. Come with me. I have something I want to show you."

The old man rose from his sitting position on the floor. He was awfully agile for a man of his age. He walked deeper into the old, abandoned mansion.

Brandi followed him with her flashlight. Finally the old man came to a stop. He turned to Brandi as he reached into his jacket.

"Turn off the flashlight."

Brandi clicked it off. They were immediately plunged into total darkness.

The old man put forth a mirror. The room was suddenly lit with an iridescent light. Streaks in the colors as of a rainbow surrounded them.

There was a jagged crack down the middle of the mirror. The old man and Brandi stood close; their heads were almost touching.

He pointed to the mirror.

"Look, my child. Look there." His voice was lulling, hypnotic.

Brandi leaned forward. The mirror took on a life of its own. On one side of the mirror there was pitch-black darkness. In that darkness Brandi saw the face of Chase Ajani reflected.

On the other side of the cracked mirror there was a brilliant, twinkling light from that of the North Star.

Brandi peered into the mirror, both fascinated and frightened by what she was seeing.

"You see, child. You were born with a choice. You made one when you eluded Ajani. He couldn't force you over to his side. It had to be your choice."

How did the old man know about that?

Brandi now remembered she had called out the name of the Lord after remembering her mother's words when she'd given her the Bible. That was what had helped her escape Ajani's grasp.

The pieces were slowly falling into place.

The old man waited, knowing she was sifting through the events in her mind. He gave her time. Then he said, "As I was saying, you were born with a choice. You must now make a life-affecting decision. The choice is yours. It is time."

The old man turned his back on her.

He walked away, deep into the building, surrounded by that iridescent light. Brandi turned to look at the light in time to see him fade away.

All that was left in his place was a lone shining and brilliant star. The same one that had shown in the alleyway the night she and Fish had had their talk. The North Star.

It was the same night, she now realized, that something had happened to Fishbone. Something had taken place that had changed him. That same something had rendered him different.

As she stared at the star contemplating the disappearance of the old man, her heart leaped into her throat.

As the realization of who he might be dawned on her, a look of utter, absolute amazement crossed her face. She took a tentative step in the same direction. She wanted to go with him. His very presence was so regal, so magnetic, but above all else it was so pure, so inspiring. It compelled you to want to do what was right.

She shook herself. It couldn't be.

She cried out from the depths of her soul. "Please! Please! Don't go! You haven't yet told me who you are. What is your name? How can you come and go like that?"

Brandi saw a flash of white, silver streaks of light, and then a vaporlike mist appeared before her.

Out of the mist the old man's voice spoke. *"His name is written. And you, my child, are welcome in his kingdom. It is your choice. The rebirth is inside of you. Seek and you shall find."*

And then the mist vanished before her very eyes.

Chapter 56

After her meeting with the old man Brandi went on a mission, rummaging through the trunk of her car as though her life depended on it.

In many ways it did.

Her trunk was filled with stuff she had thrown in it over time. She didn't care, she patiently went through everything because she had to find that Bible.

She remembered the salesman running her down to give it to her when she had bought her Lexus. She knew she had thrown the Bible in the trunk.

She had never wanted to see it again, so she knew she couldn't possibly have moved it. What could she have been thinking?

She would have remembered if she had moved it because that Bible was like her personal haunting. No matter what she had done to try to get rid of it, it was always still there.

She now had a sneaking suspicion that that was why her mother had given it to her in the first place. She had given it to her so the importance of it would never be far away from her, even when she didn't know it.

Finally she spotted it. She breathed a sigh of great relief. You would have thought she had found a cache of buried gold. In reality she had found something of much greater value and importance.

She took it out and looked at it.

She wondered how such a simple-looking book could carry so much power.

It had gotten dirty from living in the trunk of her old car, and then her new car. She wiped off some of the dirt and dust with her hand carefully, lovingly.

She slammed the trunk closed. She walked around to get in the car.

She sat in that car all night long reading the Bible until the break of dawn. Her eyes were glued to the passages written in red.

It was as though they had come to life and invited her in for a private look. She had never been so captured by anything she had read in her entire life.

She felt like she was swallowing living water. She stared for a long time at the rising sun.

Later that day found her standing in front of the remaining members of the Conquerors.

"Today we're going to do this differently, ladies," she said. "Please sit down."

They did as they watched her silently.

"You are all aware that I called a Peace Conference with the leaders of the other gang factions who could make it possible for peace to happen. We've reached an understanding. We've reached a bound agreement as well as a pact for peace."

Brandi paced. She glanced briefly at Tata and then at the empty spot where Tangie would have been had she still been alive.

Hesitantly she faced the truth painfully.

"I want you to know the truth of something about me. I had this hunger for control and power. It was like a thirst that I couldn't quench. Recently I was faced with a choice. That was when I realized that an empty victory was no victory at all."

She blinked back her tears as she stared out at the sea of faces that had trusted her faithfully, and had put their lives on the line for her and her plan.

Haltingly she said, "What I'm trying to tell you is that I love you all."

She paused once again, hesitating. "I love you but I'm getting out of the life. I hope that all of you will, too. I just can't do this anymore."

One of the Conquerors spoke out. "Why are you leaving the life, Brandi? In this life it is what it is."

There was a chorus of agreement from some of the other girls.

Brandi nodded. "Yeah. I know. That's why I've got to get out. I can no longer accept the fact that it is what it is. Because what it is is what it shouldn't be."

Her voice lowered to a whisper. "I've made my choice. Believe me it's the only one I've got. It's the only one I can make. For me there is no other choice."

The girl spoke again on behalf of the group. "Yeah, well, we're gonna respect that because you've been good to us, Brandi. But I know I speak for the sisterhood when I say we're gonna miss you, Brandi."

She would miss them, too. She would miss them so much more than they would ever know. Little did they know she didn't plan to let them go.

She had a new plan, one that this time she planned to present to the Lord Jesus Christ, and in her private closet she would list each and every one of their names individually to hold up before him, seeking his grace as well as his mercy.

She had learned that he was like that if people would just give him a chance.

Let him who is without sin cast the first stone.

Brandi hit a hand to her chest.

They all followed suit. Some of them remained nonchalant. Others were sad. And still others contemplated the truth of her words and decision, weighing them in their own lives.

Brandi gave them the signal to rise.

They did.

When they were on their feet she walked to the front row. She hugged each girl in turn.

It was to be her last good-bye.

Chapter 57

Jackie was sitting in the recliner looking at television. She looked over and smiled at Fishbone. It had been a good many years since they had spent any real family time together.

Lately that had changed.

Fishbone had been visiting more often. They'd been having dinner together, grilling steaks in the yard, as well as playing cards and stuff like that.

Jackie was happy to have her brother back in her life. She smiled at him. Her heart was bursting with the news of his leaving gang life.

Their quiet reunion was interrupted by a special newscast from a newsroom in L.A. "Today we learned there has been a pact that will be a first in the history of the gangs. It has been announced that a Peace Conference was called among the leaders of the gangs, and they have insisted on as well as called for a halt of the violence in this astonishing turn of events.

"There have been unconfirmed reports that Brandi Hutchinson, leader of the Conquerors, and Fishbone, whose real name is not known but who is the leader of the L.A. Troops, are the brainchilds behind the conference."

The newscaster, in an unusual gesture, shook his head, smiling unbelievingly at what he was reporting. "For the time being, peace seems to have been restored in the South Central neighborhood. In other news today . . ."

Jackie clicked off the television. She walked over to her brother. She gave him a big hug.

"Welcome home, Michael Parker," she whispered softly.

Fishbone smiled at his sister, and then he hugged her just as tightly.

Both Brandi's family and Q's family were back in their respective homes. Brandi had gone to pick up Q and take him for a walk. He was so glad she had found a way to set things right.

While he was gone and on the last night they had spoken, he had thought he might never see her again.

She had picked him up that morning and now they were hanging out in the Square where Ari's girls were jumping double Dutch, and the boys were out on the court playing basketball.

Brandi had jumped up off the bench.

"Q, watch this."

She jumped into the double Dutch game and started jumping and doing her thing, showing off for Q.

Q gurgled in excitement.

The Mister Softee truck chimed in the distance. Only now it would do what its designated job was, and that was to serve ice cream to the kids in the neighborhood.

In a strange turn of events Left Eye had been found dead in her sleep. At eighteen years old she had gone to sleep one night to never wake up again.

She had died of natural causes.

Chapter 58

Later that evening Brandi stood on the front porch of her parents' house, looking through the screen door. Charles saw her shadow and rose from his chair. He stood looking at her without making a move to unlock the porch door.

Brandi cleared her throat and as tears welled up in her eyes was the first to speak. She had gotten rid of her car and every other material possession she'd ever accumulated from her gang activities including all of the money.

The only thing she arrived home with was what she had left the house with, minus her car that she had sold. On her back was her backpack with a few of her original clothes stuffed inside of it.

If you wanted to be born again, then you needed the heart as well as the spirit of a newborn baby.

She looked at her daddy, tears shimmering in her eyes. "I was wondering if I could come home, Daddy?"

Charles unlocked the screen door without a word. He took his daughter in his arms.

Rita walked into the living room to see them hugging. She walked up to them, her eyes brimming with tears. They each reached out for her to include her in their embrace for a family hug.

Finally they broke off and took seats in the living room.

Brandi's daddy was the first to speak. "Brandi, you will always be welcome here. I'm sorry for what I said."

Brandi bowed her head in shame at her actions, and how they had led up to his actions. "I'm sorry, too, Daddy. Thank you for saying so."

She swallowed hard before continuing. "I have to tell you I don't know how much trouble I'm in but there could be some."

Charles nodded his head. "Whatever it is we'll deal with it. We're a family, you know."

Brandi smiled her gratitude. "I know that now."

She looked over at her mother, who was sitting anxiously staring at her.

"Thanks, Mom."

"For what?" Rita asked, surprised.

"For not giving up on me."

Rita couldn't help it. The tears spilled freely down her cheeks.

"I've been thinking that maybe when everything has been sorted out and once I've paid whatever debt I'm to owe, I could go to a community college or something. Of course, I don't have any money or anything, so you and daddy might have to help me. But I can get a job."

Charles and Rita both smiled in her direction. Glad to have their baby girl back in their fold.

"Do you mind if I go up to my room now?"

"Of course not, baby," Charles said.

Brandi stood up and headed for her room.

Later that night Charles and Rita talked in their bedroom late into the night about all that had happened.

Charles was the first to speak on it. "Something happened to Brandi. She's different."

Rita took his hand, covering it with hers. "I know. Whatever it is let's not question it. You know they say never look a gift horse in the mouth."

Rita glanced at the old trunk where the Bible had resided. She looked at the dresser where the picture of Brandi now hung in a new frame. The old shattered one in the pail with the cross on top of it was gone. Brandi smiled out at her from her golden frame that was all in one piece.

Charles pulled Rita close to him for a hug. "I love you. You know that?"

Rita snuggled closer. "Yeah, I know."

Brandi sat in a chair by her window listening to the sounds outside, staring out at the shining bright North Star that seemed to have parked itself directly over her bedroom.

The computer was silent. So was the stereo system.

After a few minutes she went over to her bed and got on her knees, her heart full.

"Now I lay me down to sleep. I pray the Lord my soul to keep. If I should die before I wake I pray the Lord my soul to take. Amen."

Brandi had discovered there was a real power. And it was definitely the one to bow down to.

Chapter 59

Shortly after Brandi moved home she was driving her daddy's car down the freeway. It was a beautiful day, and the wind was whipping through her hair. For the first time in a long time she felt a sense of inner freedom.

As well she acknowledged the fact that she would spend the rest of her life seeking forgiveness from the Lord Jesus Christ for her past actions.

But it was as it should be because it was what it was, and she knew that. She couldn't expect to walk away without a payment, but being stand-up as well as ready to face the consequences she was discovering offered their own kind of freedom.

At the same time that Brandi was having her reflective drive along the freeway so was Fishbone. He was experiencing as well as discovering that same sense of freedom that was overcoming Brandi.

He pulled off the freeway as he spotted a little flower stand. He pulled his car over to the side and walked up to the wooden makeshift counter.

There was an abundance of flowers in every array and color. Behind the counter stood the old black man that Brandi had met in the abandoned mansion when the Conquerors had taken shelter there while in hiding.

He smiled as Fishbone walked up to the counter.

"I wanna buy a lily, man. One white lily."

"That is an unusual choice for such a young man," the old man said with a hint of a smile in his voice.

He put the lily on the counter, wrapped it, and tied it with a red bow, handing it to Fishbone.

"The lily is the symbol of new birth," the old man said to Fish.

Fishbone took some money from his pocket. He handed it to the old man.

The old man shook his head, refusing the money. Fish looked at him strangely.

"It is a gift. Go in peace."

Fishbone smiled his silent thanks. He picked up the lily from the counter and headed toward his car. When he reached the car he turned to look at the old man questioningly.

"What's your name?"

The old man stroked his goatee before answering. "I be called Gabriel."

Fishbone uttered the name softly under his breath, "Gabriel."

He stood there for a second, then said, "Thanks, Gabriel."

Fish gave him the back-at-you sign, then he smiled and drove away.

Gabriel smiled, too. He watched him drive away. And then he and his makeshift stand with the lilies disappeared.

Chapter 60

Brandi slowly drove up the long, winding road to the cemetery gates. They seemed to loom in front of her. She hesitated. She gazed through the gates at the tombstones before they slowly opened and she drove through.

The cemetery was old and totally quiet, as though a hush had fallen over it. There wasn't even a bird chirping.

She drove over to an area with a plot of fresh dirt, and then pulled the car over to the side. She stepped out into the crisp air.

She walked over to the grave, glancing at the wooden marker with Tangie's name on it. The grave was still open, and the dirt hadn't been thrown on the casket yet.

There were colorful flowers piled on the sides of the grave. Brandi stood there looking solemnly down into the grave.

The arrival of another car drew her attention. She looked over to see Fishbone climbing out of his car.

As Fish got closer to her she could see that he was carrying a single white lily. He stopped, looking around the gravesite.

He handed Brandi the lily.

She took it, putting it to the tip of her nose and smelling it.

A sad little smile crossed her face.

Fish put an arm around her shoulder. "Come on. Let's go."

They walked away from the grave together. Brandi stopped in her tracks.

She looked up at Fish. "Wait. There's something I need to do."

She broke away from him and ran to the car. She opened the door, reached into the glove compartment, and pulled out the Bible her mother had given her.

She slowly walked past Fishbone back to Tangie's grave. She stared down at the casket. Then she leaned over, throwing her Bible into the grave. It landed with a thud on top of Tangie's coffin.

Brandi turned away with tears in her eyes. Fishbone walked over and looked into the ground to see the Bible lying on top of his sister's coffin.

As he took Brandi's hand he saw the little boy standing across from them on the other side of the cemetery.

The child treated him to one of the warmest, brightest smiles Fishbone had ever seen.

Fishbone nodded his acknowledgment.

The little boy disappeared. He was a grown man now, and he had been set free by Fishbone's willingness to change.

That little boy could rest in peace.

Hand in hand Brandi and Fishbone walked away from Tangie's grave, each filled up from their individual experiences.

And then the most beautiful thing happened.

Music.

Music flooded their minds simultaneously as though it were a precious gift being handed to them, and they heard the words:

> *"Give me one moment in time.*
> *When I'm more than I thought I could be*
> *Then in that one moment of time*
> *I will feel, I will feel eternity"*

freedom of those lyrics was awash in the spirit of their
A breeze blew over them.

The Bible sat in its place. In its time, just as it always has been, where it needs to be, when it's supposed to be there, on top of Tangie Parker's coffin.

Jeremiah 29:13: *"And ye shall seek me, and find me, when ye shall search for me with all your heart.*

STREET VENGEANCE

EVIE RHODES

ABOUT THIS GUIDE

The questions and discussion topics that follow are
intended to enhance your group's reading of
this book.

Discussion Questions for *Street Vengeance*

1. Who is Brandi Hutchinson?

2. What events molded and shaped Brandi's thinking?

3. Why did Q run from the police?

4. What elements led to his thinking just before he put his foot on the gas pedal leading the police into a chase?

5. How did the rap concert they attended affect the mind set of Brandi, Q, and Tangie?

6. Did Brandi have a right to her bitterness?

7. Should Q have done something differently?

8. Were there other avenues Brandi could have chosen as opposed to the one she did choose?

9. What about Charles & Rita's Brandi's parent's attitude? How did their attitude contribute to Brandi's plight?

10. What about Brandi's feelings regarding the Generation?

11. Are Brandi's insights correct regarding the breakdown from generation to generation?

12. What inspired the type of loyalty that bonded the women together?

13. What was the turning point for Brandi?

14. What was the turning point for Fishbone?

15. Why did they turn it around?

Author's Note

The story in *Street Vengeance* very much lends itself to the plight that other people are facing today. It is my sincerest hope that the mirror of this story offers one important element the one that always seems to be missing: hope!

I too have a dream—it is for the winds of change. If you listen closely enough you can hear it coming.

Evie Rhodes
P.O. Box 320503
Hartford, CT. 06132
Email: *evierhodes@evierhodes.com*
Web Site: www.evierhodes.com